Playing It Safe

MARCIE PARSON

authorHOUSE®

AuthorHouse™
1663 Liberty Drive
Bloomington, IN 47403
www.authorhouse.com
Phone: 1 (800) 839-8640

Published by AuthorHouse   07/15/2016

ISBN: 978-1-5246-1828-5 (sc)
ISBN: 978-1-5246-1826-1 (hc)
ISBN: 978-1-5246-1827-8 (e)

Library of Congress Control Number: 2016911205

Print information available on the last page.

Let me properly introduce myself; speaking in the manner of a lady. My name is Ava Dulaye Johnson. I am twenty-six years of age. My skin is the color of caramel. I'm 5' 6" wearing two inch stillettos. A sister with green eyes that weigh 145. My cup size is a 42b, 28 around the waist and 40 around the buttocks and thighs. Nice, huh? Indeed it is. My hair is shoulder length; most of the time I wear extensions; especially when the jobs demand it. My call name is Advantage. Now, you may wonder what are these jobs that demand that a woman have certain qualities. Still wondering...? Well, it shouldn't be that hard to figure out...

I was born in Mississippi. The land of the rebel flag, KKK, and other such indescrepancies. I'm an eighties baby, so I didn't have to deal with too much prejudice. Hell, the first encounter I had with prejudice I was walking to the store with my sister (who was 13 at the time) Stecha and my two cousins Ronao (11) and Pateka (4). We took over babysitting Pateka for my aunt once my older sister YoSavon realized we were old enough to handle it. YoSavon always called the shots about everything. Now that YoSavon had purchased her first car (a green '95 escort, 4-door with a wing) she was basically out of the picture more than she was on the scene. At least, not on our scene. Which happened to be a well-paved, one-way street leading to one of the grocery stores. Leaving my aunt's apartment complex was a field that a private school used for their sports and games. We crossed the street. Stecha holding Pateka's hand. Once we were across, we started the small incline up a very small hill. The private school to our right started at the bottom of the hill with the parking lot for the students old enough to drive and ended with the next intersecting street at the top of the hill where a traffic light control traffic. The school was about 1\8 of a mile long. We walked on the left side of the road opposite of the school. Besides, the store was on the left side, midsection of the school, directly across from it. We were about 150 feet from the store when we heard vroom, vroom, vroom come from the muffler of an old chevy truck; we didn't get a chance to look back. Before we knew it, the rust pink colored truck with back bubble hips were in front of us speeding toward the traffic light. One white boy at the wheel with his left arm out the window showing us a fingersign; the polite way of saying fuck you. The white boy on the passenger's side of the vehicle was screaming, "whoo- hoo" along with the two white boys on the back of the truck. The two white boys on the back threw a whole lot of notepad size white sheets of paper above our heads. They then started to beat on the roof of the truck and screamed, "whoo-hoo" in unison. We stopped walking all of us except Pateka picked up a sheet of paper it read: "Coon, coon, black baboon should've died in your mother's womb." It was stamped with the picture of a monkey. We did not ever experience, first-hand, a racial moment. We heard our parents and grandmother talk about how ignorant and evil the white man is. I was 14. So, we were old enough to understand what happened. All of us, except Pateka. When we made it back to my aunt's complex. I stood in the parking area and noticed my surroundings. The tan bricks, the L-shape in which the apartments were made. The gate looked like prison bars. We were constantly kicking the gate down. The opening that lead to everyone's mailbox and my aunt and her neighbors apartment. The opening on the opposite end of my aunt's stored the laundry room. The swimming pool that was packed with dirt because a little boy drowned in it. My aunt was at work. She worked the front desk at a Super 8 hotel. I unlocked the door. The large gray curdorouy sofa was to the right of the door in front of the large double pane, floor to ceiling windows. An identical loveseat sat vertical to it. There was a fake palm tree between the loveseat and entertainment center. A long rectangle table seperated the sofa from the center. The table was beige oak with three different, equally portions of glass in it. Pateka was the only child then, so pictures of her at different stages of her life were on the walls. A gray recliner marked the starting point of the dining room. The dining room contained a black-legged with gold trimming metal dining table. The roof of the table was all glass held down by suctions. Four black and gold chairs sat around the square shaped table. The whole apartment was tan carpet except the kitchen and bathroom. The kitchen was directly across the dining room. The bathroom was in the hallway to the left. You could see my aunt's bedroom door from the recliner and Pateka's room was beside my aunt's room. We all had our own bag full of junk food that my aunt already had in and on the refrigerator. I sat on the sofa and dropped my bag beside my right foot. Ronao had the remote in her hand; listening to Pateka tell her what kid show she wanted to watch. Stecha was in the kitchen taking her contents out of her bag. She turned her head to the side and said, "Man, that was fucked up." I said, "Yeah, if I had a gun I would've shot at them motherfuckers." Ronao said, "Me too!"

as she sat the remote down after finding "Barney" for Pateka to watch. Stecha said, "That's why I can't stand white motherfuckers they be calling us coon and shit and them motherfuckers can't get wet without smelling like a damn dog." Ronao and I agreed. Ronao sat in the recliner and kicked her feet up and said, "Man, fuck that shit roll that blunt up." I said, "Nigga, yo' ass would be rolling it, but you fucking don't know how." Stecha didn't smoke. She turned around with her arms bent, hands on the counter and said, "For real, that shit pissed me off. How in the fuck they gone say we shoulda' died in our momma's womb? Shit, black folks are the shit. Damn near all of us are fine. We look good." I stood up to throw the cigar stuffing out the door, "That's why they hating..." Stecha continued, 'We age slowly. When they get old you can see their fucking veins through their skin." I responded with, "I hate to see that shit, Ronao go get that sac out of Pateka's top drawer, the one closest to the door." Ronao got up, halfway down the hall she said, "I hate crackers." Stecha said, "I hate I was born in MS." she turned around to finish what she was doing. Ronao came back with the weed and gave me the sack. "Ste.." I said, "Don't let that shit get to you. This is the first time you experienced some shit like that, but it won't be the last." I began to seal the blunt by licking, tucking, and rubbing. Ronao asked, "Are we smoking in here or in the laundry room?" I said, "the laundry room; San, will be home in a hour we don't need that shit to be in here when she get off. Come on. Ste we'll be back." "Alright." Ste nodded. In the laundry room. I sat on top of a washing machine with the lighter stuck to the blunt. Once I was satisfied, I inhaled on that bitch and passed it to Ronao. I exhaled, "Ronao, man when I get old enough to chooose what career I want I'm not going to deal wit too many white people." We were young, but we definitely had a mentality that exceeded our age. "I feel you, but that shit is going to be hard in this country ass white boy, red-neck ass state." she said as she pulled on the blunt and held it in her mouth; the smoke inflating her jaws. "Yeah. maybe, maybe not, pass the weed bitch." I snatched the weed from Ronao in a way that let her know I didn't mean any harm. "Ritch, you always hold on to that shit like it's a fucking dick and ain't one of us even know how to begin a fuck." We both laughed. Ronao looked at me her eyes starting to get tight, "Ava, for real though, what are you going to do when and if you graduate?" I started talking while I was blowing out smoke. "If I graduate?! If I graduate?! Bitch, I'm gone gruduate fuck that shit. I don't know, but I'm definitely not going to work for some fucking hotel. Fuck that, I always wanted to assassinate motherfuckers." I passed Ronao the blunt after I hit it one more time. She looked at the blunt and said, "What's assassinate?" I jumped off of the washer and said, "You know when you kill bitches for money, babe. I'm high then a motherfucker." Ronao laughed. "I'm serious, though. I could do that shit especially if the price is supercalifragilistic." I joined Ronao in her laughter. Ronao stopped laughing, hit the blunt and look me in my eyes. "If you ever do that shit for real; Ima' do that shit with you." She passed the blunt. I said, "Damn, at first, you were hogging that hoe. Now, you're hitting it twice and passing, but, hey I'm not the one to complain." "Did you hear me?" Ronao asked. "yeah, bitch I heard you. We'll see. I'm gon put that bitch out. We'll smoke the rest of this shit later on, aight? You high?" I asked Ronao. "Yeah, I'm straight." she said. "Let's bounce then." I said. We exited the laundry, passing the stairs that led to the upper apartments. As we passed each apartment door, I imagined myself behind each one of them murdering each neighbor in a different way. The first door; poison. The second door; silently between the eyes. The third door; slean throat slice. The fourth door; suffocation. The fifth door (my favorite); choking with a guitar string. I wandered what Ronao was thinking about.

1-Hello

TWO YEARS AFTER GRADUATION, I'M damn near twenty-one. I never thought I'd still be living in Mr. whip me a.k.a. Mississippi. Call me crazy. I don't love the state, but I do love most of my relatives and I do consider one or two hoes a friend. Not really. Well, I'm not working at some fucking hotel. I wouldn't credit a Mexican restuarant as a notch higher. In fact, I'd give a notch or two down. The money isn't great, but it helps my boyfriend keep me fresh. I know you didn't think I was going to say pay the bills... and ain't! I don't believe in dating without rating. Ambrose is a good man. Does he cheats? I care less as long as he straps up and get paid. He gets upset everytime I say this. He's 5'8". Dark-skinned brother, sexiest lips I have yet to see (besides L. L.) He's built nice and a great lover. I met him at a Community College. I was taking my general courses. Na'Mar is studying to be a Crime Scene Investigator. In fact, He graduate \s next fall. He paint cars, also, at his father's car shop. He makes a pretty penny. Monday - Wednesday he cuts hair in our home. So. we're doing okay. I live in an one bedroo. Rom house. It has a living room, kitchen, laundry room and of course, a bathroom. What? I don't need anything more. It's just the two of us. No children involved. Stecha is now 19, a work-a-holic. She has a little girl. A nice brick house with three bedroom. We visit each other 6 days out of the week sometimes 7. Ronao is 17, now, about to graduate high school. Hard-headed as hell and hot in the panties. "Those folks have left your table." My co-worker LeBo'me told me as she pushed my right shoulder. "Huh, oh, okay, thanks. I hope they left a tip; they worried the shit out of me, girl." She laughed, "Well, there's only one way to find out; go clean up their shit." Le BoMe said as she headed toward the kitchen area with a plastic pail full of silverware. Le BoMe is what you would call a blue-black color. She's a pretty girl, though. Her lips are just now beginning to lose it's pinkish color from smoking blunts with me after work. Thank God! I hate pink lips. She's about 5'2" or 5'2", ha, ha. She's short, she weighs about 175 to 180. Sweet girl before she met me. She didn't even curse. As I cleaned off the table, I grabbed the twenty dollar tip and slid it in my apron. I smelled him before he came. He put his arms around my waist and kissed the back of my neck. Though, I knew who it was, it came as a shock. "Are you about to get off?" I turned around sliding gently out of Na'Mar's grip, "Baby, I told you about getting freaky with me while I'm at work; are you trying to get me fired?" He held his head down, licked his lips, looked up and smiled, "I haven't seen you since this morning, I'm just happy to see you. Can't you tell?" Na'Mar took a step closer to me. We were standing so close that I could feel his rock hard erection. "Na'Mar!" I said, I felt myself getting hot. Le BoMe walked in carrying a plastic pail similar to the last one. Except this time the pail was blue and the silverware were clean and wrapped in napkins, "My, my, my. Am I interrupting something here?" "No." I said blushing, stepping out of Na' Mar's wrath. He turned his back to Le BoMe so that she wouldn't notice the obvious. "Hey, Na'Mar." "Le BoMe." Na'Mar said as he slid into a booth. "Well, are you about to get off?" he asked. I said, "In about 30 minutes. I still have to clean up." "I'll wait. Give me a menu." "Hell no, I just cleaned that table. You want something to drink?" I asked, grabbing his arm and leading him to the smokers section. "Yeah, an Iced-Tea." "Alright. Just make sure you tip me." He smiled. I looked back to make sure he was looking at my ass as I walked away... Yep, never fails. I had me head down, smiling that Ambrose is always picking me up from work even when I, seriously, asks him not to. Sometimes, I want to ride with LeBoMe, smoke a blunt, turn a few corners; you know?

I thought about that. As I made my way to the kitchen, I bumped into a man dressed in an expensive suit. "Excuse me." I said. I looked up and noticed this man was a Puerto-Rican. He was the same height as Ambrose and very attractive, I might add. "It's okay. No need to apologize. Tienes bonita de ojos." "What?" I asked. "You have beautiful eyes." He said. I noticed his right hand cupped my left elbow. I pulled it away. "My name is David." (pronounced Dah Veed) "Hello. Now, if you'll excuse me." I made my way around him. "Senorita, como te llamas?" I ignored the last shit. I'll admit he's fine, but so is that thirsty brother of mine.

In the kitchen, Hector was mopping the floor. He's about 5' 6" with a light skin complexion. He has a thin mustache. Hector was wearing a pair of just about faded gray-black jeans. He wore those jeans everyday. Almost. "Sup, Ava?" Hector asked, throwing back his head. "Gas prices, baby. Say, Hector, What does combing the llamas mean?" Hector gave me an enstranged look and bunched up the space between his eyebrows, "Hell, if I know. Does it mean you're about to quit, again, and go work in the desert? Because if you are, I need to tell Jesse..." "Hell naw, I just thought you might know what it means since you're Mexican and shit." Hector stopped mopping and placed his head on the backside of his hand which was resting on the top of the mop. "Oh... shit, you mean como te llamas. ha. Combing the llamas. ha. What's your name, amiga. That's what it means. Why?" I was placing two lemons on the top of Ambrose's tea glass. "No reason. It's a long story. Well, thanks. I'm about to finish cleaning and I'm out of here." As I started towards the silver metal push doors with a circle window, Hector called, "Let me guess, Iced-Tea, two lemons; Ambrose, right?" "Right." I said and gave Hector an one-sided smile. "Ava." Hector called. "I am Mexican, indeed, but I'm definitely not shit." I stopped walking, turned around, and placed my left hand on my hip, "No, Hector you're not shit but, those pants are close to it." Hector looked down, "Cold, Ava, muy frio." I laughed as I exited the kitchen.

The expensive suit was still where I left him. "Are you waiting for someone?" I asked. "Because we are about to close." "Actually." He said, "I came in here hoping to get directions." Right then, Ambrose walked towards us. Once he was standing beside me, he placed his right arm around my waist and took the tea with his left hand. Then, as I knew he would, he kissed my left jaw and said, "Thank you, baby; just how I like it. You always give it to me just how I like it. Hi." Ambrose directed towards expensive suit. "I'm Ambrose. I take it you know Ava." "No, I don't. I just so happened to wonder in here hoping to get directions." "Oh, yeah." Ambrose inquired. "Where to? Maybe, I can help you out there, um..." "David" Expensive suit said extending his hand. "My name is David." Ambrose took his right arm from around me and grasped David's hand. "Nice to meet you David." They released one another's grip. "Now, where are you trying to go, David?" David placed his hands in his pockets revealing the Rolex he was wearing on his left wrist. "The Revolving Door Casino. Maybe, you've heard of it?" Ambrose sipped his tea, "Heard of it. That's Ava's and Stecha's mother second home. I'm just worried the apple don't fall too far from the tree. Know what I mean?" David showcased his beautiful smile, Ambrose continued, "The directions are a bit confusing from here. If you have a few minutes to spare, we'll escort you there, first class." I looked at Ambrose. "I'd be honored and in your debt." David said, pulling out a paper thin wallet, full of one-hundred dollar bills; extending two of them to Ambrose. "Whoa." Ambrose said, "The honor is all mine. The debt is all yours." Ambrose said, refusing the two hundred dollars. "Well." I said, "Since, you gentlemen have this situation settled, be so kind as to excuse me. Some of us still have work to do."

As I walked away, I couldn't help but think about how Ambrose rejected the two C-notes. Hell, if he didn't want it, he could've took the shit and gave it to me. I could've bought that Dooney handbag I've been saving for and still had some change left over to buy a half ounce for RoNao and I. I would've smoked two of those blunts with LeBoMe. Shit, if I would've have known we were on baller status, I would've been quit this refried bean, burrito ass job, again. Ambrose must've sensed something was wrong because he crept up behind me scaring the shit out of me. "Damn, baby, are you finished, yet? You've been cleaning this same table for five minutes. You're going to rub a family in this motherfucker." I took my lips out of the automatic pissed off knot they were in, let out a sigh, and said, "Yeah, let me clock out." Not looking at Ambrose, I walked pass David who was sitting in the pick up area with his left ankle on his right knee, and his left arm(elbow) on his left knee. I went behind the cash register and started to press in my employee pin number. After that, I grabbed Ambrose's (now empty) glass that was sitting on the counter, next to the cash register, wiped away the water ring it left and headed towards the kitchen. Hector was standing over the sink cleaning one of the Woks. "Hey, girlie. You're leaving?" "Yeah, after I clean this glass. It's been a long day for a Sunday, Hector."

Hector smiled one of his toothy smiles, wiped sweat of his forehead with his forearm and said, "Yeah, chica, a long day. At least, you had some help. I was the only fucking cook, all day. Jorge claimed he had an emergency. The only emergency I can think of is Lolita." "You're so stupid, Hector."

He placed both of his hands in the small of his back and stretched. "Yeah, I know, don't worry about that glass, I'll get it. Go on, before Ambrose wants another iced tea and I'm not about to make another gallon." I kissed Hector on his cheek. "Thanks, Hector. I'll see you Wednesday." Hector looked at me confused, "What do you mean Wednesday?" I tossed my rag into the sink, "Off days, baby. Goodnight."

I strolled back into the pick up area. Ambrose and David was standing by the exit door. Before we left, I turned toward the kitchen, "Don't forget to lock up, Hector. I faintly heard Hector say, "Yeah, I know, thanks chica, goodnight." "Goodnight." We all said together as we left the restaurant...

This man's lifestyle is exuberant, I thought, as we left the building. As we entered the parking lot, three cars filled the spaces. LeBoMe left about ten minutes, ago, without saying goodnight. If she would've been here there would've been an additional space occupied with LeBoMe's navy blue Pathfinder. Since, she had already left the premises, that left Hector's cranberry colored Durango, my champagne colored Honda Accord with twenty inch rims, I might add, and David's car. I should've guessed from David's footwear, apparel, and watch that his style in vehicular movement would be outlandish. He began a slight jog to the Jaguar. (As if we would leave him if he wasn't behind the wheel the same time as Ambrose. I tried not to gawk at the Jag'. Ambrose opened the driver's side door and pushed the switch to unlock all the doors. By the time I sat down, Ambrose had already closed his door. Now, he's truly a gentleman. He used to, continuously, open my door for me. It took six months of beckoning him to stop before he relinquished the idea. That's so 80's. It's a modern world and I'm a modern girl. I gave a deep sigh as I closed the door and relaxed in the seat. "Can we ride in silence, tonight? I'm in no mood for music. I just don't feel like hearing it." I insisted. "Come here." Ambrose placed the knuckle of his pointer finger under my chin and turned my face towards his. We stared at each other for a second. He licked his lips. I placed my hand on his left jaw and our lips met. Before I knew it, I was indulging myself in his sultry kiss and taking advantage of the softness of his lips. I felt my hormones over react and remembered we were in the parking lot of La Cocina de Comida. "Mmmm..." I said and laid my head back on the headrest with my eyes still close. "You okay, Love?" Ambrose asked. He brought the car to life and switched on the headlights. "Yeah, now, I am. I wonder if Stecha called me."

"There you go. Not today, baby, damn. You worked a double. It's almost nine thirty. Leave Stecha where she is. He was two seconds too late because I was, already, pulling my purse from under the passengers seat and searching for my cellular. Damn, 32 missed calls... 9 from Stecha, 6 from RoNao, 10 from various friend girls, 2 from mama, and, damn, I couldn't believe it, 4 from YoSaVon. You have to understand YoSaVon calls me once a month since she moved to New York. Hell, sometimes she didn't return my phone calls but, to receive 4 calls from her in one day. One would consider themselves on V. I. P. status. Immediately, I hit the 1 button that dialed YoSaVon's cellular and placed in my earpiece. After two seconds, I glanced at my phone to see if my battery was dead from not being charged all day. Nope, 3 bars left. Finally, the phone began to ring. Damn, after two rings, I got the fucking voice mail. YoSaVon believed in the kiss rule. Keep It Simple Stupid. Her voice mail said, "YoSaVon." beep... "Ava, hit me up! ya dig?"

Ambrose stopped at a traffic light and glanced in the rearview mirror to make sure he didn" lose expensive suit. "Ava, what do you think of David?" "I don't know; there's not much to think of him. I don't know him, Ambrose." Ambrose looked at me, swiftly. Then he put eyes back on the road. "I didn't say you knew him. I was just asking what do you think of him. I mean... I'm saying when we got acquainted it was a formal handshake. No business card or anything. You'd think a top-cat dude like that would have a business card; if he's in the legal business." Ambrose voiced. "Damn, Ambrose, can you not be an investigator, for once? I'm off work and you're no longer at school." I said, looking out of the window. Ambrose rebounded, "...and don't think I didn't see homeboy checking you out. If I weren't there, he, probably, would've been another one of those unknown numbers on your celly." "psst.. Whatever. I'm not going through this shit with you, tonight. I should be bitching about you turning down that money like we are doing it big." I said, lighting the cigarette I took out of my apron and rolled the window down (just a bit). Ambrose tightened his grip on the steering wheel. "I knew that shit was coming. We're not fucking bumming, either, Ava. What do I look like taking money from a man? Huh? Man, sometimes I don't know about you. Seems to me your heart follows a dollar and your ass goes everywhere your heart goes." That shit made me mad. "If that's so true then why am I with you? Huh, Ambrose? Why am I loving living in an one bedroom house, huh? Why? Ambrose, why?" Silence... "That's what I thought. Now, please, let me rest." He placed his hand on the inside of my left thigh and started massaging. "Baby, you crazy I can be about you and… You got upset about me not taking the money. Well, it's kind of damaging to a man's character, you know?" I pulled on the cigarette. "Yeah, Ambrose. I know and I apologize, forgive me?" Ambrose ran his hand to my mid-section and gave it two pats. "Yeah, I forgive you, pussy." I smiled, reached over and kissed him on his right cheek. The rest of the journey to the casino was in complete silence. Ambrose made a loop around a section of parked cars. David and he exchanged each other's gratitude and that was the last time I thought I would ever see expensive suit.

What&s Really Happening?

THE PHONE WAS RINGING WHEN Ambrose and I entered our cozy, little abode. We by-passed our spacious living room which is surrounded by mirrors on three of the four walls. There is a long, hotel style dresser pushed to the right, once a person enters the house. A window centers the dresser. A stereo sits on top of the dresser. I always believed: less is more. I, also, refused to purchase furniture for this room. We considered this room and either/or. Either, I'm working out or Ambrose is cutting hair. That explains the fold out chairs in the corner and the linoleum floor. Ambrose tossed the keys in a basket on the mantle. "Don't answer that, baby." Ambrose said as we made our way to the bedroom. "Damn, can we eat, first?" I kissed Ambrose on his cheeks and took the Subway bags away from him. "Yeah, baby. Be the good man that you are and get us some plates. Would you?" I asked Ambrose holding a bag in each hand. As soon as he stepped in the kitchen, I tossed the bags on the bed and turned on the T.V. The t.v. was sitting on top of two identical dressers as the living room dresser. They were stacked one on the other. The top dresser contained Ambrose's items and the bottom one, mines. The phone was still ringing. Ambrose entered the bedroom with two plates that were still wet from him rinsing them. "Man, answer the phone. Whoever it is, obviously, wants to talk." Ambrose said. "Okay, baby, since you are pressuring me." I said reaching for the receiver. "It do." "It do what, bitch." It was Stecha. "Damn, girl, did you have to pull a double?" I sighed, "Yeah, girl, what's up?" "Nothing. I wanted you to go to the mall with me, today. Mom asked about you. She said you, probably, had to pull a double. Why do you leave your purse and celly in the car? You be tripping." Stecha said. I rubbed the back of my neck, "I on know. It's a habit. How's Mom doing?" "She's straight; playing broke, again. She had me buying her everything." I laughed, "Girl, she is a trip. Oh, YoSaVon called me." "What?" Stecha said, "What did she want?" I looked at Ambrose and noticed he was growing impatient. "I don't know. When I called her back I got her voicemail. Shit. Look, I'll call you, tomorrow. I'm off. Alright?" "Ambrose's giving you that look, huh? Tell him I said what's up with his punk ass." "Girl... you are stupid. I'll holla. Kiss Sympathy for me. I love you. Later." Stecha has never been the type to say she loves you. You just have to know that she do. With that, I hung up the phone, ate, watched T. V., made love with Ambrose, bathed with Ambrose, watched more T. V., and fell asleep in Ambrose's arms.

The next morning, I awoke alone in bed. Ambrose left a note on his pillow for me. It said that he left early to visit his father before he went to school. For me to enjoy my day, he loves me, and he hoped I would be home before the feigns start prowling. I stretched, smiled, yawned, and closed my eyes. Right when I was getting comfortable to take a nap, someone blew their horn outside. I groaned and stretched, again. I threw my legs over the side of the bed, pulled on my shorts, slid my feet into my houseshoes, rubbed my eyes, and made my way towards the door. Stecha was smiling at me; wearing shades. "Damn, you're still sleeping?" "Yeah and so are my neighbors. So, turn that music down." I said, squinching my eyes that were not yet adjusted to the sunlight. I stretched and yawned, again. "Matter of fact, just turn off your car and come inside." Stecha drove a blue Impala. Stecha got out of the car. All I could think was 'Damn, my lit' sister is jazzy.' She usually wear stilletos. Today, she was wearing an orange, open sliced shirt (that could've been two strings), khaki shorts with an orange belt, and black, strap around the ankle stilletos. She's lighter than I am. 5'1" or 5'2" in those heels. Maybe, 5'3". She weighs about 120 to 124. Her hair is thick, healthy, and streaked. She had her hair strawed today. She have brown eyes. She's beautiful. As she closed her door, she said, "You did not notice my rims; What's up with that?" "They tight, Ste. Come in, girl." Ste' turned around to admire her most recent purchase, "Yeah, whatever."

Once we were inside, I went to the bathroom to brush my teeth. "Where's Sympathy?" I yelled from the bathroom. "Mom got her." "Oh." I said. Stecha was watching T.V. "Damn, come make this bed up." "Sit in a chair." "I am but, damn, you were supposed to been up, dressed, fed, and ready to go." I walked out of the bathroom wiping my mouth with a face towel. "Didn't you bathe last night?" Stecha asked. "Yeah." I said. Stecha threw the remote on the bed, "Well, clean up this bed, wash your ass, and change ya' clothes. I'll be right back." I thought she was gone when she stuck her head back in the door, "...and bitch, fix ya' hair." "Lock my door!" I yelled. I heard her say, yeah, whatever. I knew she was going to get us something to eat.

When Stecha came back, I was ready. "Damn, can we eat?" Stecha asked. "In the car." I said, feeling rejuvenated. "Shit, it took you long enough to come back. So, where to, first?" I asked, as we drove off... "Stecha, go by Le ebo's so I can smoke this blunt." "Alright." We rode five minutes to the projects Le ebo lived in. Stecha had to show her license and let the guard copy her license plate. These projects would be nice if the thugs didn't loiter in the parking lot. They were two story-brick apartments. Three apartments per building; about twenty buildings in all. Space in between each building for clothes lines. It, also, had a playground and a basketball court. We got out and knocked on the door. Le ebo opened the door, holding her youngest child on her hip. She's 23 years old, black with some pretty big eyes. "What's up, ya'll?" "Unlock the screen and see." I said. We entered the apartment, sat down on her black sofas, and looked at her large ass, empty fish tank. "When are you going to buy some fish for that tank?" Stecha asked. "You buy me some." Le ebo said. "Shit..." said Stecha. Now, this is how we talk to each other all the time. "Put it in the air, Ebo." I said. "Hold on. Let me put Tre' in his pen." Le ebo said. "Girl, pull that pen in here; don't leave that lit' nigga by himself. Anything can happen." Stecha stated and turned on the radio. I fired up my blunt. Le ebo came out of the kitchen with her blunt lit. We got high, of course. Stecha don't smoke. We shot the shit about a good hour and left. This was a 'no baby allowed day' for Stecha. So, we left Le ebo at home and said we'd come back. She knew we wouldn't and so did we.

On our way to the mall, my phone rang. "It do." "You're fucking right, It do." "YoSaVon, I'm very flattered." I smiled. Stecha started reaching for my phone. "Let me talk to her. Let me talk to her, Ava." "Damn, Ste. Yo, Ste wants to pollinated ya' ear." They did the sisterly thing for about 5 minutes before Ste returned my phone. "It do, baby." "I want you to come visit me next week. I'll pay for everything. I need to talk to you about a job offer. Bring Ambrose." Yo said, like I didn't have a job. A life, period! "Girl, I can't do that. I have to give my boss two weeks notice before I can take off. What? Do you want me to get fired? Then, Ambrose is in school." "Well, when can you come? I know your hate Mississippi ass isn't trying to be a hick forever. Look, this is idle chat, baby. So, let me know what's the total?" "Yeah, alright." YoSaVon paused and then finished by saying, "Just don't take too long. Tell Mom, I said I love her and tell the rest of the family the same. Holla back at me Saturday; no earlier than 6 rising and not later than 7 setting, got me?" "Yeah." I said, visualizing Ambrose's reaction. "Good." YoSaVon said, "It's done." I hung up daydreaming, cursing myself because I knew if I called right back, I would get her voicemail and I didn't ask her what type of job it was. I'll just have to remember to ask her about it Saturday. "What was that about?" Stecha asked. "I don't know." "What do you mean, you don't know?" I lit a cigarette, "Yo want me to go to Atlanta soon. She said she have a job for me and before you ask, I don't know what type of job it is." We were in the mall's parking lot. "Well, are you going?" Ste asked. "I don't know. I have to..." Stecha finished the sentence for me, "... see what's up with Ambrose." "Already, baby." "Yeah, well, I'd go." Ste' said backing in a parking space.

In the mall, we window shopped. Ste' bought a bad apple bottom dress. I admired the Dooney and Burke hand purse, once again, and sighed. I started to think about how Ambrose turned down that extra money. Money... I wondered about the job YoSaVon was offering. Was I qualified? Damn, there are a lot of voids in this choice. What will Ambrose say? Will my boss let me take a couple of days off? So many questions and no answers. We went by mom's and picked up Sympathy. RoNao was there. "Hey, Momma. How are you feeling? I talked to YoSaVon, today." I told my momma as I kissed her on her cheek. She was sitting on the couch with Sympathy in her lap. RoNao sat on the loveseat opposite my mother with one leg on the couch, smoking a cigarette with her shoes off. I kissed Sympathy on the cheek. She threw her arms around my neck. Sympathy was now in my arms. "Oh, yeah." Momma said, "How is she doing? I haven't heard from that girl in a while. She's so business oriented." I looked at RoNao. She flipped me a fingersign. "Don't ya'll start that shit. I'm trying to relax and I don't want to hear that foolishness, today." Momma said. SteCha laughed. She was sitting in a dark blue, leather recliner. "Well, YoSaVon is doing okay. She sent everyone her love. She asked about you in particular, Mom." I said, hugging Sympathy. Children always warm one's heart. I love that little girl so much. "What's up, RoNao? What it do, baby?" "It do. It do. I'm ready to graduate. I'm ready for my presents." Stecha turned her nose up and said, "Girl, please. You better ask them niggas for a present." RoNao started putting on her shoes, "Man, whatever." "Yeah, whatever." Stecha said. Mom put her legs on the sofa and started changing the channel, "Didn't I just tell ya'll I was trying to relax? Don't start that shit." I gave Sympathy to Stecha, who said, yeah, whatever to mom. "Alright, lit bitch." Mom said. RoNao and I, silently, laughed at Stecha. "Let's go in the backyard. I want to show you something." RoNao said. "Don't be smoking those trees back there.", Mom said. "Mom, don't nobody smoke leaves.", I said. Mom said, "You know what in the hell I'm talking about.

RoNao and I stood in the backyard smoking a blunt. Courtesy of RoNao. "You think Yo' is coming to see me graduate?" "I don't know. She's so fucking unpredicatble." I said. RoNao brought her eyelids close together, as if, she was holding back tears. "Yeah, well, as long as you're there; that's all that matters. Don't nobody else seems to care about me, but you." "That's not true, Ro'. You know how Ste' is." "I'm not talking about Ste. I know she's a natural bitch. I'm just saying my own mom won't be there and that hurts." A tear fell from RoNao's left eye and rolled down her cheek. Her mom had been in prison, now, for 11 years. She's serving a life sentence for murder. My mom has been taking care of her since she's been 5 years of age. I couldn't and wouldn't say to her, 'I know how she feels' because, honestly, I don't. So, I said the only thing that came to mind, "Pass the blunt before you put snot on it with your crybaby ass. Naw, for real, though. Buck up, girl. You know if your mom could be here, she would. So, stop feeling sorry for yourself and besides, Mom loves you like her own." RoNao wiped the tear, "Yeah, I know. It's just... Nevermind, you wouldn't understand." "Well, I can't say I won't but, you're right. Right now, I don't. Just be strong and..."

"You know what? I'm so tired of motherfuckers saying,'oh, just be strong or; oh, keep your head up. Man, fuck that!" I exhaled my smoke, "Well, if you're so tired of people saying keep your head and be strong; you should be tired of talking about it.

In the house, Ste was falling asleep. Sympathy made her way back to Mom. "Whoo.." I said, upon entering the house. Snapping my fingers and doing a little dance. "Stop all that damn noise." Mom said. "Ya'll been smoking them trees. Looks like ya'll are sleep walking." Stecha woke up and began stretching. "Oooh. You ready?", Stecha asked. "Yeah, baby." I lit up a cigarette. RoNao gathered all of Sympathy's stuff. Maybe, because the trees make people hyperactive. Ste gathered up Sympathy, "Thanks, Mom. I love you. Here.", Ste said giving mom fifty dollars. She turned to RoNao, "I can't wait to come to your graduation. Good job, slut." Mom swung at Ste and missed because Ste anticipated mom hitting at her and moved. "Stop all that damn cursing. Ya'll ain't got no respect." "Later, Mom." Stecha was out the door, opening the back door to her car, and strapping Sympathy into her car seat. I grabbed RoNao's hand, bidded her later on, and promised I would call her, later. I kissed mom on the cheek and told her, I love her. RoNao walked me to the car and leaned in on the passenger side, "Don't forget to call me, later. Ste' are you, really, coming to my graduation?" Ste put on her shades, looked in her rearview mirror, checked her hair and said, "Hell yeah, You know I be bullshitting with you. I... Well, you know. You're cool." I gave RoNao twenty dollars, a dime sack, and we bounced.

The Answers

AMBROSE WASN'T HOME WHEN I got in. So, I made him a meal of fried chicken, spaghetti, corn, and cornbread. Ambrose loves ice-cream. So, I had him a bowl of vanilla ice cream with Reese's in the freezer. I took a bath. While I was drying off, I heard Ambrose's car outside. He have a silver, souped-up Cadillac. I ran to the door. When he opened it,

I gave him a big kiss, wrapped my arms around his neck, kicked my right leg in the air while standing tip toe on my left foot. Ambrose closed the door. "Damn, baby. What's the occassion? It's not our anniversary, Is it? Because if it is, I have to.." "No, it's not our anniversary, silly. I'm just happy that you're home. How was your day?" "Good. I had to paint a car for dad; early this morning. Some dude wanted an emergency job done to his car. Mmmm... you smell like chicken." We laughed. I led Ambrose to the kitchen. He kept raising my towel, "I don't which to eat, first." "Neither. First, you're going to bathe." I said, leading Ambrose into the bedroom. He sat in a chair while I took off his shoes. We exchanged glances that made me think, 'fuck the food and bath, take me!' I'm a lady, though. So, I held out. After Ambrose bathed, he went to the bedroom. I prepared our food. When I entered the bedroom, I noticed a lump under our cover when I know I straightened that bed up, well. I gave Ambrose his plate, went back into the kitchen to get our drinks. Still there... The lump is still there. Okay, of course Ambrose didn't notice it. He found a movie he was into. Then, he began to indulge himself with his dinner. I sat our drinks down and ran my hand across the sheet to smoothe it out. What the? There's actually something under the cover. I pulled the cover back and there was the Dooney and Burke purse I've been admiring in the mall. My insides began to tingle. I grabbed the purse looking for the insurance card to note it's authenticity. "Oh, baby. Thank you, so much. But, how did you know?" "Come on now. I know my girl. I saw you gawking at that purse in the mall. I told you I made some extra money, today; helping dad out. So, I thought to myself: I can put this money into our savings account or I can do something to make myself happy." "Oh, baby." Ambrose held up a finger.., "...and nothing makes me happier than seeing you happy... So, Happy Anniversary." I sat down thinking, 'damn how I love this sexy, black, considerate ass brother. "Baby, it's not our anniversary." "Everyday I'm with you is like meeting you for the first time. I love you, Ava. Did you find that insurance card?" "Yeah." "Not that one. There's another one in there." Ambrose set his plate down, put his hands on my knees, and kneeled in front of me. I looked at him like he was losing it. When I unzipped the inside compartment, Ambrose said, "Will you marry me, Ava?" I said, "Yes. Yes, Ambrose, I'll marry you. Yes, baby." The ring was 14 karat gold with a 2 karat diamond. What a night! You can imagine the events after this episode. Let's just say... We had an excellent night. Excellent.

The next morning the phone ringing woke us up. Ambrose answered the phone in his morning voice; not even, opening his eyes, "Hello, hold on. Hmmm... It's for you, get rid of them." Them? "Yeah, it do." It was RoNao and Ste on three way. "I thought you were going to call me, last night?" RoNao started the conversation. "She forgot." Ste said. "What's up? Are you dressed, yet? Let me guess... Hell naw, Anytime that nigga answer the phone. I bet he told you to get rid of us, too, huh?" Ste asked. I sighed..., "Girl, y'all are a trip. What's up?" "Shit, on my way to school. I only got two classes, today. So, I'll get out early." RoNao said. Ste interrupted, "Well, good you can go to the mall with me before I go to work. I got a feeling Ms. Thang won't be joining us." "Huh?" I said. "Hold on." "Hold on for what, bitch?" Ste asked. "Damn, Ste, chill out." RoNao insisted. "You chill out." Ste said. "Look ya'll, holla at me, later. Stop, Ambrose. Oh, and by the way, I'm getting married." I hung up in their faces. Why not give them something to think about. I bet they had their mouths open for a second. He he. I love it.

Ambrose didn't go to school, today. I didn't try to convince him, otherwise. After we ate and bathe, I called Momma. I told her the good news. She congratulated me and asked me if he had a brother. That was her joke of the day. She told me to make sure that's what I wanted and that she, 'already knew'. Big Mouth Winches. I tried to call YoSaVon; as usual, voicemail. I didn't leave a message. I told LeBoMe and Le ebo. They congratulated me. The rest of the day Ambrose and I made love, ate, made love, watched T.V., bathe, and made love.

Damn, I can't believe it's Wednesday. Ambrose was already gone. I was, transitively, awaken by the alarm clock. It was set to go off at 8:00 a. m. I had to be at work at ten. Damn, two hours to get ready. At 9:45, I was headed towards La Cocina de Comida. At 9:50, I was in the parking lot. So, was LeBoMe. She waved me over to her truck. She didn't unlock the doors until I was reaching for the handle. When I sat down LeBoMe said, "Wake up call... You smoking?" "Hell, yeah. Girl, are you crazy?" We smoked about five minutes before Hector stuck his face on the passenger's side window. I rolled the windows down. "Damn, y'all smoked out. Open the door. I, already, clocked y'all in." Hector remarked. "Thanks, Hector." We said, as

Hector got in the back seat. We passed Hector the blunt and let him play catch up. LeBoMe started to feel comical. She turned around in her seat to face Hector. "Your lip is long; like a dick.", LeBoMe said. I snickered. "Naw, I tell you what's long like a dick.", Hector said, pulling at his worn out, gray-black jeans. "My dick." LeBoMe and I jumped out of the SUV.

We were in the bathroom washing our hands, spraying on perfume, and putting Visine in our eyes. Hector burst in, "Jesse is here. Give me some Visine." "Damn, Hector. Where is he?" I asked. "In the parking lot, talking on his phone. I locked your doors, LeBoMe." Hector said. "Give me some of that perfume." "Hell no, Hector. Just wash your hands and chill out." LeBoMe said, putting her smell good back in her purse. When we emerged from the bathroom, Jesse said, "I thought this was a ghost house. Maybe, I should switch positions with Hector. He's getting all the action. Ladies, don't I pay you enough?" "Ha. ha. Jesse. Very funny." I walked past him to the coat rack that held the aprons. I grabbed one and put it on. LeBoMe, soon, followed suit. "So, Jesse, what do we owe for the pleasure of your pressence?" LeBoMe asked. Hector scurried off to the kitchen. "Can I check in on my employees and my money?" Jesse said, as he went to the safe below the cash register. I placed my hands in my apron's pockets, "Speaking of employees... I need to talk to you." "Ava, are you about to quit, again?" Jesse asked, placing his money into a deposit pouch. "Damn, is this Ava quit week?" I asked. LeBoMe begin to put the usual two hundred dollars into the register; ignoring us. "Sure, Ava. What would you like to discuss? No, you're not getting a raise! I was only kidding." Jesse said. "Jesse, I don't want a raise but, I do need a week off. I want to visit my sister." "I don't know, Ava. We're, already, short in staff. Let me think about it." Feeling defeated, I said, "Jesse, come on. I need to know, today. What if I can find someone to work in my place?" I was thinking of RoNao. "She won't be able to work until 3 p.m. but, I'll give you my word; She's reliable. You can even meet her today, Jesse." Jesse started scratching his chin, "Alright. Today, huh? I'll be back at 3:00. If she's not here, the answer's no. If I feel I can trust her, green lights, Ava." "Thank you, Jesse. You won't regret it." Jesse started to leave; He turned around like he knew we were high. LeBoMe and I looked at each other. "Oh, yeah. Congratulations, Ava." "How did you know?" Jesse smiled, "It's not everyday that a girl gets a rock like that. Lucky man." I blushed. Jesse stayed five extra minutes while we all celebrated the occassion over pink lemonade. "Alright, people, there's work to do and money to make; get busy."

Now, the big whammy, convincing Ambrose. RoNao was so excited to have a temporary job. Mom made it clear that she couldn't work past nine p.m. on weekdays. Green lights, Ava; Jesse had said. Now, if Ambrose said okay, I'll be leaving next Saturday. I got off and cooked Ambrose's favorite; neckbones, rice, collard greens, corn bread, and pecan pie for dessert. Ambrose walked in the kitchen and kissed my cheek. "Mmm... all my favorites. What's up Ava?" "Nothing, baby. How was your day?" I asked putting a sample of neckbone into Ambrose's mouth after blowing on it to cool it. "Mmm... that's good. If you can't do nothing else you sure know how to cook. Oh, you wouldn't believe this... Inspector Howard had us looking for hair and fiber particles; get this: on a red rug." "A red rug?" "Yeah, who would decorate their house with a red rug? I get nauseated just thinking about." Ambrose said sampling more of the neckbones. "Everyone was so frustrated and busy looking for particles that they didn't notice the blood soaked in the rug but, guess who did?" "My baby?" "You're damn right, ya' baby. That's who. Our team got five extra points towards our mid-term exam." "Oh, yeah? I'm proud of you. Now, let's get you cleaned up for dinner."

I was washing Ambrose's back when I decided to ask him about Atlanta. "Ambrose?" "Yeah, baby." "Don't you want to go on a vacation, like, next Saturday?" He looked over his shoulder, "No." He turned, completely, around. My eyes scanned his body. "So, that's why you made neckbones tonight, huh? We can go after I graduate. So, we'll go in June, okay?" I threw the sponge I was using to scrub his back into his chest, wrinkled my lips tight, dimmed my eyes and walked to the bathroom door. Ambrose jumped out of the water and grabbed me from behind; wetting my backside, "Girl, what's wrong with you? You know I can't vacation, right now. I have to finish school, Ava." I turned facing him, "I know; it's just YoSaVon..." Ambrose let me go and grabbed the large towel I had for him and placed it around his waist. "I should've known YoSaVon had something to do with it. Why can't she come visit you? She hardly calls. She hasn't been home in, what?, two, three years?" I was silent. Ambrose said, "Man, whatever." He shut the bathroom door in my face. When he came out of the bathroom, he was fully dressed. He wouldn't look me in my eyes. He was standing over the oven fixing his own food. He was staring at his plate when he said, "You're grown. You do what you wanna do. I'm not going with you, though, Ava. I can't." That was all he said to me that night. He even slept with his clothes on. He didn't even hold me. So, I held him, instead.

The Call

I T SEEMS LIKE EVERYONE CAN feel when something is wrong. Thursday came and went. All day everyone was asking me if I was okay. Am I alright? I looked at them liked they crazy. I didn't socialize, too much, with Hector or LeBoMe. I, even, worked all day without getting high. Ain't that some shit? When I got off of work, I went straight home. I didn't cook or bathe. I took off my clothes. Well, I had on my t-shirt and panties. I ate ice-cream and cake, watched T.V. under my cover (except my neck, head, and my right arm with the remote control in my hand) and fell asleep. Ambrose ordered pizza when he got home. We ate. I fell back to sleep. I, momentarily, awoke when Na'Mar got in bed and pulled me close to him. Friday morning I found a letter on Ambrose's pillow. It read: Ava, good morning, baby. I hope you're still not upset with me. I'm not upset with you anymore. So, perk-up, bathe, and cook. I, really, want to make love tonight. Love Always... Your future husband, Ambrose. I smiled, "My future husband." I said stretching and looking at my ring. "My future husband."

"Hey, Hector, what's up? Where's LeBoMe?" I said with my left hand on my purse strap that was on my shoulder. "Somebody's feeling better? She's in the bathroom." I walked in the bathroom. "Hey, girl." I said to LeBoMe. "Hey." She said, looking at me for a faint second in the mirror. She continued to wash her hands. "What's wrong with you, LeBoMe?" I asked, placing my purse on the metal shelf that was directly under the mirror. "Nothing's wrong with me. You're the one acting like you're pregnant having all those mood swings. Hell. Yesterday, you, barely, said two word to me." LeBoMe snapped. "I'm sorry, girl. I was going through something with

Ambrose." I said, wiping my hands with a paper towel. "I understand that, Ava. But, next time, don't push everyone who loves you away. Some people get offended. I had to smoke all by myself, yesterday. How do you think that made me feel? You don't care." "Yes, I do. See." I said, moving my head in that snazzy little black girl way. Producing a dime sack for LeBoMe. "My nigga. That's what I'm talking about." "It do, baby. It do."

I drove my own car to work. So, when I got into my car I called Stecha. She answered, "Yeah." "What's up?" "Shit, headed to work. What's up with you?" I hadn't even cranked my car, yet. "Nothing. Jesse and Ambrose gave me the okay to go to ATL. Ambrose..." Stecha got it bad cutting people off, "Who in the hell is Jesse?" "Jesse is my boss and Ambrose was tripping when I first asked him about it." "Ambrose trip about everything. That's no surprise." Stecha said. "Stecha, that's not true." "What? If someone calls he wants you to 'get rid of them', you can't come by the house unless, he's gone. If he's there, you have a time limit that you can stay over. You can fucking set your watch by it." Ste' said. "Well, anyway. Like I said, it's all good. I'm ATL bound." "Good for you. I wish I would go with you." "I wish you could, too." "Who's going to work in your place?" Ste asked. I opened my door and stuck my left leg out. "You haven't heard? You hear and tell everything else." "Bitch, please." "Anyway, RoNao is working in my place." "RoNao! Stop lieing." Ste' said and started laughing. "For real. Jesse hired her, yesterday. I have to go pick her up so she can drop me off at home. She start training today." I said. "Cut it out. First, you get her a job. Second, you let her use your ride. Damn, buy me some stilletos, bitch." "Hoe, please." "Anyway, I'll call you back. I'm at the place I love most. Work. Holla." This lit' bitch hung the phone up in my face.

I know she hears me blowing. "Girl, what took you so long to come out the house?" I said, stepping out of the driver's seat, waving at mom; who waved back from behind the window's curtain. Sympathy was waving, too. "You drive." I said. "Shit, you know how Mom is about me finishing my homework. I told her I would finish that one question after work." RoNao said, adjusting the rear view mirror. RoNao was, already, 5'7" wearing tennis shoes. She weighs, at least, ten to fifteen pounds more than me. She looks, exactly, like her mother. A black coffee color with two tablespoons of milk added to it, her hair is about the same length of Stecha's but, not as thick. We all are beautiful but, you know every female thinks they look better than the next. If one doesn't feel that way, maybe, they have a low self-esteem. I thought about this as I pulled down the sun visor to check out my reflection. I'm a beautiful, young lady. Hopefully, I'll be a beautiful, older lady when that time comes. Black women don't tend to age quick. But, a hard life will give you a hard to look at face. "Blow at Mom and Sympathy." I said, looking at how our mom looks like she could be our sister. As we drove off, I threw one finger in the air to the guys I grew up with in the neighborhood. There were at least two people out on every block in a quarter mile radius. Younger females dressed in the hippest apparel; mostly, high school students. They had their hair cut short or styled by some stylist. Some of them, already, had a baby at home. Then, there are the lit' boys trying to mack on these females. Most of them hung in groups of four or more. The females did, too! Damn, they are some lit' hotties. Too young but, hot. We passed the shade tree mechanics. Children riding bicycles. Everybody seemed happy it was Friday. RoNao pulled over and talked to some guy. I assumed was her most recent boyfriend. They talked about future plans, RoNao's new job, and they kissed. I turned my head, looked out the window, and rolled my eyes. "Alright, RoNao, don't be late to work on your first day. You'll make me look bad." I said, looking for a C.D. to put in the C.D. player. "You still have to take me home. Bring me my car in the morning at eight o'clock because I have to be at work at ten. If you don't think you can do it, let me know, now. Because I will drop you off and pick you up, tonight." I stated, putting the C.D. case under the seat and grabbing my purse(so I wouldn't forget it). I placed my purse in my lap. RoNao stopped at a stop sign. She looked at me and said, "I'm not going to forget, Ava." "Good." "Damn, where did you get the purse? That shits is a gem, baby." I looked at her, pursed my lips and said, "It's not a matter of where. It's a matter of when. Na'Mar surprised me with it the night he proposed to me. My ring was inside it." "Aww.. that's so sweet." "Yeah, I know, almost sweeter than the time he put a red ribbon on his dick for Valentine's Day." I said. RoNao looked at me like she was confused, "Damn, cuz, T.M.I." "Speaking of penises, you and homeboy better not fuck in my car. Make his ass get a room. I don't give a damn where you go or what you do just don't fuck in my car, don't let that nigga drive my car, don't burn my seats, let's see... Oh yeah, make sure you're on time in the morning and make sure my gas hand stay on full. There's fifty dollars in the glove compartment, solely, for gas. Got me?" "Yeah." "Good. I know you get off at eight, tonight, because you're a trainee. I advise you to take a shower before you step out or you're going to smell like refried beans." RoNao laughed. I went into my purse and gave her twenty dollars for however she saw fit. I gave her enough to buy her something to eat, a blunt, and a beer or two. Just not enough to pay for a room. I believe if a man wants to try, he should, always, buy. I wasnt worried about that lit' nigga or none of her friends going through my glove compartment. It could, only, be opened with the ignition switch keys and she supposed to be the only one with access to that. As we got closer to my house, I said, "I want a receipt to every gas purchase you make and I expect all of my change from that fifty that you don't use on gas." "Damn, cuz, it's like that?" RoNao said, looking at me unbelievably. "Exactly like that." I said sternly. "Shit, I'm letting you..." "I know. I know and I appreciate it. Straight up. Therefore, your wishes are my commands." When she pulled in front of my house I got out and closed the door. I knocked on the window. RoNao rolled down the window, electronically. "I forgot I need the keys to get in the house; just take it off the key ring." I said. RoNao handed me the key. "Thanks. Oh, one more thing; don't drink in my car, alright?" "Alright." I hit the top of the car twice, "Get there, baby." I watched as she drove off. When I made it to the bedroom the phone rang. "It do." I said. "Yeah, Ava." It was RoNao. "Yeah." I said. "Thank you for everything. It really means a lot to me." RoNao said. "Yeah. Well, just give them a good performance. Now, let me go, girl. Enjoy your night. Later." "Later."

Ambrose came home an hour later than usual. My arms were folded, lips puckered, and my right foot tapping. "Where have you been?" I asked; following Ambrose to the bathroom. "Looking for you. I thought you were pulling a double. So, I went by your job, saw your car but, no Ava. RoNao told me everything." I grabbed him from behind, stood on my tip-toes, and sniffed his hair. "Sorry, baby." "Yeah. Well, if you were so worried about me, why didn't you just call me cellphone?" Ambrose asked. "Ion know; giving you the benefit of the doubt. I, also, had to cook and bathe." "Girl, you look and smell something good." Ambrose said as he turned around in my arms and kissed me. Tomorrow is Saturday; So, no school for Ambrose. Unfortunately, I have to work. "So, what's on your agenda for tomorrow, baby?" I asked Ambrose, holding back the urge to suck on his bottom lip. "Well, I have to help out dad at the Car Shop. I have two cars to paint. An

Impala and a box Chevy." He said. I was thinking: Damn, he'll be just as busy as I'm going to be, tomorrow. "...and then." "And then?" I said walking towards the kitchen to check my lasagna. "And then what, baby?" I heard him dipping his hand in the bath water; testing it. "Baby, my water is cold. Why is my water cold, baby?" He asked, coming into the kitchen, dripping water on the floor from his fingers. All I could think was men. "Well, it's been in there a little over thirty minutes. Since, you're late you, now, have to run your own water." Ambrose walked back to the bathroom. I heard the water draining. He called from the bathroom, "Well, it's not fair being that I was looking for you. It's your job." "My job?" I asked. "Yes, your job. I pay the bills and you keep the house kept. Since, I pay the bills, I'm part of the house." I had my hands on my hip with a smirk on my face. "Okay. Fine, you win." It reminded me of how I laid down the rules of my car to RoNao. "Now, what is this 'and then' you were talking about, Ambrose?" I asked, lighting two cigarettes, taking one to Ambrose. I was standing in the bathroom door. I handed Ambrose the cigarette. "What 'and then'?" He asked taking the cigarette and sitting on the toilet. "You said you were going to paint two cars and then." "Oh, and then I have six cuts lined up." He said. I walked back into the kitchen, turned up an ashtray, and tapped my cigarette ashes into it. "No." "No, what?" Ambrose asked. I pulled on the cigarette. I was considering whether or not to take him an ashtray. I decided against it. Afterall, he could use the toilet or the sink. "Get rid of them." I said, using his words. "Huh?" he said. "Get rid of them. That's cutting two hours into our time." I said, laughing to myself. "Baby, are you serious?" "Hell, no! I'm just kidding." I told Ambrose. I heard him running his water for his bath. I went into the bedroom and thought about how comfortable I am with Ambrose. I thought about how much I love him. My sub-conscious said,'if you love him so much, why can't you tell YoSaVon, no; and continue to live your comfortable little life.' My conscious told my sub-conscious to shut the hell up. I sat on the bed and sat the ashtray on the bedside table. I grabbed the remote and begin to flip the channels. I wasn't even paying attention to what was showing on T.V. Why didn't I tell YoSaVon no? What am I looking for? What type of job is it? What if it required me to move to ATL, permanently? If so, could I just leave it all behind like YoSaVon did? I snapped out of my daze, listening to the "Good

Times" theme song. This shit better be worth my while, YoSaVon. It better be worth my fucking while.

Saturday morning. Another letter from Ambrose. I know it's eight o'clock because the alarm is blaring. I jumped up. I, actually, raised the top part of my body; as if, I was doing a situp. Where's my car? My hair was in disarray. My tongue felt like it grew a rug on it. I went to the bathroom. I brushed my teeth and washed my face. I yelled to the top of my lungs. Then, I looked in the mirror and told myself, good morning. I smiled at myself like a big kid. Someones's knocking on the door. They're knocking like crazy. I should've known it was RoNao's ass. She walked past me and apologize for being late. I told her not to sweat it (even though I was sweating where my ride was as soon as I go up.) "Aye, you goine have to chill for a minuter while I get dressed. There's a blunt, well, half a blunt in the ashtray. Take it to the head." I went to the bathroom and groomed myself. About forty-five minutes later, we were headed towards momma's house. I went inside. I still had thirty minutes to spare. I spoke to Mom and kissed her. RoNao sat on the loveseat. She kicked her shoes off and dozed off, almost, immediately. Five minutes after watching "The Golden Girls" with my mom, my phone rang. "It do." I said. "You're fucking right, It do." It was YoSaVon. "Yo, I was just about to call you." I lied. I, actually, was going to call her when I got off of work. "What's up, baby?" I asked "You know what's up. Yes or no?" She said. Her voice was sort of cold. She asked me that like an obese lady with her hair in a bun; sitting at a desk with her glasses on the top of her nose. It felt like she was a pimp. It was just cold. I looked at mom; she was staring at me with a glow in her eyes. "Mom, Yo' said hello." "Tell her, I said hey, baby." Yo asked me what was the answer again. I was thinking, 'what the fuck?; acknowledge your mother. So, I did the bitchy thing there was to do. I handed Mom the phone. "Hey, baby. Oh... I'm alright." That was mom's opening to a ten minute conversation. I know Yo' was steamed, but I didn't care. Family is everything to me and my mom and nieces are at the top of the list. When mom handed me the phone, no one was on the other end. She was pissed. Good. That'll teach her that I don't take orders. If it teaches her nothing else, it should teach her some fucking manners. I didn't call her back, immediately. Hell, I'm not going to call her back until I get off work. Before I left Mom's house, I left a note for RoNao to be ready at 3:30 to 3:40. I told her to be sitting on the porch. RoNao was snoring. She had her mouth wide open. I took a deep breath and blew in her mouth real hard. She opened her eyes. She looked shock and started coughing. I ran to the door, touching mom on her shoulder; who was laughing. RoNao got up and chased me, but didn't go past the door because she didn't have her shoes on. I hurried to the car because she disappeared. I knew she was putting on her shoes. I put the car in reverse and laughed. I saw RoNao jump off the porch and chase the car. I laughed harder as I stopped at the corner to watch for oncoming traffic and pedestrians. RoNao caught up at the corner and started beating on my window. "Stop hitting on my window, hoe!" I said. "Ima get you, bitch!" RoNao started laughing, "Motherfucker!" I backed the car and directed it in the direction I was headed. I looked in the rearview mirror and saw RoNao walking back to momma's house.

After work, I went straight to Momma's house to pick up RoNao. She was waiting on the porch. When she dropped me off at home, she slapped me on the ass, extremely, hard. I sat back down in the car. It was reflexes that stationed me back in the passenger's seat. We tangled for a minute or two. RoNao said, "Hey, Ambrose's home and it looks like he gots company and a lot of it." "Yeah, but it's not company. It's business." As I headed towards the house, RoNao said, "Forgetting something?" Her left arm was stretched out of the window with my purse and celly in her hand. I took my items and slapped her hands, real hard. "Ow... bitch!" RoNao said, rubbing her hand. "Hey, same routine as yesterday. The money's in the glove box. There's seventy dollars in there. Twenty for you. I want my..." She finished. "I know you want your receipts." "I see why you're a good student." I tapped on the roof of the car, twice, and she was off. I called her on her cell phone. "What's up, Ava?" "See if that nigga of yours will wash the car, huh?" "Yeah, alright. Is that it, your highness?" I liked the sound of that. "Say it, again." "Say what, again?" RoNao asked. "Your, highness." I said. "Girl, please, bye!" "Bye."

I took a deep breath because I knew there was a lot of brothers in our livng room. Some will be reading magazines or, at least, pretending to. I prepared myself for what was expected inside. When I entered the house, Ambrose and his customers, looked up. I heard someone say,'damn, she's fine.' I pretended I didn't hear it. Ambrose gave me a toothy smile. "How was your day, baby?" Ambrose said. "All the skeezer talk is, officially, out the window. Naw, I'm just playing, baby." I walked over to Ambrose and kissed him on his cheek. In unison, they all said, 'ooohhh...' Ambrose said, "Cut it out." I walked into the bedroom. I put the idea of taking a shower in the back of my mind until the house contained Ambrose's and my presence. I tried to watch T.V. but, the music was too loud in the living room. I asked Ambrose to turn the music down. While I was watching "Cheaters", my cell phone rang. "It do." "Do it, now?" YoSaVon asked. "It do." "So, what's your answer?" she asked. "I'm en-route to Atlanta." I said. "How soon?" "Saturday, I'll be on I-10." I told YoSaVon. "Good. Call me Saturday morning, okay?" "Okay. So... You're not mad about earlier?" I asked. "Hell, no. That's my mom, nigga.. Are you crazy?" "Well, I thought you were because you were no longer on the phone." "That's what you would call business. That's the city-life. Call me, Saturday. Alright?" YoSaVon said. "Already." I said, ending the phone call.

Before The Trip

"ATLANTA! ATLANTA! DAMN IT, JUST hit me. I thought Yo' was living in New York. I'm serious. The shit just, now, registered. What do you think about it?" I asked Stecha, as she showed the guard at the apartment complex Le ebo lived in, her driver's license. "You should be use to me, by now, old man. You make me show my license, everytime." Stecha said putting her license back in the wallet that matched her purse. As she crept towards 'Ebo's apartment, She said, "I don't know what to think of it. Maybe, she just got business there. If she's living there, she sure didn't tell anyone." We got out of the car. Le ebo's door was open. So, we just walked in.

Le ebo was coming down the stairs with a blunt between her index and middle finger. "Ya'll ready?" Le ebo asked. "Hell naw, ya'll ain't smoking that shit in my car. Ya'll can roll that shit in it but, you can't smoke in my ride. A vacuum cleaner will pick up seeds, sticks, and the leaves but, that damn smell stick to leather. Uh-uh. Fuck that." Stecha said, sitting down;

indicating, we might as well do the same. "Where are your kids?" I asked Le ebo. "They grandmother got 'em. Thank God." Le ebo pulled one the blunt, once more and passed it to me. I hit it and said, "Damn, this shit taste good. Where did you get the? Nevermind." I twisted my body and faced Stecha. "You still didn't tell me shit." I asked Stecha. "About what?" "About the trip to Atlanta." "I told you, I don't know what to think. Maybe, she wants you to sell some ass. Le ebo laughed, "What are ya'll talking about?" We gave her a rundown of the offer YoSaVon offered me. "Pass the blunt, Ava." 'Ebo said. "Girl, this tree is so good my lips were chopping it down." I said. "What do you think, Ebo?" "Shit, I'm like Ste. I don't know what to think. Take that ride and find out." I was thinking,'damn, thanks for nothing.' I couldn't get upset with them, though. I mean, I'm asking them questions they couldn't possible answer. Still, I was expecting them to say something more than,'I don't know.' Stecha talking about, sell some ass. If that's what she needs me for, she can forget about it. I'm not going to be unfaithful to Ambrose. I'm not saying I wouldn't date but, I'm ot letting anyone, except Ambrose, enter my body. YoSaVon knows my standards. She knows I have very high morals. I hope she wouldn't embarrass herself by asking me to join an escort service. I don't knock anyone's hustle; don't get me wrong but, there's just some things I wouldn't do and selling ass is one of them.

We stopped at Shoney's to get something to eat. We sat at a table to prevent arguing about who was going to have a booth to themselves. "Damn, that washboy is fine." Le ebo said. "Yeah, he is cute." Stecha said. They both looked at me. "What?" I said, looking down at my plateful of fruits. Showing favoritism towards the grapes. "Oh, you can't acknowledge a fine brother, anymore? Every since punk ass put that ring on her finger, she no longer see evil." Stecha said. Le ebo laughed, sucking on a strawberry; holding it by the green stem. "What the fuck are you laughing at, 'Ebo?" I asked. "That girl can laugh if she wants to." Stecha said. "I didn't say she couldn't. I just want to know what's so damn funny?" I said. Le ebo threw her strawberry on the floor, threw her right arm behind her chair, stretched her left leg and slumped down in her chair. "I mean, if the shoe fits, wear it. If it doesn't, take it off." Le ebo said. We were still high. "Save the parables, Le ebo and get to the point." I said. "All I'm saying is, why not admire the finer things in life. Married or not. Marriage don't stop them from looking." Le ebo said. I thought about when Ambrose was cutting hair and said all the skeezer talk is over. "Ya'll hoes don't know yourselves shit about Ava... I'm not the one to be peer pressured into doing anything I don't want to." "We're not applying peer pressure. We're just telling the truth." Ste said. "I don't need ya'll to tell me shit. You see, evrything ya'll are saying, I, already, learned." "Temper. Temper." Le ebo said, sitting up in her chair; grabbing a cut cantaloupe. "Temper, my ass. I get engaged and you hoes place me in a nun's covenant. I never been a hoe and just because I have a ring on my finger doesn't mean I have to prove to have hoe tendencies. So, back up off me!" Stecha had her arms crossed, her head tilted, and a smirk on her face. "Why are you getting offended? Can't nobody even play with your ass, anymore." Ste' said. "Man, I'm just not in the mood to play, right now. I'll be back." I said. I went outside to smoke a cigarette. Le ebo joined me. We didn't talk; just smoked. I'm glad I didn't tell them what I, really, thought. Stecha hasn't had a steady boyfriend in a year. She's had one (here or there) but, I wouldn't call them, boyfriend material. Yeah, she's a bitch to us but, we're used to it. She just believe in dogging a man out. Her motto is: break his heart and pockets. She did Sympathy's dad so wrong. I can guarantee it's going to take a very special lady to make him love, again. Get this, he's still in love with Stecha. Poor dude. Le ebo's boyfriend (baby daddy) ain't shit. He just dogs her out. He cheats on her, faithfully. Is, currently, cheating on her and, in my opinion, will always cheat on her. She is a beautiful female (like I said, earlier). Her boyfried is just one of those type brothers that is never satisfied with two females. So, you know what I wanted to tell them, right? You're damn right. They're just jealous!"

RoNao still has my car until Wednesday. I try to give her a little leeway and freedom. She has to get use to being responsible for accessories like that. It turns out, she likes working at La Cocina de Comida. Everytime we talk, it's about something that happened at work. It gets old but, hey, if she likes it; I love it. She, also, talk about how mom wants her to take her everywhere. The Revolving Casino is her favorite place to go. I just hope RoNao knows that she's going to pay me back for the gas money I've been giving her. Since, I'm home, I might as well call her and let her know. Le ebo and Stecha continued the day without me. No, the conversation at Shoney's is not the reason why I'm home. I'm just tired. When I get off work, I'm exhausted. I'm off. So, I asked Stecha to bring me home. They kept explaining and apologizing about the Shoney's incident. I was so high; it went in one ear and out the other.

I sat on the bed; watching T. V. I lit my blunt and called RoNao. "What's up?" RoNao asked. "The piper." I said. "What?" "The piper needs to be paid gas money, baby." "Oh, girl, I have every intention on paying you everything back." "Naw, not everything; just the gas money." I said sucking in smoke. I picked up the remote, changed the channel, and looked at the blunt like it was edible. Thank God for weed. Indeed. Indeed. "What are you doing?" RoNao asked. "What I always do?" I said feeling the effects of Mary J. "Bitch, put it out. I'm on my way." "I'm not putting shit out. Just bring a 'gar. Matter fact, bring two, ya' dig?" "Alright, give me five minutes." "Bitch, don't speed; putting tickets on my registration. Take ten. Ro?" "Yeah." "Bring me two oatmeal pies, a fudge round, a snickers, and grab a bag of Doritos, Cool Ranch." "Damn, cuz. Can you say major case of the munchies." "Major."

YoSaVon was on the sixth floor in the posh neighborhood of Buckhead. The penthouse was lavish. Every room was designed in white; even the dishes. Not to exclude the staircase that leads to the studio bedroom. She stood in front of the floor to ceiling, wall to wall window that overlooked expensive hotels. "Well, what's the report on our new employee?" He asked. YoSaVon held the white coffee mug in her left hand and ran her fingers through her long hair. Her hair, nearly, touched her buttocks. She was wearing a long, black, cotton trench coat that fell right above her ankle. She had on a black scarf to accentuate her coat and outfit. She wore black slacks, a black long-sleeve turtleneck (that was tucked in her black slacks) with a black patent-leather belt. Her black stilettos were six inches and very thin. YoSaVon was the lightest in skin of her sisters. She is, also, taller and weigh 20 pounds more than Ava. She continued to stare out of the window. "We can't call her an employee, just yet. Now, can we?" YoSaVon answered. "Well, sure we can. Who would turn down an offer such as this? If she seems skeptical, offer her a bonus, hmmm... You assured me you would find the right girl for the job or should we say, profession?" He asked, wearing identical clothes as YoSaVon; except, masculine. He was wearing a black pair of Stacy Adams. A black pair of Ray Bans was tucked in the neck of his V-neck sweater that topped a black turtleneck. YoSaVon sipped her black coffee and Hennessey. She turned and faced him, "I'm positive she's the right one. It's just a matter of persuading her."

"You forgot my fudge round." I said, as I rummaged through the white plastic bag with a yellow smiley face on it. "So, sue me. Roll up." RoNao said. "Huh? Do I look fourteen? Are you eleven? Don't say nothing. I'll answer those two questions and respond to your 'roll-up' statement. I don't think so. Self serve." I said, as I lit up the half of blunt that I was smoking on when I was talking to RoNao on the phone. I passed the blunt to RoNao. She hit the blunt with her left hand and was licking the cigar with the right hand. "Girl, you're licking like a kitten. Suck that thang, girl." I said, bringing my knees to my chest and wrapping my arms around my knees. Smiling like a chester cat. "That's what you going to be doing in Atlanta. Why do you think I asked you to roll up? Practice." "Girl, don't play with me. If she even thinks for one second that I had a thought to get down like that, she better think again!" "I was just fucking around. Maybe, she wants you to sell drugs or something like that." "I'm not about to push drugs, girl!" "Well, it's probably a legit ass job." "Yeah." "Girl... Boom. I hate to blow you up but, when have you ever know YoSaVon to be legit?" I hit the blunt and thought about it. YoSaVon's first driver's license was a fraud. One year, she kept super glue on her fingertips. I asked her, why the glue? She said, just in case. No one knows what YoSaVon does for a living but, we do know she is living a great life. She paid for Mom's house, bought Stecha's Impala, and paid for my Honda Accord. Since, Mom don't drive, YoSaVon puts fifty thousand dollars in mom's bank account, every year. Only the F.B.I. and the I.R.S. knows where she is getting her money and, maybe, not even them. "I wish you could come with me, Ro." "Yeah, me too! You gon' be aight. You might even see Nelly and Ludacris." I burst out laughing and smoking at the same time because I had just inhaled some smoke. "Girl, Nelly is from St. Louis." "I know. That doesn't mean he won't come through A.T.L. A lot of famous people come through Atlanta." "Yeah, well, I won't be looking for any of them. I, already, miss Ambrose." "Awww... poor baby. Do you need me to take you to the bus station or is Ambrose is going to take you." RoNao asked. "I'm not riding a fucking bus? Are you crazy? You're joking, right?" "No. I just thought you were going to let me keep your car until you got back. So, I can get back and forth to work. You know Stecha..." "Stick that shit. I'm renting a car. Yo, said she would pay for everything and I intend on letting her." "Word." "Already. Guess what I'm renting?" I asked. "Hell no. Too wide of a selection; just tell me." "Escalade." "Straight up!" "It do, baby. It's already lined up." I said. "Damn, you gone have to let me push that when you get back." "Hell, no. My name, alone, is on the insurance for that. Sorry, doll. But, no." I said. "Why not?" RoNao asked. "Damn, I thought I just told you why. Besides, your name, Stecha's and mine is on the Accord. "What about Ambrose's?" "Nah... because his dad own a car shop. They fix, detail, paint, and sale for retail. If he tear my shit up, I'll, easily, get another one. Ya' dig?" I asked. "Yeah." RoNao said. She stood up and stretched. I began to eat on the snacks. So, RoNao didn't offer the blunt to me until I took a break from eating. "You know what, Ro?" "What?" "I'm glad to be getting a change of scenary. And, who knows? This might be the job I've been wanting all my life."

After I cleaned the house, I lit incenses. I placed one in each room. I had to wake RoNao up. She was, almost, late for work. I hope she makes it on time. I started from the living room (spraying air freshener) and ended in the bathroom. I bathed and cooked a chicken tetrazzini with broccoli and cheese and dinner rolls.

Ambrose came home as soon as I was taking the dinner rolls out of the oven. I heard the front door slam. He came, directly, to the kitchen. I was putting the oven mitts back on the hook that was glued to the wall. Ambrose grabbed me from behind, smelled my hair, bit my shoulder, and rubbed my personal part with his right hand. "Mmph... You're such a good woman. I don't know what I'd do without you. I couldn't wait to get home; knowing you'd be here." Ambrose spun me around and pinned me against the refrigerator. We kissed. Ambrose put his forehead on mine and said, "I love you, baby." I told him that I love him, too.

After Ambrose bathed and we ate, we made love. Ambrose sat naked with his back against the bed's headboard. I was between his legs. Ambrose was flipping the channel and left it on HBO. "Baby." I said. "Hmmm?" Ambrose said. "Do you love me?" "With all my heart." "Forever?" "Forever." Ambrose said. "Well, good because I want to ask you something." I said. "Oh, Lord. Here we go." Ambrose said. I reached over the side of the bed and grabbed my T-shirt. When I did Ambrose rubbed my ass. I put my shirt on and moved to my side of the bed. "Titanic's coming on." Ambrose said flipping the channel. "I hate that movie. Old girl was so selfish. She should've shared that wood with ol' boy." He said leaving the channel on a dating show. "What's up, baby? What did you want to ask me?" Ambrose said, never taking his eyes off the T.V. screen. He lit a cigarette. "Baby, do you feel like going to get me an ashtray?" I took our plates to the kitchen, too. "Thank you, baby." He said "Un huh." I said, giving him the ashtray and thinking motherfucker trying to avoid the questions and what's that bullshit talk about the Titanic?. He used to love that movie. He even shed a tear or two. Then, he is watching a dating show. I love dating shows. Love them! He don't hate them but, he'd rather watch the news than a dating show. I lit me a cigaretted. See, I have to ask them (questions), cautiously. I don't want to argue with him. I'm not going to bring the topic up, just yet. Ambrose's real smart with a memory like a hawk. He knows I want to ask him some questions. I just want to see how long he will not mention it. He looked at me and gave me a half smile and faced the T.V., again. Bastard. Good looking motherfucker. I didn't know what to say. So, I smoked. After, the second dating show went off, I decided it was time to pay Ambrose back for ingoring me. I live for payback. The first thing I did was, I got out of bed with just my T-shirt on, walked directly in front of the bed and bend over in front of him. I was pretending to look in my drawer for some shorts. Now, I had to find out if he was looking. So, still bending over, I turned my head to the side and said, "Baby, do you want me to bring you some boxers?" Yep, he was looking. In fact, he was staring. "Huh?" Ambrose said. I stood up, still facing the drawers and smiled. I turned around. The smile no longer present. "Boxers? Do you want a pair?" "Oh, naw. I'm okay." See, it's different when you're walking around naked and when you're walking around with just enough on to do a strip tease. I find T-shirts to be the most resourceful. "Come sit down and watch T.V., baby." Ambrose said. When I sat down I made sure the shirt covered my personal part. Then, I laid flat on my back and stretched; showing off my assets. Ambrose jumped on top of me. "Un-unh, What are you doing, Ambrose?" "Baby, I..." "Baby, I, nothing. Get off of me." "Why?" Ambrose asked. "Because you should've answered my questions." "Baby, I'ma' answer your questions. Just..." I gave in.

Aftermath, we layed in bed, staring at the ceiling. The blanket was pulled up to my neck and it, barely, covered Ambrose's knees. One of his legs were bent. He had his right hand behind his head. I turned to my left; placing my hand between his shoulder and chest. I wrapped my right leg with his right leg. With my index finger on my right hand, I played with his chest hair. I was thinking 'everything about this brother is sexy.' "Baby, if the job in Atlanta is good and promising and I have to move there; Would you be willing to relocate?" Ambrose moved his hand from behind his head; threw his arm along my back, lifted me up, and raised himself. He lit two cigarettes and gave me one. "I haven't graduated, yet." Ambrose said. "I know. I'm saying, after you graduate?" "I don't know." "You don't know. What do you mean, you don't?" I asked, facing Ambrose. "Like I said, I don't know." He said. "I guess you don't love me, then." "What is that supposed to mean?" He asked. "Exactly what I said." I said. "Oh, Ava, that's such bullshit." "Is it? If the shoe was on the other foot, I would do it for you in a heartbeat." "Yeah. Well, you don't have as many priorities as I have." Ambrose said, getting out of bed, stumbling into his boxers. He went into the kitchen. He emerged from the kitchen with two can sodas. "What, do you think your occupation is more important than mine?" I asked, accepting the soda. "Did I say that?" Ambrose asked. "Basically, yeah." "No, I didn't." "Explain what you are saying, then." "All I'm saying is I have ties here. My customers that get that hair cut. Hold up, don't interrupt me. I'm the sole heir to my dad's car shop. Plus, Ava, I want to start my career here." Ambrose said. "Career here.." I said, mimicking Ambrose. "Man, come on. How much money do you make cutting hair a week? 150 to 300? I'm not saying anything about your dad's shop because I know you make good money painting cars and I know you're an only child; which makes you king of the throne whenever your father passes. But, that freaky ass old man got, at least, thirty to forty years in his tank." I said. "Anything can happen, Ava." "Duh.. like I don't know that. Shit, you could go before him and then you're talking that non-sense like you just have to start your career in Mississippi. Just because you graduate here, don't mean you have to start here, Ambrose." "I know that, Ava." "Besides, who wants to be a detective in this prejudice ass state. You're going to send a lot of innocent brothers to the pen and let a lot of guilty crackers walk." "What in the fuck are you talking about?" Ambrose asked. "I'm talking about Mississippi. I hate this fucking state. I never wanted to live here. I hate that I was born here. I want to leave, Ambrose!" "It's not so bad." "Bullshit, it's not so bad. If it's not so bad, why did you become a detective? Because Paston is doing time for some shit he didn't do?" I paused because I knew Paston was a touching part of

Marcie Parson

Ambrose's life. Paston is Ambrose's cousin. He is serving a life sentence with parole for the murder of his boss's wife. Paston found the body in the backyard of the Victorian house while he was pulling up weeds around the flower patch. He freaked out, ran into the house to call the police and was accused of her murder. She was stabbed with a garden spade. Paston was seventeen at the time. He and Ambrose were like brothers. I think the husband did it. I think he hired Paston just for that reason. Ironic, huh. A spade committed a murder with a spade. At least, I'm pretty sure that was the inside joke for the white community at the time. Nevertheless, that's, exactly, the leverage I needed to convince Ambrose to depart from dear, old, prejudice Mississippi. I continued, "No matter how hard you work or how good of a job you do; to them, You're still a nigga. Ambrose sat down on the bed with his back to me. He lit another cigarette.

"So, what do Ambrose think?" Ste cha asked as we browsed the jeans on the 50% off rack, in the department srtore in the mall. I sighed, "Nothing yet. The more I think about Atlanta, the more excited I get. You ever wanted something so bad you could taste it. "I said closing my eyes for a brief second and sniffing the air, holding the jeans to my chest and exhaling deeply. "Yeah, bitch, but you look like one of them hoes in the movies, closing your eyes, breathing all hard and shit. What's wrong with you?" Stecha said "I'm serious" I said, putting the jeans back on the rack. "I know. I felt like that about Sympathy's dad. Once, I got him I realized he wasn't what I wanted. Even though, he was good to me and still is. Something was missing. I can't put my finger on what but, it wasn't there." "Yeah." I said, thinking your cold ass heart wass there but, I don't know. No one knows that a relationship like the people involved in it. "I asked him would he move there after he graduate if I accepted the job." "And?" "Nothing. he didn't say nothing." "Damn, that's cold." Stecha said walking towards the register with about ten pairs of jeans on her arms. Five little pairs for Sympathy. "Tell me about it." I said. "I mean, YoSaVon called you out of the blue with this mysterious job, expect you to drop everything, you expect Ambrose to drop everything, you expect Ambrose to drop everything. What's really fucked up in that ya'll are engaged to be married. Girl, what you need to think about is what is really important to you. "Stecha said. I thought about it while we were at the cash register.

32

At Mom's house, Stecha said, "Look what I bought you mom." displaying a pair of jeans. Stecha bought herself an identical pair. "Ooh... mama gone wear this out, Friday. All I need, now, is a shirt." Momma said, looking at me half-expectantly. I tore my purse on the sofa beside her. She smiled and went into my wallet, then took fifty dollars. "This ought to be enough." she said putting the money in her pocket. "YoSaVon called me today. "mom said. What did she want?" I asked. "She told me I had a package at Western Union. I need one of y'all to take me to go get it." She said. "Well, you know RoNao has my car. Where is her and Sympathy?" I asked "She took Sympathy to Baskin Robbins." Stecha was busy pulling her and Sympathy's jeans out of the bags to showcase them to mom. There. "Stecha said You're missing a pair." I said scanning her receipt that she had in her hand. It only took me a split second to glance at the receipt and notice she was charged for one pair of jeans twice. "How do you know?" Stecha and mom was staring at me because the only thing I could see is the back of the receipt. "How do you know?" Stecha asked again. "Just check your receipt and your clothes." I said calmly. "Oh, they gone give me my money back." Stecha said grabbing her clothes and Mom's jeans tossing them back in the bag. "come on y'all I can take you by Western Union while we're out. "Stecha said." And I can get get me a shirt whirt while wea're in the mall" Mom said me. I thought here we got another hour in the mall. Stecha said, Why didn't you tell me when we're out there?" "I don't know." I said Honestly I was not paying attention. I was thinking about what was more important to me. Ambrose or my will to do asw I please. To finally, fulfill my needs.

Stecha and I sat on a bench as Mom stood in line at Western Union there were two young girls here. They were pointing behind Mom's back and laughing. Stecha hit my arm. I was already on it. I told you that my mom look young. They probably thought she was in her late twenties. Stecha and I stood behind them in line. The first girl said, "Girl, why is she talking like she's somebody's grandmother?" Stecha said, "Because she is somebody's grandmother, problem?" Girl two said, "Not unless you want it to be." Stecha laughed, "Want it to be. Want it to be, bitch." Mom put her money in her purse and turned. She moved between me and Stecha. "What's going on?" Mom said Stecha gave Mom the keys to the car and said, "Nothing old friends. We'll be outside in a minute." "Oh, okay." Momsaid taking the keys and she walked out the door. Stecha snapped her head back in the directions of the two girls. "Next time y'all are out in public I advise and who is with y'all to have manners because you never know with who is watching what. and bitch I'm as an honor student. So, you are asking the wrong one if they want a problem." "I'm an honor student too! What? "I said turning my head head back and forth between them. They didn't say anything. "These bitches ain't putting anything on the blackboard, lets go." Stecha said. We walked off, I turned around they were talking underneath their breath to each other with their arms folded. "Wipe the chalk off your hands, schools over, hoes" I said reaching in my purse for a cigarette and a lighter.

 "They watched him as he crossed the street leaving his car. The profile had described him efficiently. 5'11, brown hair, blue-eyes, thin and narrow nassal passage, slightly wide nostrils. 185 to 190 pounds and most importantly very dangerous. They left out that he was attractive. He looked both ways before he entered the hotel. His name was Johnathan Albert Johanneson. He's been married 15 years now. 3 children former Secret Service; currently, Congressman. His marriage is on the rocks. His wife cheats on him with a fellow congressman and he cheats on her with various women. His reason for being at this hotel wearing shades, a fake mustache, and a fake skin to make him appear to be balding is to rendezous without one of his mistresses. The reason why they're there is for the three hundred million dollars they were paid to hit him. At first, this was a hard feet to accomplish because he's so careful. He denied room service on all occasions. He make sure everything he need to accommodate his stay is in the room prior to him arriving. From their understanding, he is always carrying a pistol. He keeps a a twenty-two strapped to his ankle at all times(even during intercourse). He's smart. Too damn smart! They thought about executing him the sniper way like they've done so many others, but he's always in a crowded place. He's a master of disguise and he's never in the same vehicle. His ability to stay alive is incredible. It's a damn shame they had to kill him. He would've been a great partner to add to the firm. The only opportunity they had at penetrating him was publicly. They are against public mutilation. That's why they needed Ava. The congressman have a thing for black women with pretty eyes. YoSavon tried once, he brushed her off. If they took a chance publicly, they would risk being discovered. They couldn't take a chance with a female from an escort service. They would have to murder her, at once; breach of trust reasons. YoSaVon is the prettiest female with their firm. If she couldn't get close to him, none of them would. They watched the hotel for 8 hours. He never came out. The maid (which was with the firm) said he didn't check into his room. At that very moment, a man in a car rental uniform picked up the keys from the front desk and took the car. They left.

"Hey, Ava, are you excited?; this being you last day at work for a week." Hector asked, looking over his shoulder while standing over the wok cooking shrimp fried rice. I just looked at Hector as I leaned on the metal table with my arms crossed. I had my right leg across my left leg. "Hey... What's wrong with you, chica? Why are you giving me the cold shoulder?" "Sorry, Hector. It's not you..." "I know it's not me. What's wrong with you?" Hector asked, stirring the rice as if he were flipping pancakes. "I don't know what's wrong with me. I haven't been the same since..." I let the last sentence linger in the air. I haven't been the same since Ambrose didn't answer the questions about moving to Atlanta. I still haven't decided which is more important: my dreams or my man. I kept thinking that it was a sad predicament because my man should be top priority. I, clearly, wanted them both. I love Ambrose but, I hate Mississippi even more.

"RoNao, you understand all the guidelines about my car?" I asked. RoNao said, "Yeah, Ava, for the umpteenth time, I understand. Dang. When are you picking up the Escalade?" "Tomorrow morning. Stecha is coming to get me. I tried for you but, mom said, no cutting into school time. Damn shame. I wanted you to ride with us to Apple's, tomorrow night. In the big 'Lac. Thursday is ladies night. Hey... we gone be up in that bitch like whoa!" "Ugh... Ava, tell mom you want me to spend the night at your house." RoNao said. "Hell naw! What do you look like staying at my house like I got kids? You better ask Stecha if you can use her as a scapegoat." "Man, Stecha be tripping. Why ya'll can't wait until Friday?" RoNao asked. "Because Stecha has to work Friday evening. I'm leaving Saturday. So, I'm spending time with Ambrose, Friday night. All night." "T. M. I., cuz." RoNao said. "T. M. I., my ass." I pushed RoNao off mama's porch. "You asked. I'm telling you." I grabbed her cellphone out of the chair she was sitting. "You want to go?" I asked. "Yeah." she said. "Call Stecha, then..." gesturing for her to take the phone. RoNao and Stecha's conversation: Stecha, "Bitch, what?" RoNao, "Hey, Ste-" "What, bitch?" "Where's Sympathy?" "Sleep. What?" "Aye..." RoNao looked at me. I was moving my right hand in a circle tell RoNao to get on with it. "Nevermind." RoNao said, slamming her phone shut, tightening her eyes, and balling her lips up. "You punk!" I said, shaking my head. "Man... fuck that I just won't go. Ste is such a.." RoNao said, getting saved by the bell. Her ringtone went off; playing Young Joc's "It's Going Down". It was Stecha. "Answer your damn phone." I demanded with my left hand on my hip. "Hell, No!" RoNao said. "Give me the damn phone." I snatched the phone from her and opened it. "Bitch, don't be hanging up in my face." "I didn't, hoe. That was RoNao. Ay... that shit rhymes." I said. "How cute. Where's that punk bitch at?" "She's right here." I said. "Well, give the bitch the phone." "Let me ask you for her. She don't want to get back on the phone. You scared her. Haha." "If that hoe ain't used to me by now. Girl, fuck it." "Anyway, she want you to ask mom can she spend the night over you house, tomorrow. So, she can go out with us." I stated. "Tell the bitch to ask me, herself." I gave RoNao the phone. "She said, ask for yourself." RoNao said, "Ay, you'll ask mom if I can stay over your house, tomorrow. So, I can go out with ya'll?" "Naw., bitch." Stecha said and hung up the phone.

The Champagne colored Escalade was a beauty. I loved it. It cost me five stacks just to rent it for ten days. Not including the deposit and insurance. Stecha, RoNao, and I pulled in front of Le ebo's apartment. No one got out to knock. I was feeling too classy to be blowing the horn. Stecha called her and told her to bring her bitch ass on before she left. Le ebo, finally, emerged from the house; six minutes later. "Bitch, what took you so long?" Stecha asked, turning to face Le ebo. "This bitch! Clock out, your bitchiness is not needed, tonight." "Naw but, my styling tips are. You are too damn black for that blue eyeshadow. Take that shit off and switch to off-green." Stecha said. Le ebo did as Stecha asked. I bet Le ebo was thinking,'Stecha is so up-to-date on trend." We rode around town about two hours, broadcasting the 'Lac and our undefined beauty. By the time we made it to Apple's, it was eleven thirty and the line was extremely long. "I'm not waiting in that long ass line with these heels." RoNao said. All three of us looked back at her and laughed. "Did you think we were? Girl, get with the program." Le ebo said. I grabbed RoNao's arm. "Look, you're going to lead us in. The guy at the door is Marco. Touch him on his chest with your right hand. When he leans over, you whisper Titsil in his ear." I said. "Titsil?" RoNao asked. "Yeah, too important to stand in line and don't ever repeat that, bitch." Stecha said. "Got me?" "Yeah." "Let's go. We're the grand finale."

Indeed, we were. when we walked in the club it was like everything moved in slow-motion. All the dope boys, businessmen, and young entrepreneurs stopped what they were doing and indulged themselves with our presence. The only other females in the club were all Titsil. We all had an unspoken understanding. Each cliche had their own little section of the club. Every baller was viewed as A. P. (anybody's property). No titsil bought herself a drink. Under no circumstances, did a Titsil smoke or danced in the club. We were there to be pretty. Pretty and that's it! We would play pool; only one game per Titsil. Most of the time we just socialized. The only time we would dance is when the D.J. cleared the floor and announced, 'Premium Cut Only'. Marco would stand at the (now chained) dance floor and wait for the password to enter. Some females would try to enter by whispering 'premium cut' to Marco. He will reject them. How embarrassing. Why would they think the D.J. would announce the password out loud. The minimum we would stay on the floor is five minutes. The maximum we would ask them to chain the floor is thirty minutes. "Well, well, well.. if it isn't the honor student." Girl one from the Western Union said. Le ebo had, already, picked up the hand fan and began to fan herself, slowly. There are, always, four fans on the table. The first fan means things are getting heated up. Two fans means security. That's right, you can get kicked out of the club behind a titsil. That's one reason why we love Apples. Three fans at one time is to let other titsils know back up might be needed. That only happened once. Each titsil had to, respectfully, pay five hundred dollars, each, for damages. Debating the matter lead to immediate termination. Failure to pay within the issued date meant the same; disqualification. There was an anti-titsil group. They were banned from the club. All four fans means there's an unwanted brother at the table. Marco or someone from his entourage will (politely) ask the brother to leave the table. A titsil is obligated to keep two outfits at the club at all times with a pair of stilettos to match both outfits. It's your responsibility to keep them changed, fresh and dry cleaned. Usually, one cliche will take a month to dry clean the clothes. Then, the next cliche will be responsible the next month and so on, and so on... RoNao turned to girl one, and smiled. "That's right. It's me, tonight. I'm too cute. So, if you'll be so kind as to excuse yourselves. Surely, you've noticed we are previously occupied." Girl two said, "Bitch, fuck ya'll being occupied!" I stepped in, holding RoNao's arm. I knew she was desperate to punch someone. "Ladies, you are, clearly, outnumbered. Now, you either leave this table or you leave this club." Too late. Stecha began to fan herself. "Well." I said. "I tried to give you the benefits of the doubt. It seems my associates here do not want your presence at the table or in the club. With that being said; goodnight, ladies." At that moment, two of Marco's goons escorted them out the door. "Damn." RoNao said. "How did those guy know? That was smooth as fuck!" RoNao said. Someone ordered us some Dom Perignon, Grey Goose, Hennessey, Gin, and Patron. RoNao looked around. "Don't do that." Stecha said. As we drank or sipped, we explained The Rules of T.I.T.S.I.L. to her; beginning with: no cursing, at all, in the club. The rest of the night was spent in club bliss. We all shot a game of pool. Two brothers joined us at the table (which seats eight) for thirty minutes. They knew the rules. One kept looking at his watch to see how much time they had left. We visited other titsils, as they did us, and introduced RoNao. The D.J. even called premium-cut only. Almost. all the titsils danced about ten minutes. It was good. The dance floor was left unattended for some time because some of those people did not ever get off the dance floor. Men and women, alike. I just don't see how some women don't mind sweating. That is so unlady like. After the club, we were all invited to Ruby Tuesday. We all declined except, the excited RoNao. We made her change her mind.

RoNao called me about ten thirty the next day. "I'm on my lunch break." she said. "I'm on my smoke break." I said. "What's up, RoNao?" "Okay... So, I want to know why you and Le ebo are living below your means?" "Below our means?" I said, holding smoke in my lungs. "Yeah, I mean what we did last night was like a fairytale. Why ya'll won't move into a house like what Stecha got?" I thought about what she said. To be honest, the weed just had me daydreaming. "Hmmm... It's not like we can't. It's just that we're content where we're at, right now." "Well, can Le ebo move? I mean, she don't work." RoNao said. "Girl, she's getting more money than the mayor. That's the truth. Check this out, I woke up this morning and the Escalade was missing but, Ambrose's 'lac was still outside. So, I called him, right?" "Right." "This brother took the Escalade to school. Talking about stunting." "Well, he left you the keys the 'lac, right?" "That's a dumb question. I'm not answering that." "Well, when you get back from Atlanta, I want to go back to Apples." I exhaled some smoke and looked at the blunt. "We don't make appearances. like that. Shit, you will know about the next time we go. Alright?" "Yeah." "Well, I have errands to run before I make my way to the mall and visit mom. You'll, probably, be there when I come by mom's. I'll holla at you, either way. Even if I have to call you. You'll hear from me before I leave... and RoNao?" "Yeah, Ava." "Save some of that money you're making. Don't let Mom or that nigga rob you. I'll be gone five days. So, I'm leaving you 250 dollars for gas, okay? You don't have to pay me that back. I'm leaving you sixty dollars to take my car to get tuned and, remember, do not let that nigga drive my car. I'll know if you do. I got eyes everywhere. You wouldn't believe." I said. "Oh yes, I will." "Look, I'm blowed. I'm about to watch T. V. and take a nap." "What time are you leaving, tomorrow?" RoNao asked. "Probably about two towards setting." "Oh, well. Be safe, okay? I love you, Ava." "I love you, too, Ro! Ciao." "Ciao"

After visiting Mom and the mall, I returned home and packed my suitcase; then I opened it and checked off the items on my inventory list. I smoked a blunt. Then, I checked my list, again. I cooked a nice dinner of steak, macaroni and cheese in chicken broth and bread crumbs, sweet peas, and croissants. Ambrose called me when he was headed home. How convenient! I ran his bath water with bubble bath, milk and baby powder. You have to apply the baby powder and milk, first or it will dissolve the bubbles. Then, I took the rose petals(I bought them like that; just petals) and spread them from the front door to the bathroom. I had two wine glassed in the bathroom. The Chardonnay was on ice. I lit the candles in the bathroom. I went to the kitchen to get an ashtray to place in the bathroom. I put four cigarettes and a lighter in the ashtray. I turned the stereo on in the bedroom. I put five C. D.'s in the C. D. changer. All mixed C. D.'s. I didn't want to get caugt off guard with a jumpy song. The music, to me, is the most important item of all. That is why I selected the music to be played. I checked the C. D. arrangement to make sure Natural Woman by Aretha Franklin was the last song to be played. After that, I went into the front room(that was impeccably clean) plugged in the night light and lit one scented candle and taped to the floor a note that read: follow me. Don't ever put rose petals in front of the door. They'll just get stepped on. I checked to make sure. I put the remaining rose petals in Ambrose's bath water. Check. Finally, I checked myself to see how I looked in my brand new brassiere and panty set. It was blue and black. His favorite colors. I purchased it from Victoria's Secret. I thought to myself 'it should be a sin to be this fine.' I heard Ambrose shut the door outside. Damn, those Escalades ride smooth. They creep up on you. I pulled the cover halfway back on the bed, grabbed my stilettos, and rushed to the bathroom. In the bathroom, I put some clear eyes in my eyes. Shit. I'm high as hell.

Ambrose was naked when he entered the bathroom. I was standing up, leaning most of my weight on right leg. I had two wineglasses in my hand; half full with Chardonnay. I handed Ambrose a glass. He took it and swallowed it in one gulp. I thought,'fucking savage; didn't even sip the shit. I looked him up and down. I stopped when I noticed his erection. It looked larger than normal but, I was high, remember? Maybe, it was that 'remember me penis when you're out of town.' I knew what was next. So, I gulped the Chardonnay just like my savage man did. Ambrose grabbed me, kissed me, then turned me around. He pushed my hair to one side. Then, begin kissing on my neck. He pulled my panties down and we fucked for about ten minutes. I braced myself on the sink. Then, Ambrose slowed it down and turned me around, again. We started to kiss, again. He stopped kissing me and took off my brassiere. He took a blanket and laid it on the laundry room's floor. I'm a lady. I, already, gave you too much of an insight of our love making. Use your imagination. It was so good.

We ended up bathing together. After we ate, I blew out the candles, picked up the roses, and placed them in a bowl of cold water. We were in bed. I asked Ambrose if it was okay if I smoked? Ambrose said, "I don't care. What do you want to watch?" "The Titanic." "Ha. ha. very funny. How many blunts you smoked, today?" "This is my first one." I lied, tossing the cigar stuffing into the waste basket. "What..? I can't believe that." I can't, either. I thought, breaking the weed down; stuffing the cigar. Ambrose said, "Girl, why are you lieing? There are two fat ass roaches in the ashtray." "I was just testing you detective skills." I said, looking over my shoulder. "Yeah, okay. Whatever. Lieing ass." Ambrose said, pulling at his pubic hairs. I finished rolling the blunt. "Did you just call me a liar?" I asked Ambrose with my right hand between my chest; looking appalled. "Yes, I did." Ambrose said, pulling me close to him. "But, you're my little liar." He said. It's funny how marijuana make one self conscious, curious, relaxed, and paranoid all at the same time. We were watching "Cheaters". I stubbed the cherry off the blunt and asked Ambrose. "So, if I get this job are you coming with me or what?" "I hope you don't get it." "Aw. That's messed up. Why not?" "Because." "Because what?" "Because I don't want to lose you." "Lose me?" "That's right, Ava. I love you. I know you love me, too! I just think it's unfair for your sister to butt in our life like this. I feel like she's going to tear us apart. In fact, I know she is; today seems the last day of us being an us. My heart has been aching, all day. Even when we were fu making love, Ava. It just didn't seem right. It felt like the first time for the last time." Ambrose said, looking down at his stomache. A single tear rolled down his cheek. "Oh... baby. That's not true." I said, feeling uncertain of myself. I reached to wipe the tear from his face. Ambrose grabbed my wrist mid-way. Now, he was fully crying. "If it's not true, why didn't you tell her no, Ava?" "You're my hurting my arm." I said, trying to free myself from his grip. He ignored my statement and my attempt to get free. He squeezed my wrist tighter. "Huh, Ava? Why didn't you tell her no? What are you looking for? Why aren't you happy here? Don't I make you happy? Huh, Ava? Don't I? Don't I?" I slapped him. He let go, put both of his hands on his face, and started sobbing. I ran to the bathroom and locked the door. Ambrose started banging on the door. Apologizing; asking me to come out. "Ava, come out! Don't you understand that I love you. I just don't want to lose you." "Go away, Ambrose!" I yelled, looking in the mirror. I turned on the cold water and rinsed my face off. I heard Ambrose return to the bedroom. I looked at my reflection; water dripping off my chin, nose, and eyelashes. I grabbed a towel, wet it, and dried my face. I was thinking,'Hell, Ambrose is right. YoSaVon was wrong for interrupting my calm and serene home. Can you blame her though; wanting to give her sister the opportunity to get more out of life? What was it that I was looking for? It, damn, for sure wasn't in Mississippi. And why not? Ambrose is here. My family. That wasn't enough for me. I, always, wanted more. Craved more. Hell, YoSaVon even invited Ambrose to come along. I'm questioning my love but, what about his love? He says he loves me. If he did, he would follow me to the end of the world. Why can't he make some sacrifices, too? I would do it for him. See, that's where men and women are different. Women always make sacrifices. Well, not this time. I love Ambrose. I, really, do but, if.. if I take this job, he's has to make a sacrifice. We'll see how much and how deep is his love. I've always been nice; always be the one to be lenient. When the truth is... I'm not nice, at all.

When I came out of the bathroom Ambrose was sitting on the bed; watching T.V. I couldn't tell because he was high! "Ambrose, you don't smoke weed!" "I just did." "Oooohh, Ambrose." "Oooohh, what? I'm a grown ass man. Besides, I'm not a detective, yet." We were silent while we both smoked cigarettes. "So, what are we going to do, now?" Ambrose asked. "Nothing but, wait." I said. I looked at Ambrose. When I stopped looking at him; he looked at me. I wonder if he was thinking the same thing I was: It's all on you. Everything is riding on you. We fell asleep.

The Trip

"YOU MAKE SURE YOU KEEP your cell phone on you at all times. Do you have nine, one, one on speed dial?" "Yes, Mama." "Where is that boy? Why isn't he here?" "Mama, I thought we discussed that, already. I'm going to call Ambrose, once, I get on the highway." "Well, okay." Mama said. She grabbed both of my shoulder and gave them a firm squeeze. "You call me, once, you've made it there safe and sound. Alright? Alright, baby?" "Yeah, mama." "Be careful, baby. I'm about to freshen up. Stecha's taking me and Louise to the casino!" Mama said, walking towards her walk-in closet. She paused, turned around, smiled and said, "Tell YoSaVon, I love her and thanks for everything." She disappeared into her closet. I punched RoNao in her shoulder. "Ya'll gone get enough of using me as a punching bag. One day I'm going to snap." RoNao said, holding her shoulder. "Snap, then." I punched her, again. She charged me with her head down. She threw her arms around my stomach and back. She pushed me into a wall. The wall held a large, clothe picture of some dogs sitting around a table playing cards. I started to elbow RoNao's back. Once, she had me against the wall, she started to punch me in the side of my legs. Real fast, too! I grabbed her under her arms and started kneeing her. I made sure to avoid her face. I heard Mom coming. So, I let her go. RoNao grabbed me and put me in the headlock. Mom started to yell, "What in the hell is going on in here?" RoNao looked up, saw Mama, and took off running. Mom chased her, "Get your ass back here!" I was laughing behind Mom's back. She couldn't catch RoNao. So, she turned to me. "What in the hell is going on? Are you okay, baby?" My smile faded. I was walking towards the door while talking, "I don't know what got into her." I said. "I guess she's upset because I told her she couldn't go to Atlanta with me." Once, I was close to the door, I said, "Mom, you know I love you, right?" "Yeah." "So, you know I can't lie to you, right?" "Yeah." "Well, we were just playing." I said that last sentence fast and took off running.

I met up with RoNao. She was on the corner smoking a cigarette she bummed from some cat on the block. "Let me catch that short." I said, out of breath. I bent over and put my hands on my knees. "When... girl, you got some fight in you. That's what's up." "Thanks." RoNao said, passing me the short that was left on the cigarette. We heard a loud thumping sound. The sound kept coming and it kept thumping. We looked at each other and said, "Stecha." We saw the blue Impala two blocks away. "Damn, her shit sound good." RoNao said. "Oh, bitch, don't stunt like mine don't." I said. "Yeah, yours sound good." "I know." The truth is Stecha's system is decked out. She have 2 fifteen's, 2 twelves, 2 amps, and tweekers all over. Ay, my shit is still hitting, though. I could, easily, match that; but, why bother? I plucked the cigaretted away. Stecha stopped, rolled down her windows, and put her music on mute. "What's up, hoes? Ya'll working the block, early. Ain't it?" Stecha asked with a smirk on her face. "You know, it don't make sense if it don't make money. I'm checking on my hoe. How much money you done made, bitch?" I said to RoNao in my best pimp voice. Stecha threw two dollars out of her car window. "Un-unh, baby." RoNao said, "You're in the wrong neighborhood with that shit. Ain't no two dollar hoes around here." "Can't tell." Stecha said, then directed her attention towards me. "When are you leaving?" She said. "Two towards setting." I said. "Bitch, you ready, ain't it?" Stecha said, taking off her shades. "Hell, yeah! Where's Sympathy?" "Pateka has her." "Girl... Pateka's only ten." "Duh... bitch. Like I'd leave my baby with a ten year old. Santina's at home." Stecha said, "I'm about to take Mama to.." "..the casino. I know. She, already, told me." I said. RoNao saw her friend guy and walked off. "Yeah, but, I bet she didn't tell you why I'm taking her and not RoNao." Stecha said, hitting her pipes. I thought about why RoNao wasn't taking Mom. In fact, that's why! I hit her in the arm. Anyway. "Why?" I asked non-chalantly. "Because, I have a date and we're meeting at The Revolving Door restaurant and pub. He is going to dine and wine me. The very next date I'm asking that nigga for a stack. I need to know how deep his pockets run." "A stack ain't shit! Ask that nigga for six stacks. Who is this brother, anyway?" "Damn, Sis. Can I take it slow? I'm making love to this nigga's pockets. You want me to fuck his pockets." "Right. Who is this brother?" "Do you remember 'keep track of time' at the club?" "Them cats at the table with us?" "Yeah." "Stecha, you know A. P.s are off limits as far as dating." "And what?" "And when he hit the club he will still be considered A. P. That's what. Ya'll won't be able to make it known that y'all are a couple in Apples." I said. "A couple. That nigga started off as anybody's property and he will continue to be A. P., got that? All I need is two weeks to get twenty bean beans. He gets no sex. Nothing! Can you dig that?; And T.I.T.S.I.L. can continue to drain liquor, pool games, and dinner at Ruby Tuesday out of him, okay?" "Yeah, okay. I just hope he's not expecting a relationship. You're playing with fire Ste'." "What is this? Why are you giving me the third degree? I, always, handle myself well; haven't I?" Ste said, snapping her neck. "Yeah, Ste'." "Well, don't start drilling me, now. If that cat gets out of line, I got something that will set his ass straight." Ste said. She placed her car in the park gear. Ste reached under her seat. The next time I saw her right hand it was holding a small gun. The weapon was a twenty five. The handle was pearl. "Click. Click, nigga." Ste said pointing her gun at me and squeezing the trigger. I jumped. "Bitch, don't play with me with a fucking gun. Are you crazy?" I asked. "Chill out. It's not loaded." "I don't know that. If you were someone else, I would've knocked your ass out." I said, pointing my index finger at her. "Yeah, whatever. You're lucky I'm no-one else because you don't want none." Ste' said. She placed her gun into a holder. "Hold up, then." I said with a smile throwing my head back. Stecha got out of her car. "You ain't saying nothing. What's up?" Ste' said. RoNao walked up. "Look what I got?" She showed us five hundred dollars. "Where'd you get that?" I asked. "That's what I thought." Stecha said, getting back in her car. "Girl, gone somewhere before I sic Ro' on you." Stecha laughed, "That hoe ain't gone do shit." "What are y'all talking about?" RoNao asked. "We are talking about that five hundred dollars that you need

to donate to charity. You small time hoe. Pick them two dollars up, bitch."
Ste said, hitting her pipes. "Man, I'm tired of you, always, talking bad about
me. You're a negative ass bitch." RoNao said. "Are we getting serious here?
Because if we are, you lit' skeezer, let me know." Stecha said. She turned her
car, completely, off. She opened her door and emerged, once more. "It do."
RoNao said. "It do what, bitch?" Stecha said, pushing RoNao's head. I
jumped in between them. "Man, Y'all chill out. What's wrong with y'all?" I
said with an arm on both of their chest. "Ain't nothing wrong with me. It's
this humorless ass broad that's something wrong with and don't act like
Ava's stopping you. I'm right here." Stecha said. RoNao swung. Stecha
backed up and went around me. She punched Ro three times in her face.
Ro grabbed Stecha's hair. "Bitch, let go of my hair." Stecha said. RoNao
punched Stecha in the face. Stecha grabbed RoNao's hair and pushed her
on the hood of her car. "Let go of my hair." Ro said. "Let go of mine." Stecha
punched RoNao. RoNao punched Stecha. Stecha banged RoNao's head
against the car hard. RoNao started crying. They tangled. I broke it up.
RoNao was still crying. "I hate you, bitch!" A crowd gathered. RoNao's
boyfriend put his arm around her and they walked up the street. Damn, I
felt guilty. I should've never initiated that but, I was just playing. I was just
about to ask RoNao for two C-notes back. Stecha is mean as hell but, damn
she can hold up. Stecha was smoothing out her shirt. She looked at me and
asked what. "You're wrong for that shit." "Ain' wrong for shit. She needs to
grow up." Stecha ws back n her car fixing her hair in her rearview mirror.
She checked her make-up. "She'll get over it. If she don't, fuck her." Ste' said.
"See, that's what I'm talking about you-" "Naw, you ain't talking about shit.
Talk to your motherfucking self." Ste' said and pulled off. I had to back up
so she wouldn't run over my feet. She pulled in front of mom's house and
blew the horn. Mom scuttled out; oblivious to the events that just happened.
Ste' stopped the car and rolled down the passenger side window. Mom said,
"Well baby, I know you're grown but, you're still my baby. So, please be safe
and know that I love you. Don't forget to call me when you get there, okay?"
"Okay, mama. I love you, too!" I said. "Come here. Give me a hug." Mama
said. When I stuck the top part of my body into the car to hug Mama,
Stecha hit her pipes. I looked at her like 'bitch, if you do.' She looked at me
like 'and if I do, then what?' I held mom a second longer just to dare her. I
told them both I loved them. Stecha said, "Yeah, Whatever." She hit the

accelerator allowing no further verbal communication. Mom didn't and would not ever find out about that fight. That would be the first thing I tell YoSaVon. I waited around for RoNao to come back to Mama's house. Ambrose was waiting at the house for me. I called him and told him that I was waiting for RoNao and that I would be there within the hour. RoNao came in and walked past me. "RoNao?" I said. "What?" She stopped and turned around. "Look, I apologize for starting all that drama, back there. I was just playing." I said, shaking my head side to side; looking down at my hands. "I didn't mean for it-" "To what? Get out of hands? Well, it's been out of hands with us. She don't like me and I don't like her." RoNao said, walking to her room. I stood in her bedroom doorway. "That's not true, Ro'. Stecha's just-" "How do you know, Ava? You're always backing her up. Even when she's saying something negative about you, you just brush it off." "That's because I know she don't mean any harm. Everybody's different. You can't expect everyone to have the same personality." I said. "I don't expect everyone to be the same but, she's never nice. Not even to people who are nice to her. Look, how she did Sympathy's dad. I hate to say it and God knows I don't wish bad luck on no-one but, one day that shit is going to come back on her.

"Ambrose. Ambrose, wake up, baby." I said, rolling him over and sitting on top of his pelvis. He awoke, slowly, and place his left hand on my butt. He placed his right hand behind his head. "Mmmm.... Hey, baby. What time is it?" He asked. He raised his pelvic bone and made his best attempt to stretch. It was a sexy, little move. "It's ten thirty. Let's get something to eat." "I don't want any food. I want you. What happened at your mom's house?" "Stecha and RoNao got into a fight." He yawned again, "Who did they get into a fight with?" "Each other." "Each other?" "Yeah." "Who won?" "Ambrose, I don't want to answer that. It was all my fault." "Your fault? How?" I told him everything as I paced back and forth. I walked the carpet in front of the television. Now, he was wide awake and smoking a cigarette. "Who won?" Ambrose asked again. "Stecha did but, RoNao held up." "That lit' ass woman can brawl, huh? ha. ha. I don't mean to laugh but, the shit is funny." Ambrose said. He was snickering to himself with a fist to his mouth. "Hmmph. It is now that it's over. RoNao is hurt behind it. She's going through a lot with her mom being in prison, and all. She's about to graduate and she feels like nobody cares about her but, me." "Well, I don't mean to be rude but, she's not the only one with problems. She ought to be thankful. She lives in a nice home. Your mother takes care of her like she's her own. She have all the luxuries in life any kid from a middle-class home wish they could have. She's throwing herself a pity party. I'm glad I didn't receive an invitation." He snubbed out a cigarette and looked at me like he was expecting a rebuttal. Surprisingly, I did not want to appeal it. Actually, I agreed with him. "So, how much time do we have before you hit the road?" Ambrose asked. "I don't have a certain time to leave. I plan on leaving at two. Damn, I still have to call YoSaVon. I, almost, forgot. Excuse me, baby." I said, as I walked to the front door. I went outside and pressed the number two that speed dial to YoSaVon's number. I promised Mom that I would put nine- one- one on speed dial set for one. She picked up after the first ring. "It do." "YoSaVon." "Are you making any progress?" "Certainly. I'm leaving at two." "Good. You should make it here around seven thirty." "Where are we to meet?" I asked. "In Buckhead at the Hilton hotel." "The Hilton in Buckhead." "Yes. Is Ambrose coming with you?" "Unfortunately, no." "How long can you stay?" "A week max." "Hmmm... You couldn't stay any longer?" "I doubt it. My relationship is on the line here. Ambrose proposed to me." "Congratulations. I'll see you around seven thirty to eight o'clock, then." "Yeah. Oh, Mama said thanks for everything." I said. There was a pause on the other end. "For what?" YoSaVon finally asked, "I guess the money you send her, annually." YoSaVon did something I haven't heard her do in months. She laughed. "Yeah, right. Get here." "It do." "Done." YoSaVon said. I told myself that I would call her again at five thirty. I decided that I would tell about RoNao and Stecha's fight face to face. I wondered why she just didn't tell me to tell Mom she is welcome.

"It's done." YoSaVon told him. "Great when is she schedule to arrive?" He asked. "At eight o'clock... So far, she can only stay one week." "We'll just have to work fast, then. Now, won't we? How long do you think it will take to convince her to take the job and how long will it take to train her?" "Two days to do both. That leaves us with four days to sting." YoSaVon said. YoSaVon's phone vibrated. "It do." YoSaVon said. She placed a finger to her lips; motioning for him to be quiet. It was Ava. "I know this is a little late to be asking you but, what is this job you are recommending me for?" Ava asked. "I apologize for not informing you, Ava. It's computer technology, of course." YoSaVon said and looked at him. He winked his eye. YoSaVon set her phone to voicemail before it rang, again. She didn't want Ava's curiosity to seize her, again. She didn't want to answer of Ava's question's. Not at the moment, anyway. "Computer technology?" He asked. He stood amused by how YoSaVon did not hesitate to give Ava an answer. "Yes. She studied it two years in college. Using that field as a reference will satisfy any suspicion her boyfriend wonders about. Besides, we do need her to terminate a virus."

"Computer technology." Ava told Ambrose. She was hoping that he would be happy for her. "Great. I hope you get it." Ambrose said, really, flat. There was no hint of excitement in his voice. He knew she loved computers. He just didn't expect her to get an offer to work with them. He didn't even want her to work. He rather she stay at home and be a housewife. He was (more than) prepared to take care of her as long as she lived. He planned to have her set to live comfortable after his death. "You don't sound too excited." Ava said. "Why should I be? My fiance is... Look, let's not talk about this, right now. You're leaving in less than three hours. We've had this talk, already. Let's just drop it. All we can do, now, is just see what happns." He said. He was thinking there is no way he is going to let her move to Atlanta. He, definitely, was not moving there. No matter what. If she move there, she didn't love him to begin with. She has to understand that he's the only one who will take over his father's shop. Okay. So what, his father had twenty, maybe, thirty more years in him. There's still a lot Ambrose had to learn about running a business. A pretty prominent one, at that. If he didn't pursue criminal investigation, managing his dad's shop will make him a millionaire in less than ten years. "So, where are we eating?" I asked Ambrose. I notice he was in a daze. Food, always, gets his attention. "Huh?... Is wh... La Comida de Cocina opened, yet?" "It will be when we get there." "Let's eat there, then." Ambrose said. "... and baby, it's La Cocina de Comida." Ava said. She grabbed his hand and pulled him off the bed. "Tomatoe. Tomato." Ambrose said. He squeezed my ass. "Don't start nothing you can't finish." I said, as Ambrose pulled back on the bed and said, "Oh, I intend on finishing this. You just pray I don't start again after this time."

"Damn, Ava, you look so... cute." LeBoMe said, as she place the silverware on the napkins. She was the waitress at the table Ambrose and I were sitting. "Thanks." I said, blushing. "Where did you get that dress?" She asked. I had on a now-n-later green color dress. It was strapless. I wanted to wear something that would bring out my eyes. It was tight (all over) but, not uncomfortable tight. My hair was down and full of body. My hair was knotted on top of my head. I had pink chopsticks in it (to match my pink stilettos and the large pink velcro belt that was under my breast). My eyeshadow was green. I wore pink lipstick. I had few trinkets to accessorize my attire. "...from Malcom's in the Mall." I said. "That expensive ass store! Girl... What brand is it?" "Donna Karen." "How much?" "It was cheap." I said, looking at Ambrose. I wished that LeBoMe would run off and get our fucking drinks and get the fuck out of my business in front of Ambrose. I could see if LeBoMe and I were chilling; smoking a blunt. She knows you don't ever ask how much something costs in front of a man. "How much?" Ambrose asked. He lit a cigarette. I looked at LeBoMe like, 'bitch, go get the damn drinks!'. "I want a Coca-Cola, light on the ice, and Ambrose wants an iced-tea with two lemons. I said to LeBoMe. "Are you ready to order, yet?" "No, just go get the drinks, please. My throat is dry." "Okay. I will be right back." "So, will I. Excuse me." I said to Ambrose. I was walking close behind LeBoMe. When we were out of Ambrose's eyesight I pulled her in the bathroom. "Bitch, what is wrong with you asking those bogus ass questions in front of Ambrose, like that?" I said. I was leaning so close to her. I swear our faces were two inches apart. "My bad." She said. "Your bad? You know the game, girl. When was the last time you had some dick, bitch?" "I don't know. Why?" "I suggest you get some because you're slipping, bitch." This dude has a memory like a hawk (when he wants). I sat down and smiled. "How much did the dress cost, Ava?" I wasn't going to lie to him. Hey, He asked. "$398.59. It was on sale." I said. I turned my head and watche LeBoMe bring our drinks. He never took his eyes off me. At least, he waited for LeBoMe to leave before he asked, "You just don't believe in budgeting, do you? You can't shop at J. C. Penny's or Dillard's, can you?" "As a matter of fact, I can and I do. Is it a crime to treat myself?" "Depends on where you got the money." "From you, of course." He was drinking when I said that. He, almost, spit his drink on me. He swallowed and started coughing. He grabbed his napkin. About thirty seconds later, He asked, "From me?" "Yeah, from you." "How?" "Our joint account." I said with a grin on my face like a kid at McDonald's playhouse. "Damn, baby. Why are you so bad?" He asked grabbing both of my hands and kissing them. "I was born this way."

I remember when I was in the eigth grade. My mother insisted that I took J. R. O. T. C. Why? I don't know. I guess it was, maybe, because YoSaVon took it. Hell, she stuck with it until she graduated. I must admit I liked the marching, the drills, and the cadence but, I couldn't stand the instructor. He walked around with an air of seniority. He walked stiff and talked stiff. I used to daydream about ways of destroying him. His mind and career; I wanted it gone. One day, I stole a letter from a boy. He wrote a love letter to his girlfriend. I practiced John Doe's handwriting for two weeks. When I felt I had his handwriting down packed, I wrote a letter in John Doe's handwriting. In that letter, I wrote about the horrifying, lewd, and lascivious things that our J. R. O. T. C. instructor had down to John Doe. I accused the instructor of molestation. The letter was supposed to be like a diary entry. I dropped it in the principal's mailbox. Well, needless to say, our instructor was suspende the remainder of my time in J. R. O. T. C. (eigth grade) and the boy... Well, I didn't like him, anyway. Why do you think I choose him? Randomly? No, he was a kiss ass. Let's just say, people still question his sexuality. It was a major blow what happened at the school. It even made the newpaper. My Mom happened to find the boy's letter that I was practicing with. One day, I was doing my homework. My mom sitting, directly, across from me reading the fucking letter! I noticed, she kept looking at me over the top of the letter. A black car with mirror tint pulled up outside and blew the horn. My Mom balled up the letter and threw it, hitting me directly between the eyes. She left. I grabbed the balled up piece of paper that was, now, on the floor. When I opened it and saw what it was, my eyes, almost, jumped out of my head. I thought I destroyed all copies. No. No. This was the original. I knew it was the original because I wrote plan and destroy at the top and bottom of the paper. But, how? I hid this paper good. So, how did she find it? I went outside and burned the rest of the evidence that could link me to the crime. You know what, though? My Mom did not ever say anything about it. She tortured me; reminding me of the incident by calling me "oily" for three months. I had to beg her to call me Ava, again. I didn't care too much for nicknames, since then.

"Be safe and have fun." LeBoMe said, as we were leaving the restaurant. "Thanks. Tell Hector, I will see him when I get back." I said. I gave her a hug and made sure I didn't smear my make-up. "You just make sure you come back." LeBoMe said, looking at me with teary eyes. "Man.. LeBoMe, don't do that. Save the tears for the wedding." "I know. It's just that I'm going to miss you." "I'm going to miss you, too. But, it's not like I'm leaving forever. I'll be back before you know it." I said. Ambrose got in between us and said, "Yeah. So, back off, BoMe. She's not your girl. She's mine. Ain't that right, baby?" He said. He gave me three small kisses on my lips. "That's right." I said grabbing him around the waist. He threw his arms over my shoulders. I looked backed at LeBoMe as we left the restaurant. I said bye. I threw my hand in the air and waved at LeBoMe. She waved back. Jorge was standing in the kitchen door, washing his hands on a dish rag. Jorge waved bye, too. Ambrose and I drove seperate cars to the restaurant because I was determined to leave from the restaurant. We shared a passionate kiss in the parking lot. Ambrose trailed me on the highway for about forty-five minutes to the next town. There, we stopped at a gas station and shared another passionate kiss. We talked about ten minutes, smoked a cigarette, and shed a few tears. Ambrose hugged me like he didn't want to let me go. I didn't want to let him go, either. After, we said our 'see you, laters', I watched him disappear into traffic from behind the wheel of the Escalade. I sat there and cried with my head on my hands that rested on the steering wheel. I was brought out of my crying spell when my phone rang.

"Where are you?" It was Stecha. I was sniffling.. "In Jackson." I said. I was rummaging through my purse looking for my make-up kit. Stecha started laughing, "Oh, ho. I know you're not crying." "I was. Ambrose just left." "Oh, look." She paused like the next sentence was labor pains. "I wanted to apologize about earlier. No hard feeling?" She asked. "No. none. I'm used to you." "Good because I will forever be a bitch. Hey, Ava?" "Yeah." "I love you." "What... what's wrong with you? Are you okay?" "Hell yeah, I'm okay." "I love you, too, Stecha. If you, really, love me, you'll do me a favor." "What's that?" "You'll apologize to RoNao." "Apologize for what?" "Nevermind. You know, earlier, you said that she needs to grow up. Why don't you set an example by showing her how grown people squash beef and apologize." Stecha was quiet about six seconds. "Yeah. Whatever." "You know what RoNao told me?" "What?" Ste ask. "She told me that she don't think you like her too much." I said, fixing my make-up. "That's bullshit. If it's the case of my attitude, then I don't like anybody." "That's for sure but, you could be a little nicer to her. We're the only sisters she's got. She needs people to look up to not stand up to." "Yeah, you're right. I'm going to apologize. I might even buy her an outfit." "Awww... that's so-" "Don't start, bitch, with your punk ass." "How was your date?" I asked, wiping my hands with a baby wipe. I put my make-up back in my purse and started the Escalade. I lit a cigarette and started towards the highway. "It was okay. He's not my type, though. He's too stuck up. He owns three gas stations. No kids and dig this... he's an angler." "An angler?" "Yeah, girl." "What in the hell is that?" "A fucking proper name for fisherman." We both laughed. Stecha said, "Well, I just wanted to wish you good luck with the interview and to tell you to have a safe trip." "Thanks." "Yeah." "...and Stecha?" "Yeah." "I would've whooped your ass." I closed my phone with a snap. Stecha called, right back. "Bitch, please." She said. I rode the highway with a smile.

Three hours down. Three to go. I felt awful, lonely without Ambrose here with me. I'm so used to him traveling with me. I thought about all the good times we had together. The wrestling, playing video games, cooking, bathing together, our first kiss, and the first time we made love. I glanced at the time in the Escalade. It said three fifty eight. I hadn't called anyone since I left. I lit a cigarette and turned the music down. This SUV is good on gas. I'm only at half a tank. I'll refill in another hour. I picked up my cell phone from the passenger's seat. I flipped it open and hit 3. "Hey, baby. How much longer do you have?" Ambrose asked. "About two and a half to three hours. I'm already missing you." I said and puckered my lips like a child that wanted cookies but, got broccoli, instead. "I'm missing you, too, baby. So, call YoSaVon, tell her you're not coming, and turn around." "I bet you're serious, too." "Damn straight, I am! I ate four bologna and cheese sandwiches and a box pizza. Do you think I'm playing?" "No, baby. I wish I could turn around, now. But, I can't." "Yes, you can. Just do it!" "No!" "Well, it was worth a try. It was silent for a while. Then, Ambrose said, "I just want you to know that you will make me the happiest man alive if you marry me." "I am going to marry you, Ambrose." "I know, baby. I know. I just.. I'on know. It's just... just feel like everything is about to change, that's all." "Maybe, everything is about to change for the better. You ever thought about that?" "I don't see how." "What do you mean you don't see how?" "Not if you're going to take that job in Atlanta." "Really? I'm not going to take that job in Atlanta. At least, not right away. Not until you graduate." Ambrose sighed, "I'm not moving, there. This isn't an one way decision. We have to come to a decision, together." "Can't tell. You've already, made up your mind. This could be a great opportunity for the both of us. Why are you so stuck and determined to live in Mississippi?" "I'm not. There's still a lot I have to learn about managing and owning my dad's shop. That could take a year or two-" "Ambrose, let's just be real. You just don't want to move and don't plan on moving; now, or two, or three years from now. Not even if it's to save our relationship." "...and you don't plan on staying if it's to save our relationship." It got quiet for about ten seconds. I put the cigarette out and lit another. "Well, baby, let me call you back. I'm about to get some gas." I lied. "Alright, I love you." "Yeah. I love you, too." Unbelievable. There's so much love in the air but, neither of us can come to terms. We should try breathing in the love air and break for the other. It seems like a woman loves a little harder than a man. I love him, damn it. I will stay in Mississippi the rest of my life for him. If this was a test, he failed. Obviously, he wouldn't do the same for me. He, clearly, stated that he wouldn't. I sighed, looked at the beautiful ring on my finger, and put it in the glove compartment.

The Hilton was, extremely, posh. I loved. it; from the time I walked through the doors. Before I could take in the scenery, YoSaVon was in my face. "Glad you could make it. Did you have a safe trip?" She asked. She grabbed my arm and walked me towards the elevator. "Yes, I had a safe trip. Don't I have to check in?" I asked. YoSaVon signaled two bell boys dressed in identical red suits. They grabbed my luggage.. "Everything is, already, taken cared of. Why didn't you call me?" "Because it's only six forty three. I was going to call you. Once, I checked in." "That was not your instructions. Your orders were to call me as soon as you made it to Atlanta." YoSaVon said, as we got in the elevator. She held the door for the bell boys. "I know but,..." "No excuses. Next time, let's just try to be more precise." I was about to say something but, YoSaVon told me to save it. She was wearing a gray dress that stopped right below her knees. She wore a matching gray coat that stopped right below her dress. She had on off black panty-hose and black stilettos. I thought it was funny that she was wearing shades inside. Compared to my green now-n-later outfit, YoSaVon looked like a F. B. I. agent. I wondered how long her hair was, now. She had it twisted in a ponytail. The elevator came to a stop on the thirty first floor. "Penthouse Suite.", one of the bellboys said. YoSaVon said thank you to the bellboys. She gave them each a twenty dollar tip and took my luggage. "Well.", YoSaVon said. "Well, what?" "Aren't you going to get your luggage?" "You get it. Nobody told you to send them boys down without finishing their job." "Would it make you feel better if I gave you twenty dollars?" "Hell no. You gave them twenty dollars a piece. I'm doing both of their jobs. I want forty." "Fine. Just get the damn luggage." We stood in the hallway as YoSaVon unlocked the three locks and demanded that I paid close attention. "These locks have to be opened in a certain order or the alarm will go off.", YoSaVon said. When she opened the door. My mouth dropped. We had to walk up six stairs. The six steps were black, white, and gray marble. Once, we were in the suite we stepped, directly, into the living quarters. The living quarters were a combination of earth colors. The leather sofas were light green with ashtrays on each end. The ashtrays were a darker green that started on the floor and surpassed the sofa. The inn tables had to be made of solid gold. They shaped like eggs. The table in between the the sofas shaped like a bird with it's wings extended. The carpet was an earth brown tone. Directly, in front of the sofas was a bookshelf. There were writers like Edgar Allan Poe, Anne Rice, James Patterson, Shonda Rhimes, and so on... On each egg shaped inn table was a bowl of candy. Good candy, too! Candy like Twix, Snickers, etc... YoSaVon took off her coat and placed it on a coat hanger. She walked over to the bar and started to brew her some coffee. She watched as I took in the place. "Your room is to the left." YoSaVon said from behind the bar. "How many bedrooms are in this place?" I asked. "Three and three bathrooms. That way you keep your germs to yourself." I ignored her and walked past the kitchen and dining room to my bedroom. Well, my temporary bedroom. The bedroom was another jaw dropper. It was navy blue. The walls, the bedspread, and the sofa was all navy blue. I threw my luggage on the bed and started to unpack. When I finished I walked back to the living quarters. YoSaVon was sitting on the sofa, sipping (what I assumed to be) coffee from a mug and reading a newspaper. "I'm glad there's a T. V. in my room because I would lose it reading books, all day." YoSaVon didn't look up from the newspaper. She grabbed a remote, while sipping her coffee, and pushed a button. A large, plasma screen television descended from the ceiling. It had to be, at least, ninety-two inches. She hit the button, again, and the televison went back into the ceiling. "Damn, I could stay here, forever." I said. "You wouldn't want to. It cost too much." "How much is this costing you?" "It's not me anything. It's costing the firm five thousand a day." "Fuck that. I would've done just fine in a Holiday Inn." "Would you like something to drink?" "Yes. I'll get it, myself." I went to the kitchen. I came back with a Coke and a cigarette lit. "Still smoking?" YoSaVon asked. "Yes. So, when is this job interview.?" I asked; sitting down. I took off my shoes. YoSaVon closed the paper and sat it on the inn table. She looked up and said, "Now." I laughed. "Now? What do you mean, now?" I asked. "Let's get some things straight. You are not here to be interviewed for a job with a computer company. I need your help." "My help with what?" "With an assassination." I tilted my head to the right and left and waited for YoSaVon to laugh. She didn't. So, I laughed, instead. "You gotta be fucking kidding me, Yo?" I said, plucking the ashes off my cigarette. "Yo, you're kidding, right?" "Have you ever known me to kid?" My hands started to shake. "So, you've been lieing to me?" "Technically, no." "Why me?" "Because you're the only one I believe can get close to the mark. You have to understand, Ava. I wouldn't have called you if I thought there was someone more suitable." "This is bullshit. You brought me all the way here for this bullshit?" "Look, I know you're in a state of shock but,..." "Fuck this. I'm leaving." I stood up and turned toward the bedroom. Like a cat, YoSaVon was in front of me. "Sleep on it. Give it a day. Please, don't do this. There's a lot at stake, here. Look, you'll get one hundred fifty thousand, damn it. Will you just sleep on it?" YoSaVon asked. I froze. I, literally, froze. One hundred fifty thousand. That's a lot of money to receive, at one time. My lips said, "One hundred fifty thousand." I must have said this out loud because YoSaVon said, "Yes, all yours. All cash." I went to the bar and poured myself a shot of Hennessey and chased it with a Coke. "Look, I need some time to be alone. I need to think about this." "Alright, but you must not discuss this with anyone." "Alright, not anyone. I understand." "Good. I'll call you, tomorrow morning at six in the rising." "Hell no. Don't call me that early." "Eight. No later." "Okay." "I take it you'll have my answer." "Yes. Sure. I'll have it."

Through the shots of Hennessey, I managed a seat on the sofa, grabbed the remote, and watched television. I'm still in awe at how this television comes out of the ceiling like that. About thirty minutes of watching the news, my stomach started talking to me. I stumbled to the kitchen and placed a T. V. dinner in the microwave. I grabbed some cookies and a Coke and went back to my trusty spot on the couch. I forgot the T. V. dinner was fresh out of the microwave because I burned the top of my mouth. The food was hot. I dropped the spoon on the floor. "Shit!", I said. I placed the bowl on the inn table and went to the kitchen to grab some damp paper towels. While I was on my knees scrubbing the carpet my phone rang. I looked at the bar that held my purse. My phone rang, again. I got up leaving the paper towels on the floor. It rang, again. "I'm coming. I'm coming." I said, like someone was knocking on the door. When I made it to the bar, I opened my purse. I open it, hastily. I spilled some of the contents on the bar. I opened my phone and stared at it for a second. I could hear a tiny voice saying, "Hello? Hello? Ava, are you there? Hello?" "Yellow" I said, like a drunk sailor. "Hello, Ava?" "Yeah, who dis?" "This is your mother, young lady. I've been expecting your phone call. Are you okay?" I tried to straighten up my act as best as I could. "Yes, Mom. I'm okay." "Good. Well, I'm glad to see you are okay. Have you been drinking?" "Just a little." "That's all it takes to knock you down." "I'm okay." "Well, I was just calling to check on you. You take care of yourself and tell YoSaVon I said hey and I love her." "Okay, Mom. Where's RoNao and Stecha?" "They're both at work. I'll tell them I talked to you." "Okay. Where's Sympathy?" "She's right here." "Let me talk to her." "Alright, hold on." I could hear my Mom calling Sympathy to the phone. "Hey, Auntie!", Sympathy said. "Hey, baby. What are you doing?" "Ca la wing. Gan ma bwought me a new ca la wing book." "That's good. When auntie gets back I'm going to buy you a new coloring book, too. Okay?" "Okay." "Let me talk back to grandma. I love you." "Love you, too! Here you go, gan ma." "Yeah.", Mom said. "I love that little girl." "Yeah, we all do. Let me get off this phone, Ava. You're running up my bill and you know I don't have any money." "That's what you, always, say. Besides, you called me." "Alright, heifer. You're not too grown for me to-" "Yeah, Mom. I know. I'm not too grown to get a whooping. Don't forget to tell Stecha and RoNao to call me." "Alright, baby. Be safe and have fun. I love you." "I love you, too, Mom." "Bye." "It's not bye. It's... I'll see you, later. Bye means you won't ever see me, again." I said. "See you, later, then.", Mom said. "Later.", I said. I hung up the phone. My smelling sense kicking in. I rushed to the sofa where the lasagna was warm. I took a bite of the lasagna, went to the bar, and got my cell phone. I walked back over to the sofa. Before I sat down, I thought why not just get the whole damn purse, Ava. What YoSaVon wanted me to do was, really, starting to dawn on me. What in the hell am I going to tell her, tomorrow? I can't believe I'm, actually, questioning myself about this. One hundred, fifty thousand is a lot of money. Do I, actually, have to commit murder? Why me? If there isn't anyone more suitable and I choose to take this job, why not up the ante? Who is this so-called mark? Is it a male or female? White or Black? What type of job does this person have? It must be an important person; my cut is one hundred fifty thousand. There's no telling how much YoSaVon is getting. Does this person have a family? Most importantly, If I agree to this job, how will it affect me? Can I live with a guilty conscious knowing I helped murder or murdered someone? Will I wake up at night in a cold sweat from a nightmare. How would I respond to Ambrose when he's rocking me in bed, telling me, 'it's okay. I was having a nightmare'? Could I live with the fact that I would not ever be able to reveal what I was dreaming about? Would I, forever, be looking to see this man's or woman's face in the face of a stranger that share similarities as this person? or... Could I assassinate and not be faded by it?

My cell phone woke me up. I must have dozed off. I forgot where I was for a second. I was still in the living quarters in the penthouse suite. The time on my cell phone said ten thirty. I answered the phone with a groggy voice, "It do." "Ew... sounds like someone is in desperated need of some mouthwash." "What's up, RoNao?" "Nothing. Mom, told me you asked about us.", RoNao said. "Us? Who is us", I asked RoNao. "Us, bitch.", Stecha said. "Stecha... mi amor. My life wouldn't be complete without you.", I said. "Yeah, whatever. How did the job interview go?" "It went fine.", I said. "Are you going to take it?" "I don't know." "What kind of shit is that? They, probably, don't want your dumb ass, anyway. Stupid bitch, talking bout ion know.", Stecha said. "Girl... whatever. I'm not hearing that shit. It's good to hear that you two are conversing.", I said. "Conversing? Conversing? This bitch goes to Atlanta and she can't talk, anymore. She's saying shit like conversing. Get the fuck out of here.", Stecha said. I laughed, silently. "What's the job?", RoNao asked. I had to remember what I told Ambrose, earlier. "Computer technology." "Oh, girl. That's good. How much are they offering?", RoNao asked. "I don't know, yet. I won't find out until tomorrow morning. If I decide to take the job." "And if you do take the job, what are you going to do about punk ass Ambrose? You know he's not going to leave Mississippi and ya'll just got engaged.", Stecha stated. "I don't know, yet. If I do take this job, they're going to put me on a test trial for a week. Then, let me come home to tie up some loose ends. I guess Na'Mar is going to have to get with the program." "And, if he don't?", RoNao asked. "If he don't, then, we'll just have to enjoy what's left of our relationship." "Damn, I thought my heart was cold. Yours is freezing.", Stecha said. "You can't be serious?", RoNao asked. "More serious than a high school graduation." "Damn. That's crucial, cuzzo. You need to re-evaluate your motives.", RoNao said. "Girl, I've been evaluating my life since I pulled on mom's pussy hair on the way out the womb." "You nasty bitch.", Stecha said. "Seriously, though. Ro' said a mouth full. It is time I started re-evaluating my life.", I said. "Ro said that with a mouth full of dick.", Stecha said. The line went dead.

I set the alarm for seven a.m. I was up bright and early. I showered, brush my teeth, and ate breakfast. It was, exactly, eight o'clock when the phone to the suite rang. "Hello.", I said. "Do we have an answer?", YoSaVon asked. "Yes, we do." "And?" "Yes, under certain circumstances." "Have you changed your clothes, yet?", YoSaVon asked. "Yes.", I said. YoSaVon opened the door and walked in. Her walking in like that alarm because I was headed to the kitchen. I was going to get a knife. "It's only me. Calm down.", YoSaVon said. I stopped in my tracks. I put the back of my hand in the small of my back and the other one on my forehead. I had to get myself together. "You could've warned me.", I said. I made my way to the sofa. I sat down with a lazy thud. I was wearing a white 'wife beater' shirt and jeans. My jeans were ripped, almost, everywhere. "Nice jeans. Correct me if I'm wrong but, you did say, yes?", YoSaVon said. "Corrections. I said yes, under certain circumstances." "Being..." "I want three hundred thousand." YoSaVon lifted an eyebrow. I continued... "This luxurious suite will not be taken out of my end of the whammy. If I have to delete this virus, I want seven hundred fifty thousand.", I said. YoSaVon smiled and said, "Done, but I assure you, you will not have to delete any virus. Are there any more stipulations or negotiations?" Damn, that was easy. I should've asked for more. Oh, well. "No. none." YoSavon pushed three numbers on her phone. A Chinese woman walked through the door. This lady had on all black. Her hair was identical to YoSaVon's. Their hair was in a bun. Neither of them had on any jewelry. The Chinese lady was about 5' 10" or 5' 11" in her stilettos. She had a suitcase in each hand. Both of their fingernails were painted black. "This is Dependable. Dependable meet Advantage.", YoSaVon said. Dependable looked at me and nodded her head, once. I did the same. "...and of course, you, already know me, Advantage. I'm Hemisphere.", YoSaVon said. I was comfortable in my jeans around YoSaVon or Hemisphere. There were two women in black before me. I felt out of sync. They looked like two creepy morticians. "Dependable, you can leave the suitcases there. That is all. Thank You." Dependable left. Hemisphere got up and bolted the doors. On her way back to the sofa, she picked up one of the suitcases. She laid it on the flying bird table and opened it. It was (halfway) full with papers. It, also, contained two floppy disks. Hemisphere handed me a sheet of paper. His name is Johnathan Albert Johanneson...", Hemisphere began. "...former C. I. A. agent. He's a Senator, now. We have been tracking him four months, now. He's given us the slip everytime. He's a master of disguise and considered to be one of the nation's most deadliest men. He's married but, very promiscous. He has two kids.", YoSaVon paused. She wanted to see my reaction behind the idea of washing out a married man with two kids. I didn't have any. It's not like I know him, personally. She continued, "He is, currently, in Atlanta because he is to speak at the fundraiser C. U. S. A." (Congressmen of the United States of America). "Why don't you all dot his eye, there?" "The topic has been brought up. Security is, too, tight. The fundraiser will be held at Saturday. Six toward setting. If everything goes as plan, you will be considered his guest of honor." "Me?" "Really, Advantage? Do you think you're getting paid so much money to get drunk and smoke, all day? As I was saying, you will be his guest of honor. You will lure him back to your suite, excuse yourself to the bathroom, exit the bathroom by the adjoining bedroom; where your packed suitcase will be, and go home." "Hold up. Wait a minute. Don't you think someone will recognize me luring a Senator to my room?" "No. We'll have fourteen agents working The Hiltzton, that night. The front desk clerks are our agents.", Hemisphere said. "How are you so certain that I will be his guest of honor at this C. U. S. A. fundraiser?" "Oh, my. The Senator has jungle fever. Not only does he have jungle fever; he's got it bad for chocolate girls and pretty eyes. Has anyone ever told you how beautiful your eyes are, Advantage?" I looked up from the print out of Senator Johanneson. He's very attractive. He has a Hollywood smile. "That still doesn't explain how you're so sure that I'll be his guest." Hemisphere stood up, "Tonight, the Senator will be cutting the ribbon to the newest art museum 'GaleRia' in which your presence is required. Make yourself known to him." "How am I to do that?" "Damn, Advantage. Must I show and tell you everything? Bump into him or something. Just don't leave, without you all being introduced. Follow me." We walked to the second bedroom. It was all white. "This room is considered your Barbie Doll room. None of these clothes, shoes, wigs, or jewelry is yours to keep. Therefore, if you damage anything, it's yours. You bought it. Some of this jewelry cost more than what you're being paid. So, unless you want to stick around for another job, I advise you to be very careful when handling this jewelry." I was taked aback, "Why? Why do I need the wigs?" Hemisphere sighed heavily, "The same reason why you'll need a fake name. Renee, you need to masquerade who you, really, are. Don't ever use your smoke name in the presence of no-one but, other smokers. You'll learn all the smokers, in due time. Right now, pick out what you going to wear, tonight, bring it to your room, and close the door. Make sure that is what you want to wear. Once you close this door, no-one can open it but, me or Dependable. Here, take this.", Hemisphere said. She handed me a phone. It was identical to hers. "There are two numbers on the back. Learn them and burn them, got it?" "Yes." "The first number is mine. The second number is Dependable's. Do not call Dependable unless, it's an emergency. Understand?" "Yes." "Good. Come, now and leave that door open." We walked back to the table. I grabbed a cigarette and lit it. Hemisphere handed me one of the two floppy disks. "On this floppy disk is everything we could gather on Mr. Johanneson. His likes and dislikes. Study it." "Okay." "That's, basically, it." Hemisphere gathered her loose ends, closed the suitcase, and headed towards the door. "YoSaVon", I said. She turned around. "That's Hemisphere." "You forgot your other suitcase." "That's not my suitcase. It's yours. All seven. You're worth it, either way." She turned toward the door and left. I sat down in a chair around the kitchen table. I begin to bite on my middle fingernail. I grabbed my pack of Newports and lit a cigarette. I couldn't take my eyes off the suitcase. Fuck it. I grabbed it, sat it on the table and opened it. It smelled so good. I kep thinking, 'I'm rich, overnight. I'm fucking rich, overnight. I grabbed the suitcase, went to my bedroom, and slid it under the bed.

I went back to the white bedroom. Hemisphere didn't give me too much time to get to know Mr. Johanneson. What to wear? Weird, everything is in my size. I checked the shoes. Also, in my size. I tried on one of the wigs. They were already styled. I looked in the mirror. I looked good in this wig. They all were the same color and length. Just different styles. I walked into the closet and ran my fingers across the dresses. The wig was still on my head where I placed it. One dress, in particular, caught my eye. All of them were beautiful. This one was chocolate in color. The V-cut went down to the navel. It was outlined in the shape of multiple S's. The back part was chocolate and you could see through it. Beginning at the waist line, the fabric became smooth chocolate silk. It reminded me of a candy bar commercial. When they poured chocolate on top of chocolate. I snatched the hanger off the rack. Actually, I grabbed it like it was a newborn baby. I allowed the silk to hit my bare feet. It felt good. It felt cold. It felt expensive. This is the one for tonight! I took the dress off the hanger. I put the hanger back on the rack and threw the dress over my left arm. I picked out the stilettos and jewelry and decided to go with the wig I had on. I looked in the mirror and said, "There's no turning back! Ava, I'll see you next week. This week you're Renee. Renee Brown.

I couldn't stop thinking 'what in the hell did I get myself into?' How could I get myself out? It's too late, now. Backing out now, would embarrass Hemisphere. She'll never let me live this out. I should've listened to Ambrose when he asked me to turn it all down. Now, I'm stuck. "It do.", I said. I answered my phone. It was set on vibrate. "Hey, baby." It was Ambrose. Tears came to my eyes. I clutched the phone like it was a lifesaver, I was in the middle of the Pacific Ocean, and I didn't know how to swim. "Baby? You there?", Ambrose asked. "I'm here." "Are you okay?" "I'm okay." "What's wrong. It sounds like you're crying." "I'm missing you. I'm ready to come home." I said, wiping a tear from my eye. Ambrose sighed, "What can I say? I could tell you to come home but, what good would that do? You're going to do what you want to. The only advice I could give you is to keep your head up until you do come home. I'm on break at school. We have fifteen minutes before we have to go back to class. Did you take the job?" "Yes." "It was quiet for twenty or thirty seconds. Ambrose said, "Where do we go from here?" "I come home next week; that's where. They have me on trial for a week. If they like my work, they will call me back and give me a weeks notice. It will be my option to accept the job, pack, and move. That's only if they want my services, permanently." "Did you tell them that you are engaged to be married?" "They know Ambrose." "Do you? Because all this month's notice, need your service, and permanent talk sounds like that of a single woman who made all the decisions for herself." "Ambrose, please, don't start. I don't need this, right now." "Yeah, okay. But, this conversation is anything but, over." "Okay, baby. Look, I have to work, tonight, at six. They have a strict policy; no cell phones or phones calls, at all. At least, not while you're on the clock." "That's absurd, Ava. So, there's no office phone to reach you, period?" "Not at all." "I don't believe that.", Ambrose said. "Well, it's true. Besides, I won't be in the office. I will be out troubleshooting. I shouldn't work no longer than ten. I'm in training, anyway. I promise I will call you as soon as I get off." "You better. What's the name of this company?", He asked. I didn't even think of the answer to that question because I didn't think of that question. Shit, Ava! Think quick! "Ambrose!", I yelled. I was acting as I didn't hear him. "Ambrose!", I yelled, again. I hit the phone with my hand. I could hear him saying, 'Yeah, baby. I'm still here.' I could've, easily, came up with some phony company name. Hell, I would've came up with some made up name if I was dealing with some Average blow Joe. I could not come up with some fake name with Ambrose. He will, most definitely, do a background check on the company. So, I did what came to mind. "Damn!", I yelled. "I left my battery charger in the truck. I hope my baby don't be upset." I heard Ambrose saying, 'I'm not upset, baby. I love you.' And with that... I hung up the phone and called Hemisphere. "What is the name of this so-called computer company because Ambrose is subject to call this room wanting some answers. Hemisphere, once he gets a name, he's going to do a background check." I splurted out. "Don't tilt the cradle, dear, Advantage. We will take care of that." "I need to know something, now! What if he calls the suite phone, right now?" "Tell him it's called C. S. I." "Funny, Hemisphere. You know he's studying to be a crime scene investigator.", I said. "Advantage, it means Computer Service Incorporated. It is sort of catchy, isn't it?" "Well, what if he checks on it?" "Don't worry, Advantage. Let me take care of all of that. I noticed the wardrobe door is closed. Let me guess, chocolate delight?" "Yes. How did you know?" "It's one of my favorites, too. Dependable thought you would pick peach fuzz. Well, too bad for her. Now, she owes me three stacks. Advantage, a limo will be outside waiting for you at 5:30, sharp. Try not to be late." "Okay. Hey, how am I supposed to look at this disc?" I asked. "Hit the rewind button on the remote control. Any more questions?" "None." "Good. I'll call you when the limo arrives." "Okay." "...and Advantage. The next time you call me use the phone I gave you." "Okay. Later." I climbed over the sofa by throwing my leg over the sofa's backrest. Ambrose didn't call, right back. I thought about what Hemisphere said the "wardrobe room". My room will, eventually, be Mr. Johanneson's death bed. It gave me chills just thinking about it. I made a mental note to sleep on the couch from now on. I wonder, what's in the other room. I laid on the sofa, yawned, and stretched still holding the remote. I said, 'ooohhh.' while I was stretching. I got up and walked toward the third room. The room was to the right of the bar. I knew it was locked. I thought, maybe, I'd get lucky. I wiggled the handle. Immediately, the phone Hemisphere gave me started to ring. I ran and answered the phone. "Advantage, speaking." "Is everything okay, Advantage?" Hemisphere asked. "Yes. Why?" I asked. I had to catch my breath. "Because someone was tampering with the door." "That was me." "I see. Look, Advantage. Just stick with what you know. Okay?" "Yeah." "Okay. Tomorrow is a busy morning for you. When you get in, tonight, get some rest." "What time, tomorrow? Six in the rising?" "Exactly." "What are we doing that early?" "I'm not doing anything. You're doing hand to hand combat training." She said and hung up. What a joke; I thought. As if, I need hand to hand combat training. I sat down and pressed rewind on the remote. The book shelf started to rotate. Once the bookshelf was out of view, the computer terminal was visible. This suite is out of sight. I wonder what else I don't know about. I walked to the terminal and put the floppy disk in the hard drive. I opened Microsoft Office and studied Mr. Johanneson's likes and dislikes. I had been at the computer about an hour when Mom called. "Hey, Momma." "Hey, baby. You just don't know how to call your old momma, do you?" "Mom, you're not old and I was just about to call you." "Hey, baby. If you go to that Underground Mall, buy your momma something nice." "I will." "Have you been in that room, all day?" "Yes, mama." "When was the last time you ate?" "At seven." "Ooh... child. You need to get out and get something to eat and some fresh air." "That sounds nice but, I think I'll call some room service. YoSaVon has me studying this computer language for this job and I-" I said, closing my eyes. I massage one side of my temple with my thumb and the other side with my index and middle finger. "You tell YoSaVon I said, that you need to get some food, fresh air, and a break away from work, okay? Now, you promise me that you are going to get out of that room when you get off this phone." "I promise." "Good. Well, look, I gotta go. You're running up my phone bill, child." I smiled. "Okay, Mom. I love you. Later." "Later, baby and don't forget to buy me something nice." "I won't." I got up went to my room and put on some socks. I grabbed a pair of Jordans. The baby blue and white ones. When I grabbed the shoes, black stuff was falling over my face. I grabbed the wig and, quickly, threw it across the floor. I laughed, grabbed my stomach, and slid to the floor. My back slid down the wall. I forget the damn thing was on my head. I went to the bathroom and tidied my hair. I grabbed the keys to the Escalade, both cell phones, and my purse. I put the keys to the suite and Escalade, and the cellphones in my purse. I opened the door. I had a sudden urge to turn around and admire the suite, again. I did. I took it all in. I walked out the door, locked it, and headed towards the elevator. I couldn't help but feel like someone was watching me while I was waiting in the elevator. I looked left and right. Then, I looked up to see what floor the elevator was on. When you're in the penthouse suite, the elevator by pass all other floors. The elevator picks up the V. I. P., carries that person to it's destination, and then it continues with it's daily duties. No one is watching me. I'm just paranoid. I heard the elevator's 'ting' before the door opened. When I got on the elevator, I heard someone say, 'hold the elevator'. I thought, 'what the-'. There are only two penthouses on this floor. I didn't know someone was in the other room. I was scared. So, I pushed the button to close the door. It closed just in time. I heard a male's voice curse and hit the elevator with his fist. I jumped. I could've, easily, ate in the lobby area. I promised Mama I would get some fresh air, though. People were staring at me in the lobby area. I knew it was because of my jeans. I liked the attention.

Behind the wheel of the Escalade, again. I put on a pair of sunshades, lit a cigarette, and decided to get out of Buckhead, for a spell. I drove through Dekalb and Decatur. I ate at a KFC in Decatur. I ate inside. While I was sitting down eating, a young man (about my age) sat at my table. I looked up from the hot and spicy breast I was eating. I wiped my mouth with a napkin. "What's up?", I asked. "You." "Me?" "Yeah, you. You're bold as hell. Riding through here all pretty and shit in that nice ass ride." I examined him. He was a descent looking man. He looked like he could be A. P. He had gold in his mouth. The gold were only on his top teeth. He was wearing a brown-tan Dickies jumpsuit. He had on brown Timbaland boots. He wore a white T-shirt under his jumpsuit. Damn, he looked good in that shit. "Man, that shit ain't mine. My sister rented that shit for me to come visit her.", I said. "Where you from, shawty?" "Mississippi." "You pretty as fuck! Those your real eyes, uh...?" "Ava. My name is Ava. What's yours?" "Duane." "Hell, yeah. These are my real eyes." "Man, I'ma be straight up with you. I started to rob your ass for your vehicle. I thought you were some rich, white motherfucker that got lost and popped in to get directions." Duane said. "Well, I'm definitely not white and you should be glad you changed your mind because that vehicle has a tracking device on it." "I bet it do." "I'm serious." "Me, too! Girl... If you don't learn nothing about us Georgia boys, know this; we be up on game about everything. Two minutes, all I need. I would've been located that tracking device and disarmed it." "Let me eat, man. All that damn talking my food is getting cold. You smoke?" "Smoke what?" "Cigarettes." "Yeah, I smoke weed, too!" "Well, let me eat and I'll holla at you when I get through." "Alright, Shawty.", He said; flashing those gold teeth. "Damn, do you mind?! If you're going to sit there, at least, get something to eat." He laughed and got up. "Do you want something else?" "Yeah, a two piece. Hot and spicy and get some jelly." We sat there eating and talking like we grew up together. I enjoyed his company. It was nice to talk to somebody about other things. It felt normal to chat about the normalities of life. We didn't touch the topic of assassination. When we were in the parking lot Duane asked, "Do you play billiards?" "Hell, yeah. I have an hour or two to spare. What are you driving?" "That." He said. He pointed to a Champagne color Lexus. It was souped up. "Nice car. It's the same color as my car in The Sip. What do you do besides hijacking?" "I own a car shop." "For real?" "I steal from the rich and sell it back to their ass." We both laughed. "So, are you down for some pool?" "It do." "What?" "It do, nigga. I see ya'll Georgia boys ain't up on that." "Naw but, I'm a quick learner. Follow me." We headed back to Buckhead. We parked our vehicles. "What are you waiting for?", I asked Duane. I walked to his car and sat on the hood. "For our ride. There it goes." A golf cart came out of the building and took us inside. "We should've burned a tree, first.", I said. "It's not too late.", Duane said. He asked the employee at the Billiard's shop to take us back to his car. Duane and I sat in his car and smoke some weed. "So, what are you doing in Atlanta?", He asked. "Blazing." "Naw. For real, though." "I'm on business. I'm in training for a computer company." "What computer company, nigga?" "Nosey. Check it, I'm high as hell. That's some good ass weed." "Oh, yes. Let's do this pool thang." "I'm not going in there like this."

"Aw, main. You can't maintain your high?" "Nigga, I drive high and work high. Just give me a minute." I reached in my purse and made good use of my Visine and body spray. I offered some Visine to Duane. He accepeted the Visine. "Want some body spray, too?" "Hell, naw. Excuse me. Don't think I'm trying to touch your legs." He opened his glove compartment and sprayed on some cologne. "That smells good. What is it?", I asked. "Very sexy; with two x's. That's right. You ready?" "Already." We walked back inside. Duane went to the bar and bought the billiard's balls. We went to a table in the back of the room. Duane set up the table. "So, Duane, why do you hijack when you own a shop?" "Fast money. Fast, good, and plentiful. If I don't do it, somebody else will." "That's what I'm saying; it looks like you're doing okay for yourself. Why won't you hire someone to do your dirty work?" "Break the balls. Because if someone else do my dirty work and get caught, they won't do my time, Shawty." I thought about what he said as we played pool. I wondered... If I got caught or something went wrong, would I sell Smokers out? Could I sit in prison? Duane, definitely, said a mouthful. But, (just like him) I didn't plan on getting caught. We played pool and talked about two hours. It was, almost, two towards settings when we left the building. Duane gave me a card that had several numbers on it. He wrote a number on the back. I wrote my cell number on the back of one of his cards. "Thanks for not robbing me." "You're welcome. I know you're here for a short time but, if you get bored, holla at me." "I will." "Oh, Ava. I know you got an old man. So, if you know a descent lady that's looking for an honest man, tell 'em you know a friend. I'm willing to relocate. I can, always, sell the shop and invest in another one in Mississippi. I've been living in Georgia all my life. It's time for a change of scenery. You know what's crazy, though?" "What?" "It didn't cross my mind, once, to try to holla at you. I guess I needed a friend. Someone to just kick it with. You're not what I thought you to be." "...and what's that?" "Stuck up. You're alright, Shawty." "You're alright, too, Duane." We said our 'laters' and went our seperate ways. Now, here is a cool, handsome brother that's willing to relocate for the right sister. Why can't Ambrose do that? We have been together two years and I still can't budge him. What kind of shit is that? I have other things to think about, besides that. It's still upsetting, though. Duane is cute. That gold in his mouth makes him stand out. Hell, if I knew a descent girl, I'd call her, right now. When he was giving his descent woman speech I thought about

Stecha. Stecha would run the poor man into the ground. She'd have a chisel by her side to mark the grave. She would shit and piss on him like a dog. Duane thinks he robs from the rich and sell it back to their ass. Stecha robs them all and keep it. Hmmph... Someone will slow her down, eventually. Who knows? It might be Duane. I think I will invite him to Mississippi in the near future. But, for now, I'm the guest of honor in Atlanta.

Cutting The Ribbon

HEN I GOT BACK TO the hotel I asked one of the bellboys to escort me to my room. The very idea of walking, alone, in that hall frighten me. In the elevator, I asked the bellboy did anyone occupy the other suite. He said a man by the name of Mr. Preston had the room. I asked him what did he know about him. He said Mr. Preston owned several Ihops and that he tipped good. When we made it to the door of the suite that I was staying I thank him and gave him a twenty dollar bill. I opened the door to find Hemisphere staring out of the window. She was sipping on something out of her (usual) coffee mug. "Had a busy day?", she asked. She walked into the kitchen. Then, she went to the sink and poured the rest of the liquid out of her mug. She rinsed out the mug and left it upside down in the sink. "Yo-" "Hemisphere.", She corrected me. I was sitting on the sofa; taking off my shoes. "Hemisphere, Mom ordered me to get out of this room and get some fresh air." I went into my purse and switched my phone back to ring. "Accepted. Did you, at least, study the profile I gave you on Mr. Johanneson?" I pointed to the terminal and computer that still displayed his file. "I see that his profile is visible on the screen. Which is very careless. What I want to know is did you study it?", She asked. "Yes, I did. Not only does he like sisters but, he enjoys soulfood. He loves to sail, snowboard, skiing, and-" "My dear sister, I know all these things. I'm satisfied that you've done your homework." "Thank you." "I expect you'll be dressed by five fifteen." "Hemisphere, why are you drilling me?" She sat down on the sofa beside

67

me. With a very stern voice she said, "I am drilling you so you won't forget the importance of this operation. Tracks must be covered. You left this room with seven hundred thousand dollars under the bed. You didn't take the disc out of the hard drive. Hell, the profile was still booted up on the screen. These are tracks that must be covered. Our organization is not one of sloppiness. I suggest you find a bank offshore to deposit your money in. Somewhere the I. R. S. or the F. B. I. can't infiltrate. The next time you choose to stroll around town, make sure the maid don't get a glimpse of next week's obituary. Are we clear, Advantage?" "We are. I apologize.", I said. Hemisphere stood up and looked down at me, "There's no need to apologize. Afterall, you are a rookie. Next time, clean up your filth or it will cost you." She walked to the door and placed her hand on the handle. "Cost me what?", I asked. "One hundred thousand. Be ready at five fifteen. Be in the lobby at, approximately, five thirty." "I will, Hemisphere. Did you know about the guy staying in the other suite?" "Anthony Preston, 39 years of age, single, lives in South Carolina, no kids, one dog- a British bulldog, owns nine Ihops. Mr. Preston inherited the acquired wealth from his father Irwin. He has three Ihops in Atlanta, four in Texas, and two in South Carolina. Yes, we know about him. Anything else?" "No. I was just wondering. He sort of spooked me, earlier." "Lobby. Five thirty." "I'll be there." "There's a gift for you in your room." She was gone before I could ask what it was. So, I grabbed my tennis shoes, unfastened my jeans, and went to the bedroom. On the dresser, there was a bottle of Liz Claiborne perfume. I studied that Mr. Johanneson loves the scent. I thought, 'thank you, Hemisphere because I planned on wearing white diamond. Alone again, I sighed. YoSaVon knew Ambrose wouldn't come with me. If he would've, there's no way any of this would be possible. I had no option but, to come alone. It's a good thing I did because, now, I'm richer than I think I will ever be. It's ludicrous to even think that I would save fifty thousand working at La Cocina de Comida. I don't think I will be employed there, much longer. Hell, with all the money I am making I can buy a restaurant. But, why waste money on tortillas and refried beans? I took my jeans off and walked to the bedroom that was beside the kitchen. I tossed my jeans in the washing machine. Then, I went to the refrigerator and grabbed a coke. I went to the sofa and sat down. I glanced at the computer screen. I took a sip of my Coke. I thought about how irresponsible I was for leaving that disc in the drive. I took a deep breath and walked to the terminal. Leaning over the terminal, I ejected the disc. I hit the rewind button on the Television's remote. The wall, now, showcased the bookshelf. I went back to the bedroom and placed the disc in my briefcase. I'll burn it, later. I put the briefcase in my suitcase. YoSaVon, corrections, Hemisphere will have to help me set up an offshore account. I don't know how to set up an illegal account. I will, definitely, need her help. I glanced at the clock on the bedside table. Two fifty three. One hour to spare. I went to the bar to get my phone out of my purse. Eleven missed calls. I was about to call Le ebo when someone knocked on the door. I looked out the peephole. It was a white man wearing thin, gold frame glasses, he had a tan, blue eyes, and a sharp nose. His bone structure made me think his nationality was Russian. There must be a factory producing good looking men. He held his head down and knocked, again. Though, I was looking, directly, at him, he startled me when he knocked. "Who is it?", I asked. "My name is Anthony. Anthony Preston. I'm staying in the suite next door.", He said. "Hold on.", I said. I ran to the washing machine and put my jeans back on. "Just a minute.", I said. I checked my appearance in the mirror behind the bar. I took a deep breath and opened the door. "Hi, are you the person staying here?", He asked. "Yes. My name is Ava Johnson.", I said. I extended my hand. We shook hands. "Is there a problem?", I asked. "No, except for the fact that you didn't hold the elevator for me." I blushed. "I apologize, Mr. Preston." "Call me Anthony." "Anthony, I didn't mean to be rude. I just didn't know that someone was on this hall; other than myself." "So, you were frighten. Understandable. I assure you-" "Ava." "Ava. I don't bite. Nevertheless, there was no harm done. I just thought I'd introduce myself. Maybe next time, you'll hold the elevator for me." "Sure." "Well, I'm next door if you need anything." "How long are you in town, Mr. uhh... Anthony?" "Two days. I'm just checking on my business." "Maybe, we can share a table at the restaurant in the lobby. How's dinner, tomorrow?" "Are you asking me on a date?" "No, I just owe you one for the elevator incident." Oh, well. Too bad. I'd like that, Ava but, I have to decline. You're too lovely a lady to buy such a brute dinner. My treat. No arguements. Your invitation was enough." "What time shall we rendezvous?" "How's seven?" "Sounds good." "Great. Maybe, we can share an elevator, too." I smiled, "Of course, Anthony." "Well, good day." "Good day." He turned and walked to his suite. I was thinking, 'to hell with Apples. T.I.T.S.I.L. needs to hang out in a suite.

They need to grace their beauty in a posh hotel like this. Talk about meeting true ballers. I closed the door. Damn, Ambrose. If I was single,.. Forget being single. If I weren't in love,.. I called Le ebo. We talked for a split second. She complained about her boyfriend and threatened to leave him. She and I both knew that wasn't going to happen. I told her about Duane. She told me to give him her number. I lied and told her I would and that was it. I started to call RoNao but, I knew she was at work. I called Stecha, instead. "Hey, hoe.", Stecha said. "What's up?" "Nothing. I have another date with the angler, tonight. I'm tired of his sorry ass, already." "How much?" "Girl... This nigga is cheap. I asked Stanley-" "Stanley, bitch! That sounds like a cheap ass nigga's name." I started laughing. "Girl, fuck you. Anyway, I ask this nigga for three stacks, right? So, I took mom home and meet this bitch at the bank. This nigga come out the bank smiling like it's all good. He had the nerves to walk up to the car with one of those white envelopes. You know, the envelope they put your money in. I take the shit and burn rubber in his face like I just robbed that motherfucker! Girl, when I went to pick Sympathy up-" "How is Sympathy?" "She's okay. Bitch, stop interrupting me. So, I'm in Santina's parking lot, right?" "Right." "Bitch, stop talking and just listen. Anyway, something told me to check the envelope. Girl, I was, too, through. It was only one stack in there." "Hell, naw." "Yeah. So, I call Stanley the angler and asked him what's up with that? He gone say, he thought three stacks was three hundred dollars. He said he gave me a stack as a surprise. Girl, he can save that shit.." "I'on know, Ste. He probably didn't know, girl." "He knew. I know that nigga ain't that lame. He better get with the program." "Girl, you are wild." "And loving every minute of it."

After I talked to Ambrose, I called Mom. Ambrose and I had a good conversation. In the middle of our conversation, I thought about Duane. I thought about how he was willing to drop everything for a good woman. I got bothered by the fact that Ambrose wouldn't do the same for me. I'm a good woman. I couldn't bare to hear Ambrose's voice. I told him I had to get ready for work. He wanted to keep talking. He was so excited about what they did at school that he didn't ask me about my day. I wasn't going to volunteer any information. Especially, knowledge about chilling with Duane. I had a good time with Duane. I'm going to call him before I leave Atlanta. I see why they call Atlanta- Hotlanta. The small amount of time

I spent out of my room was better than anything I ever did in Mississippi. Thanks, Mom. Thanks a lot for choosing Mississippi. Maybe, Duane will go to the mall with me when I buy Mom a gift. I love my Mom, so much. "Hey, baby.", Mama said. "How did you know it was me?", I asked. "Stecha, bought me a caller I. D. She is so sweet." What!!! Stecha sweet? Aw, come on, Mom. "What are you doing?" "Getting ready to go to the Revolving Door." "Your second home. Don't you get tired of losing your money?" "My money? RoNao gave me a hundred dollars and Stecha did, too! Besides, I win sometimes. Why are you hating, child? Me and Louise be chilling down there." "I'm no hater. You don't drink or smoke. So, how do you chill?" "You don't have to drink or smoke to have a good time. They're having a blues singer there, tonight. Louise and I are going to see him. How was your day? Did you get out that room?" "Yes ma'am. I had a lot of fun, too!" "That's good. YoSaVon didn't bother you, did she?" "She started to until I told her that you told me to get out of this room." "She better leave my baby alone. I'm glad you're paying for this call." "Mama, don't start. Do you need me to send you some money?" "No, baby. I'm okay. I make it just fine. Well, let me go. I haven't decided what I'm going to wear, yet. You know I like to look good. I want to turn some heads like a tropical storm. Just call me Hurricane, baby!", I laughed. "Yeah, I have to get ready for work." "Stecha should be here in a hour. She took Pateka and Sympathy to the movies. So, what do you think; My red, sequenced, halter-top like shirt with my black slacks and silver heels?" "Stilettos, mom." "Huh?" "We don't say heels, anymore. It's stilettos, now and I think that's a good pick." "Alright. Well, I love you, baby. I like chatting but, I love chilling. Later, babe." "Later. Enjoy yourself.", I said. "Oh, I plan on it. Good luck at work.", Mom said and hung up.

I felt like Cinderella in a wig. When the elevator door open everyone was staring at me. One lady had to hit her husband/boyfriend to stop him from looking. He, also, had to close his mouth. It was five twenty seven when I walked through the double doors that led outside. The fresh air hit me, immediately. I closed my eyes and took a deep breath. It felt how a great piece of gum would make a stale mouth feel. I opened my eyes. A little girl holding her mother's hand told me that I looked pretty. I smiled at the little girl and said, thank you. They were waiting for valet to bring her mother's car. I would've given her a piece of candy but, I believe her mother to throw it away. Besides, I left my everyday purse in the suite with my everyday cellphone. I gave myself kudos for bringing my own formal purse. The only items I had in the purse were the cellphone Hemisphere gave me, make-up, gum, mints, and six hundred dollars. Thank God the phone was a razor phone. I wouldn't want a bulge in my purse and I wasn't going to carry it in my hand. The limousine arrived. Right on schedule.

I was nervous. My legs were shaking and I felt a rush to use the bathroom. I couldn't believe 'this' was, actually, happening. I started to breathe hard. I was telling myself not to panic. I had to stay calm. Remember, you are here to accompany this man to dinner. How hard could it be? I answered myself. Very hard. Considering, I've not ever done this! There's no turning back. I gathered myself and started to count; I find it relaxing. Here we go.

A white man stepped out of the limousine. He was wearing all black; except the collar shirt he wore beneath his jacket. He was wearing a chauffer's hat. I assumed that he was the driver. Surely, Mr. Johanneson would not be driving a limousine. He stood about six feet tall. The part of his hair that I could see beneath the hat was lined, excruciately, proper. He had a goatee but, no mustache. His fingernails were manicured. He had hazel eyes. He looked to be about 175 to 180 in "I will be your chauffer for the evening, Ms. Renee." Strange. How did he know to call me Renee? He opened the door for me. I sat down in the lavish limousine.

When he entered the vehicle, he rolled down the tinted window that separated the driver from the passenger. "Advantage. My name is Corruption." A smoker. He continued, "I need to know what last name to use for you. In case, we have a guest join us. I will, also, be your bodyguard, tonight. Your agenda is to get Mr. Johanneson to attend dinner with you." "You're not going to-" "Of course, not. This is a rental. Splatters of blood last on material a long time. Tonight's sole purpose is to lead him into seduction... and no, you're not to, literally, seduce him. Your last name, please?" "Brown." "Well, Ms. Brown, welcome aboard.", Corruption said. As soon as he pulled off, my phone rang. "Advantage." It was Hemisphere, "You look beautiful. I'm glad to see that you were on time. Just remeber to stay calm. If you are asked where did you get your fortune, you inherited it from your father. Whom owned a law firm; Brown and Roberts. That way if he do a background check on you, everything will be legit. You're from New Orleans, La. Metairie. Are you with me?" "Yes." "You're an only child,

Ms. Brown." "How did you know to call me Ms. Brown?" "The champagne bottle is a video and audio system. Don't worry. You can, actually, drink it. The law firm has been closed since your father's death. Your deceased mother was named Evelyn. They died in a car wreck. An incident you care not to discuss. You're in Atlanta on vacation. You're not a big fan of art but, you thought you'd go to the opening of La GaleRia to make use of your evening gown. You're single. No kids. Today is your birthday. Smile." "What?" "Smile. Before you do, take some of your make-up off, earrings, and necklace. Look under the seat, put that T-shirt on, and smile. When you're through with the shirt, give it to Corruption. He will dispose of it. You're twenty-five, today. Leave your purse in the vehicle. When you come back, you'll have a new I.D., already, in your purse." I did everything she asked me to. Then, I started to apply my make-up, again. "Nice picture. If you're asked anything that's not covered, make it up. Make sure what you make up is in sync with everything that I've told you. I'll be able to hear everything. Your dressed is bugged." These people come up with everything. I thought this stuff only happens in movies. "Is that everything?" I asked. I was, already, exhausted. "Yes. What are your parents name?" "Evelyn and John Brown." "Where did your father work?" "He owned a law firm." "Your mother?" "Housewife, I assume." "Nice assumption. Where do you live?" "New Orleans in Metairie." "Why are you in Atlanta?" "Vacation." "Name of your father's firm?" "Brown and Robertson." "No, Advantage. Pay attention to details. Brown and Roberts." I make one salty move and Hemisphere is boiling. Hemisphere continued, "Again, where is your father's law firm?" "Brown and Roberts." YoSaVon asked me those same questions three more times. Right when I thought I was going to lose my temper, the limousine stopped. YoSaVon said, "One more thing you didn't attend college because you were rich before you graduated high school. You don't care to reminisce on your high school era because it's a touchy era. You lost your parents during your Junior year in high school. How tragic." "What's tragic the car accident or all of this drilling?", I said in a sarcastic way. "The car accident. Have fun, Advantage." "Yeah, right."

The air around La GaleRia tasted as expensive as the people attending the ceremony. Majority of the attendees were white. The black members dotted the room like polka-dots on a dress. Corruption opened the door for me. He took my hand and helped me out of the limo. In a low tone, he told me to call him Svante. He to me to press 777 on the phone when I was ready to leave. Unlike the people in the lobby at the Hilton, no one stared. I made eye contact with a couple of people, smiled, and bowed my head here and there. I walked towards the podium that was set up for the speaker of the evening. To my surprise, there was a seat reserved for me in the front row. The reservation was for Ms. Renee Brown. How did they work so quick? There must be other Smokers here. No use in trying to spot them. They could be anybody. I spotted Mr. Johanneson with a champagne glass in his hand. He's quite stunning, in person. I couldn't take my eyes off him. I'm not attracted to white men, usually. Mr. Johanneson made goosebumps form on my skin. He must have felt me looking because he looked, directly, at me. Ashamed, I averted my eyes. A waiter asked me if I wanted some Belevedere or Cristal. He said if I didn't want either, another waiter will be around, shortly. He would have other beverage options, the waiter implied. I told him the Belvedere will be just fine. I grabbed the reservation ticket. I made sure Mr. Johanneson could read my name. I sat down and babysitted the Belvedere. Everyone begin to take their seats. Mr. Johanneson (still, casually, talking) was laughing out loud like he was at a bar. He pat one guy on the back and made the guy spill his champagne. The group around him burst out in laughter. The emcee asked everyone to take their seats and asked the honored guest to please assemble on stage. The group broke up and Mr. Johanneson made his way toward the stage. There was a seat reserved for him. The emcee begin with introductions of the honored guest and thanked everyone who attended the event. Not in that order, to be precise. The first honored guest was an artist who took the podium with a grim face. He begin a long, boring speech about the history of art and where it derived from. That was the longest forty five minutes, ever. The second honoree was the owner of La GaleRia. His speech was brief. His speech included men (that looked like they walked off the cover of GQ) walking across the stage showcasing some of the art that will be in La GaleRia. Some paintings took two men to carry it. With every different piece of painting, the crowd murmured. Finally, after the owner gave the history of Senator Johanneson, the cutting of the Ribbon. I see, Mr. Johanneson lived by the K.I.S.S. rule, too. When he took the podium, he thanked everyone for coming out and asked them to enjoy their evening. After he took some pictures, shook some hands, and received the scissors to cut the ribbon. The owner announced that it was time to cut the ribbon. Before he cut the ribbon, he looked at me, again. I looked down. When I looked up, again, the ribbon was cut. It happened pretty quick. Really? How long does it take to cut a ribbon? The audience begin to leave their seats and pour into La GaleRia. On cue, I made my way inside. I felt out of place upon entering the building. Everyone was admiring the art and pointing at another work of art. I stood alone; rejecting the urge to join the tour group. I gave a deep inner sigh with my arms folded. I wanted to go outside and press the three sevens on the phone to summon Svante. I thought about the briefcase in my suitcase and changed my mind. If I don't get Mr. Johanneson's attention, tonight, Hemisphere is going to be highly upset. I planned on stalking Mr. Johanneson. I had a great plan. I was going to bump into him and act like he spilled wine on my beautiful dress. I was going to blame him and his clumsiness for damaging a dress my mother passed on to me. I was stretching my neck looking for him. "Bored or are you just appreciating good art?", someone asked. I turned around. It was him. It's about time. "Both, I guess.", I said. "You guess." "That's right. I am, dreadfully, bored and I guess this is good art." "Hmmm... I see. Actually, I'm not an art lover, myself.", He said. He placed the back of his right hand to the left side of his mouth. As if, he were telling a secret. He continued, "I couldn't tell the difference in Picasso and Da Vinci." He smiled. A beautiful smile, at that. "I'm Johnathan Johanneson and who is the lovely lady with whom I am talking?" "I'm Renee Brown. Please to meet you." "The pleasure is all mine. I take you came alone?" "In fact, I did and I'm ready to leave." "So soon? The night is still young." "Indeed, it is. But, I'm still bored." "Let's skip out of here and have a night on the town." "Mr. Johanneson, I'm insulted. Do I give off the impression that I'm an escort?" "I, too, am insulted. You just labeled me a playboy. I didn't mean any harm. I just thought... Since, we are both bored, we could keep each other company. But, since..." "Wait. I mean, what could it hurt? As long as you know, you won't be slobbing on my pillow, tomorrow morning. Besides, I have a bodyguard." He laughed. "Oh, Renee. There's no need for a bodyguard. I wouldn't harm you. I'm a Senator but, your bodyguard couldn't stand up to me. Where shall we met. I have to say goodbye to a few friends." "Let's meet outside. How long will you keep me waiting?" "I wouldn't keep such a beauty waiting long." "I'll be there.", I said walking away. "Ms. Brown.", He said. He turned around and smiled. I turned around. "Yes.", I said. "I assure you. I don't slob." He turned and walked away. On my way out, I thought damn I need my phone to call Svante. Before I was halfway to the curbside, the limo arrived. Svante opened the door for me. "How did everything go?", Corruption asked. "Fine. Where's my phone?", I asked. "In your purse with your new I.D., Advantage." "That's Ms. Brown, Svante.", I said. I had a leg on top of the car door and a leg inside the limo. "We don't need you slipping, now. Do we?", I said; getting in the limo. I was starting to feel like I belong to the Smokers, officially. Svante gave me a pleased look. He got into the driver's seat and rolled down the tinted window that separated us., "Where to?" "We wait. We will be having a guest to entertain, tonight." With that being said, Corruption rolled up the window. Immediately, the phone rang. "Good job, Advantage. Is Mr. Johanneson our guest?" "He is." "Good. Now, make sure you get a second date." "Oh, I plan on it." I was on cloud nine because I asked Hemisphere, "Hemisphere, I thought my dress was bugged." "It is." "Then, you should've known that Mr. Johanneson is our guest." "Arent' we saucy? My asking you is just procedure. Am I clear?" "Yes." "Good. Now, stick with the plan. Your guest is arriving. Under no circumstances, are you to leave your purse unattended. We don't need Mr. Ex C.I.A. snooping. Good luck." "Thanks." I wanted to feel guilty but, I was starting to get comfortable. I'm, even, starting to like this.

Today, marked the true beginning of Advantage. Today, I christian myself. I am Advantage. Today, I am and will always be Advantage. Nothing or no-one will change that. They haven't made me a smoker but, I need to have an application after this week. That's for damn sure. Mr. Johanneson walked out of the GaleRia. He had his hands in his pocket. He just stood there. A second later, a black limousine pulled up behind the vehicle I occupied. Mr. Johanneson gave a salute and began walking towards his driver. His driver emerged from the limo and met Mr. Johanneson. They took an even amount of steps. They shook hands and exchanged, friendly, smiles. Mr. Johanneson placed his hand on the man's right shoulder. How civil, I thought. It seems, as if, he treats the man equal instead of like a servant. How touching. Time to break up this reunion. They looked up when I closed the limo's door. They both walked to me. I heard the chauffer mutter, 'wow'. "Mrs. Brown, I was beginning to think you stood me up.", Mr. Johanneson said. "Now, why would I stand up such a handsome gentleman who doesn't drool?" "Flattery will take you a long way. Chauncey, Mrs.

Brown." I smiled and nodded. I extended my hand to Chauncey. He took it and kissed it. "Oh, come on, Chauncey.", Mr. Johanneson said. He pulled my hand away from the chauffer. "Find your own date. Do you have to be so friendly?", he asked Chauncey. Chauncey straightend his back and pulled the bottom of his coat-tail. "Indeed, I do, John. She's beautiful.", Chauncey said. I smiled and said, "Thank you, Chauncey. You're quite a charmer yourself." Chauncey blushed. John said, "Carry on, Chauncey. I'll be with you in just a minute." Chauncey got back in the limo. We watched him for a second until he waved. "Since, We're introducing people.", I said. I walked to the driver's side door. S'vante rolled down the window. To my surprise, he was wearing a mustache, had a bald head (at the top), and blue eyes. Surprisingly, I didn't appear shocked and I didn't miss a beat. "S'vante." "Ma'am?", S'vante asked. "Meet, Senator Johanneson." "Pleasure.", S'vante said. He did not offer his hand. "Please.", Mr. Johanneson said. "Call me, John." "Will that be all, ma'am?" S'vante asked. "It will." He rolled up the window. We walked toward the rear of the vehicle. "When do I meet this bodyguard?", John asked. "You just did." "Funny. He looks, rather, old to protect anyone." I thought, 'if you only knew.' He continued, "...How 'bout tonight, I guard your body until we depart?" I laughed, "...and who's going to protect me from you?" "Me?" "Yes, you. You have to resist my charm and I am certain I have more than Chauncey." We laughed. "Your car or mine?", he asked. "Mine.", I said. He informed his driver to leave his cell phone on. He told Chauncey he will call Chauncey thirty minutes before he was, actually, ready to be picked up. Every step he took closer to me was a step leading to his death. Just like that. Simple. Easier than baking a cake. Had it not been for Chauncey he would've been good as smoked. Snuffed out. I didn't need Hemisphere to tell me that going back to the Hilton was not an option. Besides, the man is going to die there. I don't need Chauncey linking me to the hotel. I'm clearing the path for some nationwide, front-page shirt. I didn't want to be seen with him, publicly, anywhere. I assumed he felt the same being that he is married. Atlanta is one of the leading states in entertainment. Paparazzis are everywhere. A celebrity flytrap. The only question I could think of was, 'where to?' This proved more challenging than expected. "Now, that the odd necessities are out of the way, shall we depart?", he asked. "We shall." In the limo, Johnathan loosened his tie to get more comfortable. We were still in front of GaleRia. S'vante rolled down the window, "Madam, excuse my intrusion but, where are we heading, tonight?" "That's a good question.", I said. "Do you have anywhere, in particular, that you would like to go?", I asked. "No. How about we cruise the city?", he said. Great. A night out riding and no weed smoke. "Fine with me.", I said. Svante rolled up the window. As we set off, John asked, "So, Renee, where are you from?" "Oh... A little of here and there. Is it really important?" "I just want to know who I'm chilling with." "Chilling with?" "Does that surprise you that I speak slang?" "Yes, it do." "Surely, you are not hung up on speaking proper English?", John said. I thought, 'I might as well let loose and drop the masquerade. At least, a part of it. "Man, you are tripping.", I said. "Why do you say that?", John asked. "I'm just saying."

He grabbed two wine glasses and poured us some champagne. When he placed the bottle back in the container, the phone rang. I sipped the champagne and let it ring, again, before I answered. "What's up?" "I need you to turn the bottle around. I lost visual. Make sure the label is, always, facing you.", Hemisphere said. "Yeah, alright.", I said and hung up. Not to seem, too, obvious, I drained my glass and refilled it. I turned the bottle in doing so, "I wish I had a blunt. You ain't got no weed?", He asked. I was shocked. Did I miss something? I didn't read in his profile that he smoked weed. "Man, hell no. What are you some cop or something? Are you even a Senator?" "A cop? Are you out of your mind? Excuse me, for asking. Damn. You remind me of–" "Your wife. Surely, you're not the single Senator." "Surely, I'm not trying to hide it." We both looked out of our windows. Somewhere, we took a wrong turn on weed street. "You can sit over there and act prissy, all night. But, you can't say that you don't smoke weed because if you didn't you wouldn't have gotten so heated and you wouldn't have asked me if I were a cop.", he said; nonchalantly. I said, "Yeah. So, what?" "So, what's up with the weed. Shit, I want to get high." I can't believe he's a Senator. It's even hard to believe he's white. Luckily, I knew Duane's number by heart. I asked S'vante to pull over at a gas station. I grabbed my purse and phone. I called Duane. He told me to meet him where we played pool. When I got back in the car, we sent S'vante into a store to buy beer and cigars. When S'vant came back Johnathan apologized and asked him to go back into the store and get him three bags of Doritos, a pack of Newports, and a lighter. He gave S'vante a c-note and told him to keep the change. I grabbed a napkin and his hand. I began to scrub his skin. "What are you doing?", he asked. "Making sure you're not black." "No but, my foster parents are." That explains a lot. His strong charisma towards black women, his constant use of slang, and, most definitely, his urge to skip out of boring assemblies. I think, almost, everyone have a taste for marijuana. We bought a half ounce from Duane. He, actually, paid for it. I made the hand- to- hand connection. I didn't let Duane know who was in the limo with me. But, I didn't tell him that I had a guest. I believe Duane would've want to tag alone if he thought I was by myself. Back in the limo, John rolled up two blunts. He lit both of them and gave one to me. We were riding down the highway of Atlanta, getting high, and taking different intersections. I was feeling good. I kicked off my shoes. John took off his jacket, tie, and shoes. He said, "This is some good ass weed." "Hell, yeah." "I, always, wanted to do something crazy. I can't do such perverse actions without getting recognized in the Tabloids.", John said. "Yeah. What's that?" "I, always, wanted to run down the street in the nude. Penis swinging and all." I started laughing. "Yeah. You're crazy. Do the people at the White House know that you're so silly?" "Ms. Brown, my wife doesn't know and they won't ever know. There's a time and different character for every situation." Then just like that. He switched. He smiled at me, hit the blunt, and said, "But, um... The people at The White House... Hell no, they don't know! You know I have to put up a front! That good old prep boy type shit! I should've sold drugs but, my parents wouldn't let me. Believe me, I tried. Then, I realized I was smart! That day a legend was born." He sat across from me being sarcastic as hell. Was this all an act? Just one of his characters. I thought, 'today a legend is born.' It has nothing to do with being smart. Today, I realized I could murder in cold blood and not give a damn about it. Mr. Johanneson will be the first motherfucker I set up. "So, what's your story?", he asked. He had his legs kicked up pulling on his blunt. I hit my blunt and smiled, "Inheritance." "Inheritance?", he asked. "That's what I said. My father owned a law firm. My mother was a homemaker. They both died in a car wreck and left me with everything. After I graduated, I said, 'fuck it.' I'm rich. Fuck college. Fuck it all. I'm on baller status and that's all that matters." "I'm sorry about your parents.", he said. "I hate when people say that. What are you sorry for? Did you kill them? Then, what are you sorry for? Feel me?" "Yeah, I hate that shit, too." "So, what's the deal with you and your wife?" "Come, again." "Your wife. What's the deal?" "There is no deal. She's boring, a bitch, horrible in bed, and out of the blue she stopped sucking deal. The deal is she's cared for. She's... What do you say? A homemaker. Sometimes, I think I married her because I knew where I was headed in life and I know how those shallow ass politicians are. They want whitey to marry whitey and blackey to marry blackey." "Yeah, you're right. That tired, old way is dieing, though. There's nothing but inter-racial relationships, now-a-days." "If it weren't for that I believe I would've married Jackie O'Malley. She was my first true love. Fine ass black, sister. Damn, she was fine. Her parents thought I was trouble, at first, because I used to stand on their block hustling weed. They would not ever let me talk to her. She's the reason why I am who I am, today. Everyday, I would try to talk to her and one of her parents would make her come inside." "Damn." "She was feeling me, too. I stayed G'd up. You couldn't tell me shit. I had to have her. Then, one day, I skipped school and waited for her, outside. We went to different schools." "All day?" "Yeah." "Psycho." "Whatever. She was worth it. Well, anyway. So, when the last bell rung ending their school time. I saw her, persuaded her or charmed her, if I may.", he said. He was smiling with his left hand on his chin, and nodding. He continued, "She called her parents from a friends house and told them they were studying for a biology test. We went out to the movies." "Cheesy." "Girl, whatever. The movies were the shit, back then. I don't know what you're talking about." "Finish the story, John." "Alright. So, we dated about two months without her folks knowing. No sex involved. I respected her because of that. Two months before we graduated, she told me that she got accepted into Harvard. I hadn't even applied. She told me I should. I was, too, stuck on selling drugs. I was, also, a honor student. Well, she kept hounding me and hounding me. I broke and gave in. I told her I would apply to one college. If I didn't get accepted, I was going to become a drug lord." "Harvard, right?" "Yes." "...and John, It's called a dope boy, now." "What? You think I don't know that? I'm just telling you what I said then. Anyway, to my surprise, I got accepted. We dated our whole time in college. That's it?" "That's it!" "Yeah, that's it." "Oh, hell naw. What happened?" "She got a job offer at John Hopkins as an intern. She's a doctor, now." "And, you?" "Well, my job took me elsewhere. We both had very important priorities. We loved each other, dearly. It's just..." "You don't have to explain. I understand.", I said. I was patting his hand. I was going through the same thing with Ambrose. "I, truly, love that lady with all my heart. She was mixed. Her mother was black and her dad was Irish. She had her mother's beautiful skin complexion and her father's green eyes." I looked up. He was staring at me. His eyes were shining. I knew he was holding back tears. I felt sorry for him. I didn't understand why I had empathy for him. He and Jackie should not have been so damn goal-oriented. I believe love surpasses all. "Oh, snap out of it. Let the past stay in the past." "Yeah, that's easy for you to say. You, probably, never been, truly, in love and until you do, you can take it as light-hearted as you want to. When you do get that burden, you'll see it's a heavy load to carry.", he said. We got quiet. He turned the music up on his side; letting me know he didn't want to talk for a while. He wanted to get lost in his thoughts. I was lost in mine, too. I heard everything he said. I didn't know, right then, that I would be going through it myself, soon. We smoked, rode, ate his Doritos and got hungrier. We went to McDonald's and made S'vante get out, again. These little teenage girls put their hands on the window trying to see who was inside. I asked John to put his jacket on his head and I rolled down the window. They started screaming, "It's Rihanna. It's Rihanna." One of them asked me, why was I eating at McDonald's? I told them I was not Rihanna and that I was eating at Mickey D's because I was hungry. I told them when you have money you don't try to eat expensively. You eat what you like. Trying to eat expensive (to me) is trying to prove to others that you're not cheap. You don't want to seem gullible when you, really, are. If you know who you are, you don't have to prove it to anyone else. They still didn't believe I wasn't Rihanna. They asked me to sign their bags. So, I did. I know who I am. It's amazing how one can identify another better than the person themselves and be wrong. Holla.

Since, the pool hall was closed, John asked Chauncey to meet him there. When we arrived Chauncey was, already, there waiting. I gave John some of my clear eyes. Chauncey don't know John smokes. He took enough of the weed to roll two blunts. I got his cellphone number. "I, really, enjoyed myself.", John said. "Yeah, me too!", I said. I, honestly, felt that way. I just don't see how undercover agents could become friends with someone over an extended period of time and then set them up. Betrayal, it's best served cold. I know my objective. I didn't know it could be so hard. Johnathan Johanneson; the senator, the husband, the father, the agent, the son, and now (though I know I'm not supposed to cross this line) my friend.

Who in the hell would want him dead? Why? I'm not getting paid to ask questions. I could, easily, pull out of this operation. A shame. A fucking shame. I'm, damn sure, not giving the money back. Sorry, John. Business is business. "When are we going to do this, again?", he asked. "Whenever you would like.", I said. Please, don't say, tomorrow evening. I gave my penthouse neighbor my word that we would have dinner, tomorrow evening. Not tomorrow. Hemisphere is watching and will declare it mandatory. "Tomorrow, I'm busy." Yes! He continued..., "How's Wednesday? I have to check my schedule to make sure I'm free for a couple of hours. Call me, tomorrow, aroud seven. Do I look high?" "No." "I feel like it.", he said. "Here, have a look.", I said. I gave him my mirror. "Cool. So, will I hear from you, tomorrow?", John asked. "Around seven.", I said. "God, you're beautiful. May I?" "May you what?" "Kiss you?" uh... No. Though, I know if I rejected Mr. Johanneson, Hemisphere would rip me a new asshole. What could it hurt? I hope he don't think he's going to walk his way to sex because that, definitely, was not going to happen. "Sure.", I said. I closed my eyes and puckered my lips. He grabbed my shoulders and kissed me on my forehead. "Don't forget to call." "Don't keep reminding me." "Okay.", he said. He gathered himself to depart the limousine. John opened the car's door. He placed one of his feet out of the vehicle. I grabbed his left arm. He turned to face me. "John, give me my mirror. Get your jacket and tie. And for crying out loud, put that weed in your pocket!" "Oh, yeah.", he said. He grabbed his clothes and placed the weed (that was wrapped in a one hundred dollar bill) in his pocket. He was gone. I felt alone, again. Hemisphere is my sister but, she is the same way she was when we were younger. All work and no play. "Yeah.", I said; answering my phone. "Cheers. You're worth every penny.", Hemisphere said and hung up. I turned the champagne bottle around and grabbed a cigarette from the pack John left. I lit it and gazed out the window.

When I made it back to the suite, I checked my cell phone. I missed, only, two calls. What's up with that? I took off my evening wear and took a warm shower. I shampooed my hair. I slipped into a comfortable robe that was supplied by the hotel and placed a towel on my head. YoSaVon was in the suite when I walked out of the bathroom. She was dressed in all white. She scared the shit out of me. So, I yelled. My feet were stuck to the ground. I, now, understand the horror movie dummies. I understand why they become momentarily, paralyzed from fright. This experience with Hemisphere explained the 'screaming instead of running'. "Damn it, Hemisphere! I wish you would stop doing that. That shit is becoming annoying. Why are you here, so late, anyway?", I said. "It's only ten o'clock. I thought, maybe, you would like to go downstairs and get a drink." "Yo, I have to get up, early. Can't we just drink at the bar in here? I'm tired.", I said. I lit a cigarette and turned on the T. V." "You only need four hours of sleep. I'll mix my own drink and yours, too! What will you have?" "A Rum and Coke." "You should try Hennessey and coffee. I can't get enough of the shit. I think I'm addicted." "Join the party. We're all addicted to something.", I said. Hemisphere brought me the concoction she mixed for me and sat down. She rested beside me on the sofa. She snatched the remote out of my hand. We were watching a boxing match. "Where's your drink?", I asked. "I have to wait on the coffee. Did you talk to Mom, today?" "No, you know I just got in. I haven't talked to anyone." "You've, actually, been here.", she said. She snapped her left arm in front of her face. "...thirty-three minutes and counting." "Okay, Yo. I get your point. No, I haven't talked to her." "You've, already, said that." "Smart ass. Have you talked to her?" "Yes." "And?" "When you go home, I'm riding with you. She got up and went to the coffee pot that she had the maid move to the bar. I changed the channel. "Change it back, Ava.", YoSaVon said through clenched teeth. "Not until you tell me why you're going to see Mom. It's not a holiday." "Because I love her. She's my mom and I want to see Sympathy. Now, change it back." "Okay. But, I don't believe you." "Believe whatever you want. It's the truth." "Yeah, whatever. Why can't you get a rental and we trail one another?" "Oh, you don't want me to ride with you?" "It's not like that. It's just that I smoke cigarettes and weed. You don't." "Just crack the window.", she said. She made her way to the sofa. Once she was seated, I turned to face her. "I crack the windows for cigarettes, anyway. I don't like to crack the windows when I smoke weed. I'll turn the vents on for you, though. Deal?" "As long as, I'm driving when you're smoking." "I don't have a problem with that." "If you don't turn on the vents, I still would have been able to manage. Don't you think I go to clubs?" "Hell, no. You're such a bore. I can't even imagine you dancing." "Ouch. You're right. I don't dance. Any moment I'm in a club, I'm at work. I do know how to dance, though. So, don't get it twisted." Hmmph.. It'll be the weekend when we go back to our original place of birth. I'm going to take her to Apples and test that theory. "About tomorrow.", she said. "What about it?", I asked. "Try not to break any bones." "Are you serious?", I asked. I snubbed out the cigarette. "Definitely. When you are finished, call me. I made reservations for us at a spa." "Straight up?" "Yes. Afterall, you're going to need it. If you are considered to be a permanent Smoker, you'll have to attend this class, every year, for a whole month, straight. Including, the weekends. It will not be in Atlanta, every year. You will always have the same instructor. Everyday you miss you have to pay three thousand dollars. The Corp. pay as long as you attend. Got me?" "Yeah. Who's the Instructor?" "Dependable, of course.", she said. She smiled at me. "Great.", I said. "Why do you say that? You said that like your favorite shirt got shredded in the dryer." "Because. She's stiffer than you." "More insults. I'll have you know, we are not stiff and she, actually, likes you. I think I'll call her and tell her you don't like her, though. Guaranteed broke bones.", Hemisphere said. I sat my glass down and stretched both of my arms out; shaking my hands. "No. no. no, don't do that. I was just playing. Ya'll are the life of the party.", I said. "Now, you're trying to be funny.", Hemisphere said. She raised her phone up and down, threaten me with it. The same way someone would throw a football. "Man, chill out, Yo. I'm your sister. Don't do that to me." "Yeah, you're right.", she said. She stood up and tossed her phone on the sofa. "Give me your glass. I'll mix you a fresh one.", Hemisphere said. She strolled to the bar like a female James Bond. She returned with our drinks. "There are directions on how to get there. You have to walk." "Walk!", I said. "Problem?" "No." "Okay. Bring your own beverage and towels. Everything else will be there for you. Call me if you have problems finding the place. I advise you to be on the streets thirty minutes, early. If you're late, you have to pay fifteen hundred dollars." "Damn." "Hey, you can afford it. If you don't want to pay, just don't be late." We talked about five more minutes. Hemisphere finished watching the boxing match and left. I guess since, she made the drinks, it was my duty to clean my glass, her coffee mug, and the coffee pot. After I washed the few dishes, I laid on the sofa and thought about calling Ambrose. I called the front desk and asked for a wake-up call for five o'clock. I decided against calling Ambrose. I should have called him. He was the only person that called me, today. I turned the channel to a dating show and fell asleep with the T. V. on.

I smacked my mouth, several times, before I answered the phone. The inside of my mouth tasted like a trace of liquor. I reached for the phone with my eyes closed. Who in the hell could be calling, so early? "Hello.", I said. My voice was groggy. "Ma'am, this is front desk. We are calling, as you requested.", the incoming caller said. I hung up the phone. This must be a mistake. I just went to sleep. I changed the channel to the news. Damn, it is, actually, five o'clock. I yawned and scratched my ass. At least, I don't have to wear a wig.

Twenty five minutes later, I was feeling refreshed and rejuvenated. I stood outside the Hilton; sipping an orange juice. To be early, the streets were, barely, occupied. I still had the notion that I was being watched. I looked inside every car that was within eye range. Deja vu. That Jaguar looked, exactly, like the one expensive suit was driving. It couldn't be. There has to be, at least, a couple thousand more Jag's like that. The windows were tinted so dark that I couldn't tell if someone was in there or not. To satisfy my curiousity, I walked in front of the car to get a sneak peak. Damn! I still couldn't see inside. The passenger's side window was halfway down. I walked closer to the window and a poodle started barking in my face. The dog startled me. It kept barking. A blonde lady wearing shades, a navy-blue Versace dress, and red stilettos came out of a cafe. "Are you interested in buying? God knows I'm trying to get it off my hands." The blonde lady said. "Oh, no. I'm sorry. I was just admiring the beauty of it." "Yeah, it is quite a beauty. Now, if you'll pardon me. I'm late for gym class.", she said. She smiled and tilted her shades. Ironic. If I don't get movining, I will be late for training. I adjusted the blacks straps that was attached to my gym bag. The bag was on my shoulder. I gave blondie a polite smile and took off. When I made it to the building, I had to take the stairs. How could the elevator not be working in such a nice building? With eight minutes to spare, I dashed up the stairs. I jumped some of the stairs two at a time. I know this was a setup. Dependable wanted me to be late. I knocked on the door; breathing hard. Dependable opened the door and said, "Right on time." She had a smirk on her face that made me think the 'out of order' sign was placed there by one of her goons. She opened the door, wider. She motioned for me to come in by stretching out her right arm. I was awe struck. The entire apartment was white. I walked into Winter Wonderland. Beautiful. Everything blends, so well, that you would miss the sofa. If you weren't paying attention you, really, wouldn't see the sofa. There was an extremely, large, blue mat to the left of the door. My mouth opened when I heard 'hiya'. Dependable chopped me in the back of my neck. I dropped my bag and grabbed the back of my neck. I turned around. "Always be aware of your surroundings.", Dependable said. "Your ass is going to be aware of my foot if you do that shit, again." "Oh, yeah.", Dependable said. She took a step closer to me. She was wearing a black, spandex, one-piece. Her hair was in a ponytail. She was barefeet. I was wearing Jordan's, white slouch socks, and blue spandex. I topped the spandex with a pair of rugged blue jeans and a white T-shirt. My hair was, also, in a ponytail. "Tuff girl, huh? Well, show me.", Dependable said. She walked towards the blue mat. I followed her. "Take off your shoes, socks, and your shorts. They're optional. I can use them against you, though. Hurry up, slow poke! Come on. Come introduce your foot to my ass.", She sneered. I stepped on the mat. She motioned me with her hands for me to bring it on. I poised my fist in the air. I thought, 'Yeah, right. I'm not falling for that trick. I've seen it, too many times, in the movies. I run at her, yelling and she trips me. If not, she moves to the side and push me down. I apologize but, I refuse to accommodate her with the demands she asked. I'm not falling for it. "You come to me.", I said. "Okay." She ran towards me full speed and kicked me in my chest. 'Fucking bitch', I thought. I laid on my back. I'm going to beat her ass. She offered me a hands up. I accepted and punched her in the stomach. She doubled over and tried to release my hand. We looked at each other. She made the first move. She stepped to my side and swept me off my feet. On my way down, I grabbed one of her ankles and pulled her leg; bringing her to a split. I threw my legs around her rib cage and started to squeeze. She took her index and middle finger and pressed on the inside of my thigh. She must have hit a nerve because a dull, numbing pain ran through my leg and she was free. I let go of her hand and massaged the area. She was positioned in front of me like a cat ready to pounce. Without hesitation, She jumped over my head with a no hand cart wheel, grabbed my ponytail and yanked my head. My head hit the mat with a thud. She did a quick backwards flip, landed on top of me, and was choking me. She smiled. I reached up and slapped her. She smiled, again. I began to buck my body like she was riding a horse. When her grip loosened, I slapped her arm away from my neck. She scratched me in the process. I was angry. She stood there with a smile on her face, watching me cough. I had to catch my breath. I charged her. Ha! I caught her off guard. I raised her up in the air and threw her on the mat. I looked at her and smiled. She looked at my ankles and knocked me off my feet. She jumped on my back before I could get off my stomach. Damn, she's quick. When Hemisphere walked in, she said, "That's enough, Dependable." "Oh, Hemisphere. We just got started.", Dependable said. "I said, that's enough.", Hemisphere said. Nevertheless, she continued to choke me. I saw my sister fuming. She was dressed in all gray with gray stilettos. She took off her shades and trench coat and did two backward flips, a no hand cart wheel, and a no hand backwards flip. I was damn near out of it. Then, she let go. Dependable and Hemisphere was standing face to face. They assumed fighting positions. Then, burst out laughing. "Did you work her over real good?", Hemisphere asked. "I worked her over but, not real good. She's a natural fighter.", Dependable said. "It's in the blood." "Nice shoes." "Thanks, if she's accepted I want her fifth lesson to be in heels. If she prove to be a quick learner..." "I'm sure she will. You put holes in the mat, Hemi." "Charge me the cost of duct tape." "You know Danger would never approve of duct tape." "Look. Girl, flip the shit over. If he has a problem, tell him to call me." "Hey, you're the boss." Boss? Hemisphere is the boss? I sat up and said, "Boss?" They both looked at me. "Oops. It slipped. My bad.", Dependable said. "It's okay. She would've found out sooner or later.", Hemisphere said. She walked over to the white kitchen counter and started to brew some coffee. She pulled out a bottle of Hennessey. "Take a break.", Hemisphere said. I walked over to my bag, grabbed an orange juice, my cigarettes and a lighter. "So, you're the boss?", I asked. "Not, really, the boss, per se. I'm just in charge of things. While the head honcho is relaxing.", Hemisphere said, looking at Dependable. "Do you have any more juice? We can put them in the refrigerator.", Dependable asked. "Yeah. They're in my bag.", I said. "Right... and, I'm going to get them for you.", Dependable said. "I'll get them myself." "Yes. You will.", Dependable said. I lit a cigarette. Hemisphere laughed. "Two of my favorite girls, together, at last.", Hemisphere said. "What's up with the spa?", Dependable asked. "Ten o 'clock.", Hemisphere said. I looked up from my bag. Who invited Lucy Liu? "Ya'll got work to do. Ten more minutes. Now, get busy. Don't drink all that juice. You'll get cramps.", Hemisphere said. Forget cramps. I'm getting I don't want to do this itis. We went over the basic fundamentals of martial arts. Three hours went by, quick. Hemisphere was in dreamland. She woke up when Dependable said, good job. "What time is it?", Hemisphere asked. "It's nine forty.", Dependable said. Hemisphere replied with, "Let's go." "Hold up. Aren't we going to shower, first?", I asked.

"If you're smelling fishy, be my guest. If not, we go. You can wash off all the grime at the spa.", Hemisphere said. I grabbed my bag and orange juice. I started to lit a cigarette but, Hemisphere told me to wait until we get off the elevator. "The elevator works?", I asked. "You pulled the elevator trick on her?", Hemisphere asked Dependable. "Hell, yeah. She was still on time. That's what I call a work out before a work out.", Dependable said. She didn't smile. I laughed and shook my head.

Ooh... It felt so good in the spa. We got the grand deluxe treatment. We bathed in mud, received massages, avocado face masks, and we were, currently, in the sauna. Our next trip was the mani/pedi booths. As nice as this was, I wanted to get my cell phone and call Ambrose. I wanted to hear from my family, too! I looked at Hemisphere and Dependable engaged in a conversation and wondered if they ever got lonely. I wondered if they ever thought about their family. Do they ever get homesick? I sighed as the steam got thicker and obscured us from each other. The ache brought on by Dependable was beginning to settle. I closed my eyes and rested my head on the wall behind me. I thought about John and Duane. I wanted, so much, to think about Ambrose. I was trying to force memories of him into my mind; it just wasn't happening. I tried to make myself comfortable with the idea that my sister was a cold blooded murderer and the very idea that I was trying to score brownie points to get accepted. Am I sick? Smoking John would be like getting rid of Duane. I wanted to ask Hemisphere how do she walk around with a guilt free conscious. I snapped out of my thoughts when I heard Dependable ask Hemisphere,'what did she say?' I should've been paying attention but, they're so dull; it didn't cross my mind to eavesdrop. "I didn't say anything. I'm not ready for that type of committment." Committment to who? Dependable intercepted, "Well, Danger loves you. Don't let him get away." "Shit, he can't go too far. He's a habitual smoker. I just need time to think; that's all." Hemisphere said. Oh, I'm, definitely, going to ask her about this Danger. I will ask her on the road trip home. I started to believe they were talking, loosely, around me because I called them stiff. They know what they're doing; proving they are still human. After the spa, we ate at a Chinese restaurant and listened to Dependable brag about how she could make every dish so much better. She made a proposal to cook for us in the near future.

Changing

I FELT LIKE A NEW WOMAN when I made it to the suite. I enjoyed myself with them and I let them know that I did, continuously. It feels good to be back. I lit a cigarette and grabbed my cellphone. "Damn, baby. It's good to hear from you. I thought you forgot about me.", Ambrose said. "How can I forget about you when I love you so much? How's your dad?" "He's good. I visited your mom, yesterday. She said she haven't talked to you since you started your training." "That's true." "How was it?" "It was good, actually. It wasn't what I expected. How is school?" "Same old. Same old; clues and evidence. I miss you so much. I didn't think I would miss you, so much; but, I do. I want to be inside you, so bad." "I want you inside me, too!" "Ava, are you still going to marry me?" "Yes. Why wouldn't I?" "Do you promise?" "Yeah, I promise." "I'm going to make you happy." I should've been thrilled because he said he was going to make me happy. Then, why am I getting bored with this shit? I wanted to talk to him so bad. Now, I, desperately, wanted to get off the phone. "Are you still there, Ava?" "Yeah." "Well, answer my question." Damn, what question? "You answer it.", I said. "How in the hell do I know if you made any acquaintances, at work?" "You know me better than anyone." Except me. "Ava, just answer the question." "No. They're all geeks." "Has anyone tried to get at my baby?" "No. What about you? Any new freaks?" "Girl, hell no. Look, I'm pulling into dad's shop. Call me, later. Okay?" "Alright." "Don't forget, baby." "I won't." "Later. I love you." "I love you, too. Tell your dad I said hi." "I will." Who should I call next? Stecha, RoNao, or Mom? "What's up, skank?", Stecha asked. "It do, baby." "It don't do shit. What's up, bitch? Why didn't you call me, yesterday?" "Why can't you call me?", I asked. "Bitch, you sound stupid. I always call you." "Where's Sympathy?" "She's with mom." "Where are you? I know-" Stecha interrupted, "I'm in the bathroom at Red Lobster." "What are you doing there?", I asked. "Eating, bitch." "Don't play you know, exactly, what I'm asking." "I'm here with the angler." "Damn. This is y'all's third date. Are you feeling this guy?" "Hell no. He's breaking bread and popping rubber bands." "Girl, you need to put an end to that shit. Sooner or later that brother is going to want some of your treasures." "He ain't getting any. My shit is

priceless.", Stecha said. "Yeah, okay. You just be careful.", I said. "Already."
"Have you talked to Le ebo?", I asked. "Yeah." "Tell her I asked about her."
"Tell her yourself and call her, bitch." She hung up. Before I called RoNao
and Mom, I smoked a cigarette and rolled a nice fat blunt. I thought about
Stecha and how she was playing with Stanley's head. I wonder if I know
him. Afterall, he is an A. P. Stecha don't ever think about what she does. She
just do it. After she dogged Sympathy's dad, I used to wonder did she have
a heart. She would've been suitable for this job. I knocked the cherry off my
cigarette and called RoNao. What's up, stranger?", RoNao asked. "Nothing.
This blunt." "I was just about to blow one. I'm in the backyard." "Don't do it,
yet. I want to talk to momma after I talk to you. How's my baby?" "Totaled."
"What?" "I'm just playing. The same way you left it. Are you loving ATL
or what?" "Yeah. It's alright." "Girl, you must don't get out much?", RoNao
asked. "Matter of fact, I'm about to go to the mall in a minute. I'm glad you
said something." "Oooh. Bring me an outfit back. I'll pay you for it. I'm
getting money, now." "That's what's up. Keep your baby oil, though. I got
you. Did you take the whip to get tuned up?" "Yeah. I like working at La
Cocina de Comida. Everybody is so cool. Oh, guess what? I, almost, forgot.
Mom is throwing me a party when you get back! YoSaVon supposed to come
to. I got accepted into Harvard Medical School.", RoNao said. She made
a squealing sound. "Are you serious?", I asked. "Yeah. Can you believe it?"
"Hell yeah. You're smart as fuck. Congratulations, girl. We should take
you to the Bahamas or something." "Are y'all?" "I said, we should, bitch.
You know how Mom is about traveling." "Yeah. I'll get there one day." "It
do. Aye, let me talk to mom on your phone. So, she won't trip about her
phone bill." "Alright." As she made her way into the house, she asked me
questions that were similar to the ones Ambrose asked. I gave her the same
response that I gave him. "Hey, baby." "Hey, Mom. How are you doing?"
"Oh, I'm good, baby. Did RoNao tell you the good news?" "Yes ma'am. I'm
happy for her. Where's Sympathy?" "She is sleep, child. Thank goodness.
She's been a handful, today. She needs a brother or sister or, maybe, a lit'
cousin to play with." The only way she'll get a little cousin is if RoNao or
YoSaVon give her one because I don't have any plans for children, right now.
"Did you ge me an outfit, yet?", Mom asked. "I'm about to go in a second.
Anything in particular?" "Naw. You know what I like. Just, make sure it's
not old fashioned." "Mom, you know I'm the queen of fashion.", I said. "No,

you're not. Stecha is." "Yeah, whatever." "You're damn good, though.", Mom said. "I wish they still sold hammer pants because that's what I'll buy you.", I said. "No, you'd buy them for yourself. Well, we're having a party for RoNao when you get back." "I know. She told me." "YoSaVon is coming." "I know, Mom." "Mmm... Well, I don't have nothing else to say." "Okay. I love you, Mom." "I love you, too.", Mom said. "Let me talk back to RoNao and kiss Sympathy for me." "Okay.", she said. I heard Mom screaming RoNao's name. Mom got back on the phone. "That girl must be in the backyard burning up trees. You want me to tell her something?" "Yeah. Tell her to tell everybody at work I said hi and congratulations, again.", I said. "Okay, baby. Well, I'm about to watch the Golden Girls. Love ya'. Be safe, okay." "Yes ma'am. I love you, too."

    I took off my dukes and smoked a blunt. Later, I took a shower. I put some wrap lotion in my hair and blowed it dry. An instant wrap. I took a wet towel and wiped the dead hair (that had fallen on my shoulders) away. What to wear? I put my training gear in the washing machine. I, also placed my ripped jeans in the machine and started the load. I hovered over the machine. I let the water fill halfway. Then, I poured laundry detergent into the water. I put the lid down and walked away. Normally, I wouldn't dare start a load with a small amount of clothes. But, hell, I didn't have to pay for it. I went into the bedroom and retrieve my suitcase. Bingo. Look, at my precious briefcase. It's only money, right? Wrong? It's my money. YoSaVon supposed to help me deposit this booty offshore. I opened my suitcase. I choose a pair of turquoise cabana shorts, a silver (or gray) halter top. Strings flowed from the shirt. The strings were to tie around my stomach. I found a belt to my match my attire. I wore silver stilettos that strapped around my calf muscles. I smelled good, felt good, and my toes looked good. I sprayed on Lovely by Sarah Jessica Parker. I applied baby oil to my skin. I grabbed my silver Ray Bans. My keys were in my everyday purse. I called Duane. "What's up, Shawty?", Duane asked. "Are you available?", I implied. "What's the purpose?" "Shopping." "Aw... Shawty. You know men hate shopping." "If I knew any women in Atlanta, believe me, I would've called them, first. I take it, you won't be joining me." "Naw... I'll be there. Give me twenty minutes. The Underground, right?", he asked. "Right.", I said. "What are you wearing?" I told Duane what I was wearing and how I had my hair. "Alright. I'll find you." "Duane, Why go through all that like were cavemen.

Come on, man. Just hit my cellphone. I'm going to be outside. Just don't take too long." "Yeah, alright, Shawty." I stood outside the mall's parking lot; smoking a cigarette. I started to let Duane find me inside. I threw my cigarette on the ground and stomped on it. I looked at the bottom of my heel to see if I did too much damage. When I looked up, I saw Duane's Lexus and heard the thump in his trunk. He spotted me. When he pulled in front of me, my body could feel the vibration from the sound his stereo was making. He rolled down the window and asked if I wanted to ride with him to find a parking space. I started to say no but, I thought better of it. I knew he asked for a reason. As soon as I sat down, Duane told me to fire up that blunt. He turned on his vent and found a space. I passed him the spliff. "So, who was you rolling with in that limo?", Duane asked. "I wasn't riding with anyone. He was riding with me." "What? So, that's your limo?" "Not really. Only when business deem it necessary. Feel me?" "I guess. Who was with you?" "Duane, don't take this the wrong way but, that's confidential." "So, what are you; some kind of freak hoe to the stars?", He asked. I smacked the back of his head and accepted the blunt he offered. "Hey, watch that shit!", Duane said. "No, you watch what you say. I'm a lady. I'm one man's woman." "I'm just saying you'll give Karrina Steffans a run for her money." "Bullshit. I'll have that hoe's man running to the bank giving me her money." "Yeah. You're fly, shawty. Superhead is a pro." "Good, I hope you meet her one day." "Nah... She's not my type. Women are so unpredictable. You can't tell if y'all are faithful or not." "Duane, damn. I was not cheating on my man. I was with a business associate. Stop trying to pick me, man and you men are very predictable; you can always tell when y'all are cheating." "Okay. I get you point, Shawty. I know to mind my damn business." "It's just like that. I don't ask you where and to whom you sell those stolen cars." "It's felt, Shawty. It's felt. Did you tell one of your girls about me?" "Yeah... but, I wasn't trying to hook you up with her." "Why not?" "Because she has a boyfriend. She was still urging me to give you her phone number." "That's what I'm talking about unpredictable." "Yeah. She's wrong but her old man ain't shit. So, whatever." If he only knew how stealthy I am. My emotions are like a light switch. I can turn them on and off. There are rules to lighting a cigarette to be smoked. The best rule of them all is don't get addicted because you'll miss it when it's gone. Duane was good company. I told him, I might not see him, again; not on this visit. I promised him that I would call him as much as I can. He said if he didn't hear from me, I would most definitely hear from him. I tried to buy him dinner but, he refused. He said he had to get back to the shop because he left at the spur of the moment. It seems like that's part of Duane's routine. He, always, do things at the spur of the moment. Good ol' Duane. That type of person is, always, available.

The penthouse suite was kind of chilly when I got back. I turned off the A. C. I sat the merchandise (I just bought) in the recliner. I stripped to my bra and panties. I walked to the bathroom, grabbed a robe, and threw it in the dryer. It was two forty eight. I had a couple of hours before my seven o' clock dinner with Anthony Preston. I grabbed my bags from the recliner and went into the bedroom. I placed the bags in my suitcase. Opening a drawer, I removed a pair of socks and put them on. I made my way to the dryer, removed the robe, and put it on. Nice and warm. I took the clothes out of the washing machine and threw them into the dryer. I dozed off on the sofa.

It was six fifteen when I woke up. I had to rush. I was out of the shower in less than ten minutes. I didn't know what to wear I choose a long, blue jean skirt that touched my feet. It had a split in the back that stopped at my knees. A sleeveless, black turtleneck. I accentuated my outfit with black, suede boots that stretched well beyond my knees. I put on my gold chain, gold earrings, bracelets, and a ring. I put lip gloss on my lips. I put my hair into a loose ponytail. My skin was, already, oiled but, I put some more on my arms. I smoke a cigarette. The last thing I did to myself was put on some Lovely. It was now six fifty. Anthony knocked on the door. I verified his presence throught the peephole. I opened the door. "I thought you would be gone or, at least, pretend that you were.", Anthony said. He was wearing a green collar, cotton, short-sleeve shirt. He had on a pair of blue jeans that fit his ass and mid-section, quite well. They weren't cowboy tight. He wore a pair of brown Eastland boots and a brown leather belt. This guy looked good. If only I were a whore. "My word is good, Anthony. If you'll give me one second." I closed the door, slightly, and returned with my purse. "You look nice, Ava." "Thank you. So, do you." "Thank you. Lovely, I assume." "You're right. Let me guess, Very Sexy?" "Exactly. I love the scent." We got on the elevators. I thought it would be an awkward moment. Anthony leaned in one corner and crossed his legs at the ankle. He sighed. I turned to look at him. I tried not to look at his package. "Long day?", I asked. "Yeah and I have to wrap everything up by Thursday. I'm tired I have to go to Texas next." "Why won't you hire someone to do business for you?" He crossed his arms across his chest. "Because I don't trust anyone else." We got off the elevator. Men, rarely, trust someone else to do their job. It doesn't matter how rich or poor I'm learning that a lot of men have honor and pride. Where they don't trust anyone to handle business; we, women, simply don't trust men. I was beginning to understand Ambrose's reason and loyalty to his father's shop. Then, I thought about Duane, again. He didn't trust anyone, but he was still willing to pack it all up. Besides, presently, Ambrose's father was still in charge.

"Do you want to dine here or do you want to eat at one of my restaurants?", Anthony asked. I acted surprised, "Your restaurants?" "I own a couple of restaurants.", he said. Yeah right, you own nine restaurants. "What type of restaurants do you own?" "Promise you won't laugh.", he said. "Hey, I love chicken.", I said. "It's not chicken. I love poultry, too.", Anthony said. We were walking towards the front desk. "Oh, no. Then, what is it?", I asked him. He smiled at me and asked the front desk clerk for his car keys. "International House of Pancakes. There, I said it." "What's supposed to be so funny about owning several I.H.O.P.'s? That's a wonderful restaurant." "Just an upscale version of the Waffle House.", he said. "Hey, it's your place you can call it whatever you want." We walked outside. His black BMW was, already, parked under the canopy. I waited for him to open the door for me. He didn't. I, usually, wouldn't be offended by this and I wasn't fazed, then. He unlocked the doors from his key chain. We both opened our doors and took our seat. In the car, Anthony realized his error and apologized. "I haven't had a date in so long that I forgot my manners." "Anthony, it's okay. No harm done. Need I remind you this is not, officially, what we would call a date. Besides, you owe me that one. Even?", I asked. "Even." "Well, if we're even, then you can take me back to my room." "Are you serious? Oh, Ava, that's cruel." "I'm only joking. Lighten up, Anthony. So, have you ever been married?" "No. No children, either. There's no-one but, me and Bozo." "Who's Bozo?", I asked. "My bulldog." "How old are you, Anthony?" "I'm thirty-nine and you? If you don't mind me asking. I know it's rude to ask a lady's age." "I'm twenty.", I answered him, quickly. We didn't speak for a minute. I didn't know who was more uncomfortable. Mr. Preston was old enough to be my father. He could, easily, pass for thirty or late twenties but, we both knew the truth. "Do you ever plan on having children, Anthony? I mean, who are you going to leave your fortune, to?" "That's a good question. If I find that special lady; yes, I want children. If not, then I'll leave everything to my nieces and nephews." "Cool." I was thinking at your age impregnating a prostitue wouldn't be a bad idea. "So, you have sister and brothers?", I asked. "No, close friends with kids." "Aw.. that's so sweet." "Stop it.", he said.

We pulled in the I.H.O.P's parking lot. Immediately, a worker in a blue shirt appeared behind the glass dooors. "Mr. Preston, will you be dining in your office?", the manager asked. "No, find us a comfortable spot, would you?", Anthony asked the manager. The manager nodded and led us to a table that was seperated from the rest of regular customers. We sat down. "What would you all have to drink?", the waitress asked. I smiled, "A Coca-cola." Anthony asked for a glass of water. "So, Ava, what do you do for a living? It must be something amazing. You're staying in the penthouse suite." Before I could answer his question, I heard two familiar voices erupt into laughter. I looked past Anthony and they waved at me with a smile on their faces. I felt like I was on an episode of "Punk'd" What are they doing here? I know it's not a fucking coincidence. "Hold that thought, Anthony. I have to utilize the lady's room." About thirty seconds after I walked in the bathroom, Hemisphere and Dependable came in behind me. "I told you that was you little sister. Pay up.", Dependable said. Hemisphere gave Dependable what appeared to be a stack or two; It was rolled up with a rubberband around it. "Did you call J.J., today?", Hemisphere asked. "Who's J.J.?", I asked. I tried to go into a bathroom stall but, Dependable blocked it off. "What is this? The bully patrol?", I asked. Neither of them showed any emotions. I wanted to slap fire from Dependable. She should know I'm not a punk. I turned to face Hemisphere. "If you're talking about John; no, I haven't called him, yet. I plan on calling him when I return to the suite.", I said. Hemisphere looked down at her hands. She rubbed her thumb across the free edge of her left hand and said, "I don't think you grasped the importance of this job, Advantage. You should be having a jolly fucking conversation with J.J., right now." She looked up from her nails and continued, "Instead, you're out eating fucking pancakes." I felt defeated. Hemisphere made me feel like a school girl climbing into her bedroom window after hours. To make matters worse, I was being scolded in front of

Dependable. I wanted to call Mom and tell on YoSaVon. I wanted to curse but, most of all, I want to get her off my back. "Don't be so mean, Hemi. She's only a rookie.", Dependable said, sarcastically. "You know what? Fuck this shit! You hoes ain't my momma!", I yelled. Hemisphere slapped me. My head turned to the side and my hand was on the sink. "You know what?", I continued. This time my voice sounded sinister. My head was still facing the mirror. "If you think you can do a better job, be my guest. I'll pack and go home but, the next time you put your hands on me...", I said. I looked up and stared Hemisphere, directly, in her eyes. "...I'm going to be on you like ticks on a stray dog." "Don't threaten me, Ava. I'll make you eat that shit.", Hemisphere said. "That's my word.", I said. "Your word is of no importance, to me.", Hemisphere said. She took a step closer. "You're job description does not state that you are here to enjoy yourself. Once you recognized it, the more skilled you will become. Get used to it." She turned and walked away. "A high paid rookie.", Dependable said. She threw her shoulder into my back as she walked past me. She walked so fast that she left Hemisphere behind. They are a pair to reckon with. They, really, know how to push your buttons. Dependable have some nerves; bumping me, like that. What did YoSaVon mean when she said get used to it? Am I under consideration to be an actual smoker? That would be good. Once I am accepted, I'm going to let them know I'm not a pushover. I apologized to Anthony for taking so long. He brushed it off. I noticed Hemisphere and Dependable were gone. Before we could order, Anthony's alarm on his BMW went off. We, both, rushed outside. The back window on the passenger's side was burst out. I had a clue of who did it. Anthony asked by-standers did they see anything. No one saw a thing. I saw them. Hemisphere was driving. Dependable gave a sideways smile and waved one gloved hand in the air. They drove away calm, cool, and collect. That was the end of our evening. To avoid giving the police any information about me, I thanked Anthony and expressed my empathy towards his misfortune. I took a taxi back to the hotel.

"Leave a message after the tone. beep..." "Ambrose, call me when you get a chance, okay? I love you." I took off my clothes and put on a gray jogging suit. My phone rang when I was putting on a pair of socks. I walked into the living quarters and answered, "It do." "Ava, are you driving, right now?" "No." "Where are you?" It was RoNao. "I'm at the suite." "Well, sit down." "RoNao, what's up? You're scaring me." "Okay. Look, don't panic, okay?"

"Yeah, what is it?" "That man Stecha was dealing with jumped on her." "Is she alright?", I asked. "Yeah. She got a black eye and a busted lip, though. She's staying with momma for a few weeks. She had to take off work, too. They said if she don't come in after two weeks, they're going to fire her. I hope the blackness will be gone. You know she's not going to work like that." "I know. She better put on some make up. When did he jump on her?" "Earlier, today. I'm at work, right now. Look, don't tell Mom or Stecha that I told you that. They said not to tell you until you came home. I have to go. I love you, Ava." "Yeah, I love you, too. RoNao?" "Yeah." "Did she say why he jumped her?" "No. She didn't say nothing to anyone. Last time I checked, Le ebo was to Mom's house with her. She, probably, told her. I'on know, though. I gotta go." "Alright. Call me when you get off." Some people have to learn the hard way but, I'll be damned if I let this nigga give my sister lessons on physical education. Family is everything, to me. That motherfucker better pack up and leave town. He's a walking blunt and I'm going to smoke his ass.

Some things are, believed to be, destined to happen. We, also, can speak events into existence. We can curse ourselves with the things we say. The tongue is the deadliest weapon of all. I sat at the bar smoking a cigarette. I was thinking about the things that I have said that have come to past. I remember when I was a teenager in the apartment's laundry room with RoNao. I told her that when I get older I wanted to be an assassin. Then I thought about what RoNao said about Stecha's ways catching up with her. I sipped on the Courvoisier. Hmmph. I said I would tell YoSaVon about the fight betweeen Stecha and RonNao. I don't believe I did or ever would. Someone knocked on the door; breaking my reverie. I looked through the peephole. It was Anthony. I was about to let him believe that I was gone but, I owed him one. "Hey, Ant.", I said. I leaned against the door. I still had on the gray jogging suit. The suit I put on after the restaurant. I was now barefeet, though. "Oh, my. Did I catch you at a bad time?", He asked. I took a step back to look in the bar's mirror. My hair was disheveled from resting my hand on my forehead and running my fingers through my hair; from time to time. I leaned in closer to the mirror. My eyeshadow was running down my face. The novocaine fairy must have visited my face because I didn't know I was crying. Back in the doorway, I wiped my face with the bottom of my shirt. Hey, my shirt was gray, anyway. I noticed Anthony was staring at my exposed stomach. He continued…, "I like that." "What?", I asked. "You called me Ant. That's cool. I think I'll adopt that alias.", He said. He took off his glasses and cleaned them with his shirt. He's cute with or without them. He placed his glasses back on his face. "I didn't mean to disturb you at such a bad time." "Anthony, I'm okay. Trust me. If I didn't want company, I wouldn't be talking to you, now. I'm a big girl.", I said. I punched him in the arm, playfully. "You'll be amazed at how much I can take, Ant.", I said. "What can we do to cheer you up?", Anthony asked. He had his hands on his hips. "Really, Ant. I'm okay. There's no need to go out of your way." "Are you sure?", Anthony asked. He looked over the brim of his glasses. He reminded me of an old school teacher. "Yes. I just need to rest.", I said. "Okay. Well, I'm going to be busy over the next few days. I might not see you the remainder of my time here." He went into his back pocket and took a card out of his wallet. The card was gold and trimmed in blue. "Not everyone receive one of these." "Oh, yeah.", I said. I felt privileged. "Yeah. That's because my house and cell phone numbers are on it. I've had ten of these made and you are the second person to get one.", He blushed. "Mr. Preston, I'm honored. I'll only use it in case of an emergency.", I said. He was flattered but, his eyes showed that he knew that I needed to be alone. "You can call whenever, Ava." He took one of my hands in his. "Do take care of yourself. It was a pleasure meeting you. I hope we cross paths, again." I reached for him. We hugged, held hands, and looked at each other, a second. When we let go of each other's hands I felt like I was losing a close friend. "Well, I'll be moving, right along." He kissed me on the side of my jaw. A kiss I more than welcomed. He walked off. That was the last time I would see Anthony Preston for two years.

I woke up the next morning; confused and scared. I thought I was having a nightmare. A silhouette was standing at the foot of the bed. I felt another presence laying in the bed with me. Of all nights, I decided to sleep in the death chamber. I felt like I was about to meet the grim reaper. This was not a dream. I opened my eyes, wide. A finger ran through my hair. I was on my feet, immediately. I grabbed a lamp and poised myself in the defense position. Someone clapped twice. The room came to life. I placed my right arm in front of my eyes because they were, not yet, adjusted to the light. I threw the lamp. Silence. Once, I could distinguish the distorted figures. Hemisphere said, "Sleep good?" Dependable was placing the lamp on the dresser behind me. "I told you she would grab the lamp. Pay up.", Dependable said. She caught the rolled up money that was tossed by Hemisphere. "That's twoo to one. Your way. All bets are, officially, over. At least, they are over, this month.", Hemisphere said. I grabbed my jogging pants. "Why are ya'll always fucking with me?", I said. I walked into the bedroom and locked the door. I washed my face and brushed my teeth. I opened the door, a little and overheard their conversation. "She acts like a brat; constantly, throwing temper tantrums. She don't seem to understand what type of bind we are in. She's been paid higher than anyone off the streets. If our bets weren't off this month, I'd bet you she didn't call J. J.", Dependable said. "Hell, I'd bet she didn't, either. I'll tell you who's perfect for the job. Our younger sister Stecha." "Really?" "Hell, yeah. She don't show any emotions. She lives to work and take care of her daughter. She's a true smoker. I would've asked her, first but, Ava have the prettiest eyes.", Hemisphere said. "Yeah. Well, maybe, you should've held her at gunpoint and gave her an ultimatum. If you know who knew how she was acting, she'd kill us all.", Dependable said. She? Who is she? Hemisphere continued, "If this operation goes sour, we might as well take a long vacation and stand down to the rookies." "I need a vacation but, I'm not looking for it, anytime soon.", Dependable said. They both got quiet. Hemisphere was pouring Hennessey in her coffee. Dependable turned on the T.V. and I walked in the room. Hemisphere looked up from her cup. Dependable pretended not to notice me. "Advantage, did you call J.J., last night?", Hemisphere asked. "No, I apologize. I..." Hemisphere held up her right hand. She did it so quick. Immediately, I got quiet. "Advantage, I've been very nice to you. I've given you warning after warning.", Hemisphere said. Dependable didn't turn around but, she did turn the T.V. down. "What do you expect me to do, Advantage? We have only a few days to light this cigarette. Your job is simple; yet, you can't even make a phone call. Therefore, actions must be taken against your irresponsible behavior." "Hemisphere, hold on.", I said. "No, Advantage. You should be the one holding on. Holding on to great opportunities. Your greatest opportunity started when Dependable brought you the suitcase and with this suitcase I shall make you, truly, realize the importance of the job. Nothing I've said seems to. Go get it, Advantage." I was daydreaming. "Go get it now, Advantage.", Hemisphere said. I did what she asked me to do. When I came back, the television was off. Dependable was standing up and Hemisphere was closing her phone. I placed the suitcase on the table and opened it. "Give me five bundles." "Five Hemisphere?", I asked. "Correct. You ought to be happy. The boss wanted ten." She signaled Dependable to take the money. She put three in Hemisphere's black trench coat and two in her gray trench coat. They started to leave. Dependable turned around, smiled and said, "Beats betting."

Talk about drama. I felt like I was trapped in the land of Oz. I didn't need any glass slippers. I held the keys to the Escalade in my hand; fumbling with the ignition key. All I had to do was leave. Although, I was considerd a highly paid assassin in the making, I was stressed. First, my relationship was on the brinks of collapsing; thanks to YoSaVon. I can't blame her, though. It was, solely, my decision. Then, my babysitter was jumped by her trick. That's why I'm holding these keys, now, because I wanted to go home. I wanted to fing Stanley the angler and mark his ass. I expected YoSaVon to care and be lenient towards me when she didn't even know what was going on. Fuck it. I threw the keys on the bar and bit my knuckles. I'll have time to deal with his ass, later. Lately, I've been breaking promises and not keeping my word. I've got to get myself together. As much as I love my sisters, I can't be distracted at this stage of my "great opportunity", right now. I sat at the bar and watched myself smoke a cigarette. It's time to go to work. Not only will I prove to YoSaVon but, also, to myself that I am worthy of being a smoker. Yeah, true, I said it, myself, that Stecha fit the profile to be a smoker. I am a cold hearted motherfucker, too! Game on.

"Renee, I didn't think I would be hearing from you, so soon.", Johnathan said. "Are you being sarcastic, John." I asked while standing in the kitchen splitting a cigar open. "What happened yesterday, Renee?", John asked. "Something came up." "Anything I could help with. I'm a handy person, you know." "I know." "I don't think you do." "I can imagine. Are you busy, tonight?" "Well... I'm preparing a speech for the C.U.S.A. assembly but, I think I can squeeze you in." Squeeze me in, motherfucker! You better make a gap. "John, are you trying to repay me? Truly, I apologize. Do you trust me, John?" No offense, Ms. Brown but, I trust no-one." "Well, you should believe that I am telling you the truth. Something came up. Family problems.", I said. "I thought your par.." "John, don't. I'm not an orphan. Let's just leave it at that, okay?" "Fine. We discussed all we needed to venture when last we met. What are you doing, right now?" "Rolling a blunt." "Do you have a nice amount?", John asked. "I'm not rolling a nickel sack. So, does that mean I will see you, tonight?" "Of course. Where shall we meet?" "Same place. What time?", I asked. "How's six?" "Cool.", I said. "Alright. I'll see you, then. Hey, Renee?" "Yeah." "Don't keep me waiting." "I won't. Trust me." Who in the fuck does he thinks he is? Don't keep me waiting. If I didn't fear that Hemisphere would take ten bundles from me, I would make his ass do just that. He's acting, exactly, how I want him to; like a man. His behavior is making it that more easier to blow his brains out, literally.

RoNao said not to tell Stecha I know about her run in with Stanley but, she couldn't keep me from calling her. "Hey.", Stecha said. "Hey. What it do?", I asked her. She was quiet about three seconds. "Stecha?" "Yeah.", Stecha said with an attitude. "What's up? What's wrong with you?", I asked. "Why are you asking me those dumb ass questions? Ain't shit up. You live here and a whole fucking lot is wrong with me." "Damn, Ste. You don't have to snap out, like that. How's Sympathy?" "She's good." "Good. Look, tell mom I said that I love her. I love you, too. Well, I see you don't want to be bothered. I'll call you, tomorrow.", I said. I sighed, concurrently. "Look, Ava. Don't take what I said the wrong way. Just tell me something. Did Ro or Mom tell you anything?" "No, why?" "Because.", Ste' said. "Because what, Ste?" "I'm so pissed at myself. I let my guards down and this nigga, this motherfucker, this bitch hits me." "Whoa, Ste, slow down. What are you talking about?", I asked. "Stanley. Stanley, hit me.", she said. I took a deep breath, "Did he hit you once or more?" "What does it matter? The bastard used his fist. He didn't slap me, Ava. He punched me. That bitch ass nigga punched me." "Are you okay?" "Yeah, sure. I'm okay. No. I'm fucking not okay." "Are you bruised or anything, like that?" "Yeah, my right eye is black and my nose was bust all up. I'm staying at mom's for a minute until my shit goes down and gets it's proper color. Hell, I took a week off from work. They want me back, a.s.a.p. If my eye is still purple, they hang that shit up.", Stecha said. "You're tripping. Put on some make up. They don't call that shit Cover Girl for nothing. It's for shit like that. You better cover that shit up, girl." "Yeah, I guess I could, huh? Afterall, I love my job and the supply of good, wealthy, high rolling tricks." "Damn, Stecha. Have you learned anything?" "Yeah.", she said. She was laughing, "Get all you can on the first and second date and to stay strapped." I smiled and said,

"It do." "Already. Hey, Ava? You know what, Ava? The real answer to that question... If I learned anything... I did, Ava. I, really, did. Seriously, I did." "Oh, yeah. What's that?" "Girl, when tht nigga did that foul shit to me all I could think about was Sympathy, you, mom, RoNao, and Yo'. I thought I was going to die without ever seeing my baby, again; without cursing you and Ro's sensitive ass out, again; without telling Mom that I love her, again and God knows if YoSaVon would've made it to my funeral. That piece of shit ass nigga. I'ma make him pay for that shit, though" "Girl, you just said you thought about all of us. It's a blessing you didn't get murdered. Now, if you go out looking for that nigga and kill him, everybody you just named will be visiting your ass from prison. Don't trip, though. I'll take good care of Sympathy." "Naw... I'm going to be okay. Like I say, I learned my lesson. I'll just use my Visa on that one and charge it.", Stecha said. I was shocked. I didn't believe a word she said. She was, too, calm. "Yeah, your work-a-holic ass needed a break from the baller that be rolling on the river. Shit's crazy but, I got you." "Yeah. Get me some fly body gear while you're splurging, ya dig?" "Already.", I said. "How is work?", Stecha asked. "You want Webster's definition or should I inform you." "Inform me.", Stecha said. "It's rhetorical.", I said. "Understood. Nothing remains. Later.", Stecha said. "Alright. Call me, later." "I might."

I am no better than Stecha. There I was telling her to forget about what happened to her; knowing that I couldn't if it happened to me. One would think that something like that would make her want to stop taking money from men. It only made her straighten up her game. Telling Stecha to stop playing would be the same if one told me not to kill John. It was just something that had to be done. For both of us, it was a job and there wouldn't be an exchange of sexual favors. There was no need to pretend to be angels because we didn't give a fuck about how they felt. Who said life was fair? It's beautiful being various shades of brown and black. It's fucking hideous how most white (along with other races) people consider most of us stupid. Fuck, I even consider most of us stupid. I think every race is a breed that likes to party. We all go to work with a party in our heads. If it's not a marijuana party, it's some sort of drug. We're all dealt a hand in the game of life. Some hands are better than others. We're not guaranteed to acquire a decent hand every time the cards are shuffled. If you play long enough, we all get a good hand and a bad one. John has a damn good one. I'll admit his hand is better than mine but, the last card I'm going to play will be the Joker.

I met YoSaVon at one of Anthony's I.H.O.P.'s. As usual, Dependable was present. I had a hour before my shindig with John. They were sitting in the same spot the last time they were there. They were dresssed (like always) like F.B.I. agents. I walked to the table, took off my shades, and placed them in my purse. "Here, she is; five bundles lighter.", Dependable said. She reached for her glass that contained, what appeared to be, V8 juice. "Cut it out, Dependable.", I said. We got quiet until the waiter left after I rejected a drink. "So, do you want to get the limo, again, tonight?", Hemisphere asked. "No, that's not a good idea. I'm going to take the Escalade.", I said. "That's not a good idea, either. Take the El Dorado. It can't be traced. If John decides to run a trace on the vehicle, he'll learn your true identity.", Dependable said. "True. In the a.m., we pow wow. We need you to bring Mr. Johanneson to the suite, tomorrow.", Hemisphere said. "Do you mean?", I asked. "It do.", Dependable said. Where in the fuck do she get off saying, 'It do'? That shit is a family thing. "Alright. I can dig that.", I said. "Hmph... Do you think you can turn him on that he would come back to the suite with you? You have to be very seductive, tonight, Ms. Fiance.", Hemisphere asked. "I think we all can. When I'm smoking, I am a single woman that doesn't have a pussy.", I said. I looked down at the table. "So, Are you saying you're full of dick?", Dependable asked. She looked, directly, in my eyes; smirking. "Fun's over, ladies. Now, let's get down to business. So, what time are you scheduled to meet him?", Hemisphere asked. She clicked her index fingernail (on her right hand) on the table. "At six.", I stated. "Where?", Hemisphere asked. "The same place I meet the weed man." "I need a report as soon as he exit your presence.", Hemisphere stated. She didn't seem to care how I met Duane. He had nothing to do with the operation. "And... does this weed man know anything about J. J.?", Hemisphere asked. "No, I haven't said a word to him. I wouldn't tell a relative or lover about this. So, what makes you think I would tell someone that I don't know?", I asked. "Good. Not, that we have that understood, a ring is attached to the steering wheel, wear it. If you all are going on one of your weed binges, take your car and suggest that he drive. We would like to have a visual of him. Are we clear?", Hemisphere asked. "Yes.", I said. "Tomorrow we celebrate. We're having a smoke out.", Hemisphere said. I went back to the room. I had to shower and decide what to wear. I chose a short, blue khaki skirt, an insulated, pink spaghetti string shirt, and pink stilettos. Afterall, the ring I had to wear was ice pink. Before I decided to leave, I called Ambrose. "Talk about your ghost in the machine.", Ambrose said. "Hey, baby. I love you, too. How are you doing?", I asked him. "I'm alive; not that you would know." "Baby, you could call me. I, always, call you. I, really, don't want to argue with you." "I don't want to argue with you, either. But, what else is there to talk about? Everything is fine. I'm good. You're good. What else need to be said besides, I love you and I want you to come home?", Ambrose said. His voice was one of those I don't give a damn tone. "I should be home, tomorrow. I'm learning at an, exceptionally, fast rate. I'm more advanced than they thought I would be.", I said. "Oh, I'm ready to wax that ass. Beating my dick ain't getting the job done. I want to lick that pussy." "Quit it, Ambrose. So, how is school?" "It's alright. Once, you learn, damn near, everything it gets boring." "YoSaVon is coming back with me." "Are you for real? Why?" "RoNao got accepted into Harvard and we're going to celebrate." "Harvard?", Ambrose asked. "Yeah, she's had a 4.0 average since she stepped foot into a school. She never had a B a day in her life. I don't think she's ever made a 99.", I said. "That's smart. You're smart, too, baby. So, are your sisters. That shit must run in your genes." "Must do.", I said. We listened to each other breath. "Well, look, I love you, baby.", Ambrose said. "I love you, too.", I said. "It's almost time for youto go to work. So, I guess I'll let you go. It takes you two hours to get ready." "No, it don't." "Hopefully, I'll see you, tomorrow.", He said. "Hopefully." "I want to dig in them guts." "You know I don't like it when you say that shit." "I know but, you know where you feel it." "Ambrose, bye." "See you, later. Remember?", he said. "Yeah. See you, later."

I, almost, didn't see John's black Lexus with black tint. I thought he stood me up just to be an ass. I rolled down the window. John was smoking a newport. He had his eyes held together, tight; taking his last drag from the cigarette. He plucked it away. It bounced off the El Dorado. I dimmed the lights and sat there for a second. I watched John. Through the tinted window, for a brief second, I could've swore he looked me, directly, in my eyes. I was playing a dangerous game with a dangerous man who was in a dangerous situation. They say money is the root of all evil. I say pussy is. I got out of the El Dorado. "Second thoughts?", John asked. "No, I just didn't expect you to be here, early. A girl's got to check their make-up."

John rolled up his window and stepped out of his car. He looked better in regular clothes than he did in a tux. Whoa! He was wearing a horizontal, blue, white, and black Sean John collar shirt. It was short sleeve. He had on blue Sean John pants and see through Jordans. He leaned against his Lexus and crossed his arms. He looked more like a dope boy. "Well, you look nice. I'm not like most men. I have a tendency to keep my word." John said. That was a cheap shot. "Thank you, John. You look nice yourself. Let me ask you something, though.", I said. "Go ahead.", John said. "Are you going to rub the absence of me not callin you in my fight, all night?", I asked. He smiled a tight-lip smile. "No, but if I don't say what's on my mind it would remain a thought. A bad thought. That's like having friends talk behind your back. Which do you prefer?", John asked. "I prefer to leave the past as it's defined.", I stated. I took a step closer to John. We were so close that we could smell each other's breath. How's that for being seductive, Hemisphere? I know that I affected him. He looked down and licked his lips. He returned his stare back to me. Sometimes, one can sense when a partner is committing infidelity. I wondered if Ambrose could feel what I was doing. John cleared his throat, "Well, I guess we'll be using your car?" "I guess so. You drive.", I said. I dangled the key ring on my index finger and smiled. That's when it happened. That's when I allowed him to kiss me and I enjoyed it. I enjoyed it so much I didn't know it was over. When I opened my eyes John was smiling at me. "I apologize. I didn't meant to...", John said. "It's okay. It's okay. That was alright.", I said; blushing. "Now, where were we?", John asked. "We were at the part where you drive.", I said. I walked to passenger's side door. John followed me and opened my door. "What? What's wrong?", He asked. "Don't do that.", I said. "Do what? Be a gentleman?" "No, continue to be a gentleman. Just don't push the liberal rights issue. I'm fine opening my own door, thank you.", I said. "...and I'm fine with you opening your own door. You're welcome. I'm just used to opening doors for my wife and other stucked up women with money." "Well, I have a little money but, I'm, definitely, down to earth.", I said. I got into the car. John was locking his car when Hemisphere spoke from the ring. "Did you just kiss him?", Hemisphere asked. "Does it matter?", I said. "Just curious.", she said. "Curiousity killed the cat.", I said. "Satisfaction brought him back. Let's hope that kiss make that dog curious about your catnip.", She giggled and said 'out'. John opened the door. He had a C. D. case in his hand. "What's that?", I asked. "Usher.", He said. He adjusted the rearview mirror. He popped the C. D. in and drove off. We listened to Usher and Lil' John perform "Yeah" three times before he took it off repeat. I opened the ashtray and lit one of the six blunts that I had, already, rolled. "Are we going anywhere in particular?", John asked. "Your place or mine?", I asked. He looked at me and smiled. I turned my head to the side and raised my forehead. I gave him a look that let him know I was serious. "Whatever. Stop playing, girl. You know we can't go to my place. Everyone knows me there." "You stop playing; everyone knows you everywhere. They know you at your place or mine.", I said. I was thinking, 'It shouldn't be hard to disguise yourself.' Score, for Ava! Yeah, I did my homework by learning his likes and dislikes; his do's and don't's. I wonder, if he would, really, wear that twenty two during sex. The world may never know. At least, I will never know about twenty two and his sexscapades. Hell no! So what, I kissed him back. It was business, baby. That was the most expensive kiss, ever. Would I do it, again? Yes, I would. I love Ambrose but, it like Tina said, "What's love got to do with it?" Not a damn thing. There's not a woman or man that wouldn't do what I just did. A lot of them would have sex with him or gave him oral sex, already. I heard it's being done for far less. Some drop their drawers for a hundred dollars. So, if anyone besides God wants to judge me, they better sweep around their own damn door. I know people that are in relationships that are buying pussy. Some of these hoes are fucking for free, some are getting paid for it, and some are paying for it. Yes, paying for the dick. Think about it. The ratchet man will move into your house. You pay the rent, car note, utilities, and bought the furniture. That's one thing about Ambrose; he pays for everything. Most women do all these things because we don't want to be stereotyped as a chickenhead. Fuck that! Cluck. Cluck. bitch. Throw me some corn. Some women lay up with a lazy ass man that don't look forward to having shit in life. Some men are satisfied with a hot plate and some pussy. I mean, if you look at it, either way, we still pay or get paid for it. After this jock bones you, he debones the chicken you cooked for him. Hungry motherfucker. By the way, you bought that chicken with cash or your foodstamp card. That's why I don't care if a cat opens the door as long as he know he's going top open his wallet. I can open my own damn door but, he has to open his billfold. Don't get it confused. An open wallet does not mean open legs. Maybe, an open bank account, new car door, and new house. Maybe. The game is cold and titsils will keep these niggas on freeze until they get blueballs.

Back in my penthouse suite, John and I smoke a couple of blunts. Hemisphere called the 'cell phone' and told me not to leave John alone for one second. She, then, instructed me to lead him into the bedroom and excuse myself to the bathroom where my packed bags will be waiting on me, and leave. She warned me not to come back to that room for any reason.

The Big Decision

"WOW, THIS IS A NICE room; nicer than mine. Father set you up for life, huh?" John asked sipping a brandy, straight. I was behind the bar, stirring an olive on a toothpick that was in my martini. I leaned on the bar and smiled. I revealed some cleavage. "And why not? I deserver it. Afterall, I am daddy's little girl. Do you have any children, John?", I asked. "Of course." "Well, obviously, you and your wife are having marital problems. Being, that you are here with me.", I said. John downed his liquor and sucked his tongue before asking, "Where are you going with this?" "All I'm saying is, if you were to die, today, right now; wouldn't you set your children up for life?" John turned his glass in tiny circles and stared forward in a daze. I watched as he walked to the window and gazed at the city. He answered without facing me but, I could see his eyes reflect through the glass. "You know, I never thought about death, Renee. I have, always, been the type of guy to avoid freak accidents." He turned around with a cold stare in his eyes and continued, "Do you understand what I'm saying, Renee?" "Elaborate for me, John. Layman's terms", I said. I stood behind the sofa. "What I'm saying is I like to precise about everything, Ava. Everything. In Layman's terms, if I'm not killed because I ran out of brake fluid or I'm on a plane that explodes, I have no desire to let a pretty face and big ass lead me into seduction with death. I hope to die of old age.", John said. He stared, directly, in my eyes. I was in a daze. I was shocked. He knew who I was. I stood there mumbling, silently, to myself. "What's the

107

matter, Ava or should I continue to go by your alias Renee Brown?" I had to think fast. Shit! How in the fuck did he know my real name? "Well, there's no use in playing pretend, anymore, John? So, how much do you know?", I asked. "I know more than you can imagine." "Well, what's next?", I asked. "You tell me who you're working for.", He said. "Working for? What are you talking about?", I asked. Where in the hell is Hemisphere and the rest of those smoking motherfuckers? I had to stay cool. "Who do you work for, damn it?", John asked. "I work alone." "Yeah, you work alone. Do you, really, expect me to believe that?" "Believe what you want but, I am telling the truth.", I said. One could hear the tremor in my voice. John was looking down at his hand like he was checking out a fresh manicure. "Who sent you? My wife? The government? Who? I, always, suspected my wife knew about my infidelity but, for her to stoop so low and hire a private investigator.. It had to be her. The government wouldn't have me deliver a speech and dog me out in pubic.", he said. He was flabbergasted... He was confused. He, also, filled in the blank to his question. "You know, Ava, five years, earlier I wouldn't have known you and if I did, you would've been wishing that you didn't know me.", John said. His chest heaved up and down. This motherfucker just gave me a past tense break. I don't take threats, well. Fuck this. He was lucky I weren't strapped. I would've blew his fucking brains out, right there. I would have murked his ass right where he stood. Yeah, he's lucky my sides aren't burning, right now, because I would've tossed his ass in the fire. "Well, Ms. Brown, who sent you to spy on me? Was it that bitch that I got fleas from, hmmm? I hope that she don't thinks that I don't know that she's fucking, too. But, she's not the bitch that I'm addressing. Now, is she?", John said. He walked towards me. When he got close enough to touch me, he grabbed my shoulders, shook them, and yelled, "Who sent you?" I was so scared I could not, barely, form my words. "I... that's confidential. I can't tell you that.", I said. "Yeah, sure you can. Come on... It'll be our little secret.", John said. He no longer reminded me of the nice gentleman that I saw laughing with associates at the opening of La Galeria. In his eyes, I saw a cold blooded murderer. "Yes, John. It was your wife.", I said. What? What did you expect me to say? Fuck his wife. Besides, that was the best damn explanation anyone could have thought of. He'll be dead before he finds out the truth. "I knew it. That bitch is spying on me.", John said. He had his right hand on his hip and his left pointer and thumb under his chin. His eyes looking past me. He slammed both of his fist into the table. I thought the glass on the table would shatter. John continued, "I can't believe that bitch would do this to me. I'm not the only one unfaithful in this marriage. You tell her I know about her little sex rendezvous, too. So, if she's going to court, I'm more than ready. So, what now, Ava? Are you going to be a witness? Are you going to take the stand and testify against me, Ava?", John asked. I looked down at my hand and compared them to the color of the carpet. Nice contrast. Next, I thought sad thoughts. I had to make this shit look real. I thought about Stecha's ex-associate Stanley punching her in the face. There. A tear dropped. That did it. I looked up, quick. He was buying it. "John, I..." "You what? You tried to trap me. You make me develop a frienship with and you throw shit in my face. Do you expect me to forgive you for that, too? Now that I think about it, your so-called family problems didn't make you miss our date. In fact, you were meeting my wife. Did you have to give her your most recent discovery of my wild adventures?", John asked. I didn't know what to say. So, I stayed quiet. "Answer me, damn it!", John screamed. "No, I never met her. We talked on the phone but, that's not why I didn't meet you. I really..." "You really asked me to trust you. You piece of shit! Ava, if I were you, I'd leave Atlanta and forget my name.", He said. "John, listen in the beginning it was all about the money but, now John, I...", I said. I walked close to him. I tried to cup his face with my left hand. He grabbed my wrist and squeezed it, extremely, tight before I could touch him. "You what, Ava? Are you going to tell me how you grew to be attached to me? Is that what you were going to say? You love me, all of a sudden. Well, store it in your memory for the next imbecile because I had no intentions on downloading your stupid ass. Now, that I've answered your questions. Leave, Ava. I don't ever want to see you, again." "No, you leave. This is my room and you didn't answer my question. I was going to make a statement.", I said with a grudge in my tone. I tried to yank my arm from John's hand. "There's no need to prepare a speech. As far as, your room goes. I will look up everything and make sure you're checked out." "Hell no, John. You can drop that political bullshit. I don't know Senator Johanneson but, I do know, John. Believe it or not but, I like John. I like being around you and I wasn't going to tell your wife shit. Not a fucking thing. I swear.", I said. I was on the verge of tears. Hey, I was telling the truth. John was squeezing my arm, even tighter. I, really, did not want to cry. Instead, I begged John to release my arm. "John, please, you're hurting me. I'm telling the truth.", I said. When he let his hold off my wrist, my arm was asleep. John pushed me into the sofa. I sat, unwillingly. John paced in front of me, two or three times. "Do you expect me to believe you, Ava. I mean, honestly. Do you, really, expect me to believe you?" "No." "Then, since you won't leave this room, what would you propose?" "Let me prove it to you, John." "Prove it to me. Prove it to me and how might you do that?", he asked. "Let me make love to you." I know I shocked myself. I said I would not ever cheat on Ambrose. I wouldn't but, in a time like this I would have one secret I would take to the grave. I looked up. John looked at me with a look I couldn't explain. "Right here? Right now?", John asked. "Right now but, not right here. We couldn't make love on a sofa or floor. That will be fucking.", I said. I spat out the last words. To my surprise, John said, "I can settle for that." "I can't, John. I couldn't fuck a married man. Let me make love to you in the bedroom." We were there in silence for about six seconds. "Do you need to showere?", He asked. "No. Do you?" "No.", he said. "Do you forgive me?", I asked. I wanted him to say yes. Yes, I forgive you for pushing me into the grim reaper's arms. Yes, I forgive you for pretending to be a friend. In a sense, I wanted him to say, yes, he forgave me before he died. I am going to have nightmares behind this night. I knew I would have nightmares because when I looked in his eyes I saw a friend. A friend who told me things he didn't tell anyone else. I saw a friend who made me laugh. I saw a human fucking being that was scum to someone else. "Yeah, Ava, I forgive you but, I won't ever forget. Besides, I bet Carla never thought that her money would be wasted. She paid someone to catch my eye. She didn't expect me to fall in love with that person.", He said. What? In love? This is some kind of payback trap. "I know I lied but, you don't have to throw gas into the fire.", I said. John turned his back and spoke, "I know this may sound like a lie because of the many times that you have deceived me. I promise you on my children that I am being honest." He turned around, quickly, and stood before me on one knee. He grabbed my hands. "We can leave all of this behind. I have plenty of money in off-shore accounts. I'll get a divorce and I promise you I wouldn't cheat on you. What man would want to cheat on you?" "John! What about your kids?" "They're set for life. I'll visit. Well, visit as much as possible.", he said. "Wouldn't that be considered a scandal in your line of work?", I asked. I took my hand out of his, slowly. I rested my forehead in my hand like a person trying to soothe a headache. "Who cares? It happens all the time. I love you, Ava. I, really, do love you and I promise I'll always protect you." "Hmmph... Stupid motherfucker couldn't even protect himself.", Hemisphere said. I backed into the sofa trying to hide like a nut in a shell. I watched as,

Hemisphere placed the gun (she shot John in the back of head with) into a small silver case. Dependable held the case. I was too shocked to scream. I knew it was going to happen but damn, I thought this shit was going to take place in the bedroom. I wasn't prepared for this, at all. They gave me a schedule for every move I made in Atlanta. They were upset if I was a minute late to any appointment but, they did not give me the time of John's death. Hemisphere walked into the kitchen and started to brew some coffee. Dependable was busy putting John's head in a plastic bag. She tied it with a shoestring around the neck. Hemisphere called from the kitchen, "Yo, D, you owe me twenty stacks. I told you she wouldn't scream. Ava, get up and pack your shit. We have to leave, baby. D, call room service to clean this shit up." I sat there. I was stunned. "Ava, get your purified water down ass up and go pack your shit!", Hemisphere yelled. She slammed her fist down on the counter, simultaneously. I got up to do what she asked. "...and before you do, look down at your first cigarette. You held him to my mouth, I lit that bitch, and smoked his ass. Look, bitch.", Hemisphere demanded. I looked in John's lifeless eyes. This motherfucker was just pouring his heart out to me; willing to leave it all behind for me and that's, exactly, what he did... Left it all behind because of me.

Him

"No. No." "WAKE UP, AVA.", YoSavon said. She was reaching for her V8 bottle with her left hand on the steering wheel. "Nightmares?", YoSaVon asked. She placed the juice she was drinking in the cup holder. We were on our way back to Mississippi. I exhaled, deeply, and stretched. "Yeah, I can't stop thinking about John.", I said. I reached for a cigarette with shakey hands. "Well, you need to stop thinking about him.", She said and looked into the rearview mirror. "It's not that easy, Yo." "Make it that easy." "Was it that easy for you? The man was an okay person. I just don't understand.", I said. "You don't need to understand. It's final. You did a great job and yes, it was that easy.", YoSaVon said. She rolled her window down to let some of the smoke out. When she realized the smoke crossed her face, she rolled her window up and cracked the passenger's side window. "How can you say that, Yo? You're a murderer." "A murderer? A fucking murderer?", She laughed, genuinely. She continued, "I never murdered anyone. Murderers don't get paid. I'm a professional. I take that back. Are you sure you want to ask me questions?", Hemisphere asked. "Yeah. Why?", I asked. "Because you're such a fucking baby. You, literally, can't handle the truth." "I'm not that weak. Shit, I did good for my first time. You said so, yourself." "I know what I said. You did good. You didn't smoke anyone. Do you think that you could do that?", YoSaVon asked. She glimpsed at me for a quick second. Then, she directed her eyes back towards the highway. I hit my cigarette and blew the smoke out, slowly. "I think anyone can do anything if they put their mind to it.", I said. I took a swallow of my soda. "That's not what I fucking asked you. I..." "I heard you, Hemi.", I interrupted her. "By the way, kill the Hemi shit. We're not working.", YoSaVon said. "Yeah, okay. Look, I don't want to talk about if I could kill someone or not. I want to hear what you were saying about the first time you murdered someone.", I requested. I turned in my seat with my knees bent. I had to face her. "How do you know that I wanted to talk about that? Please, turn around, Ava. You are triggering my reflexes." I turned around in my seat and threw my cigarette out of the window. "Why did you throw your cigarette butt out the window when you could've used the ashtray? Future preferences, use the ashtray.", YoSaVon said. I waved her away and let my seat back. "I thought you wanted to hear this.", YoSaVon said. "I do but, you're dragging." "Well, I'll make it quick. My first victim was Daniel Allen", YoSaVon said. My mouth dropped. "Stop lieing.", I said. She didn't say anything. "Yo, tell me you're telling a story." "This isn't bedtime and I'm not your mother. Does it look like I'm playing?" "Damn, Yo, I went to school with him", I said. "I know. Y'all had a class together. I was seventeen, almost eighteen. I, only, stabbed him once.", She smiled. "You're telling me this; smiling and shit like it wasn't nothing.", I said. "It wasn't. I told you. You shouldn't be asking me such questions. Does it come to you as a shock?" "Yeah. Hell, yeah. You murdered at seventeen and it doesn't bother you.", I said. I reached for another cigarette. "Girl, kill that white girl shit. Oh, you can't believe me. Oh, oh, no. YoSaVon. Why, YoSaVon? Why? Well, I will tell you why. Money. The same reason you helped murder John.

Money.", YoSaVon said. She adjusted the rearview mirror. "Who would pay a seventeen year old to kill a high school student. Hell, you were still in high school." "I graduated. You're asking too many questions. We should end this questionaire here. Just know this, I was a millionaire before I turned nineteen. I had, at least, three million in off shore accounts. Now-a-days, expenses (high expenses) have me at a little past fifty million offshore.", Yo said. I, almost, choked on my soda. "How many people did you have to kill to get that much money?", I asked. "Lost count. No more questions, Ava." That was all she said to me. I fell asleep.

When I woke up, we were in Mississippi. YoSaVon was on her cellphone. So, I kept my eyes closed to eavesdrop. "Yeah, yeah, everything went fine. No, she's okay. Cement, of course. No, D flew to Paris. The Ambassador. I'm sure. Besides, I have to see my family. We're having a party. That's fine. I'll meet him in Jackson. Alright, love you." She closed her phone. "You're not sleep, Ava. We have to stop in Jackson. I have to meet someone.", YoSaVon said. "How long will it be before we get there?", I asked. "Thirty to forty minutes." "Good.", I said. I doze off.

It's about time. We made it to Jackson, Mississippi. We were in the parking lot of Jackson's mall. The Metrocenter. I was in the Escalade by myself. It was still running with the doors locked and the air conditioner on. I looked around for YoSaVon. She was nowhere in sight. I opened the glove compartment, closed it, and thought about shopping. I had enough new clothes in the trunk. I had so many I could open the trunk and sell them in the parking lot. I unlocked the doors and stretched. I lit a cigarette, hit it, once, and dropped it. I thought about what YoSaVon said about using what you got. I started to pick it up. When I bent over, I saw them. YoSaVon was sitting the Jaguar with him; expensive suit. David. They were staring, directly, at me but, they never stopped talking. They didn't miss a beat. I left the cigarette where it was and got back in the Escalade. What in the fuck is going on? He... must be the boss of the smokers. He can't be because Yo' was on the phone with the boss. So, who in the hell is he? The bastard knew (all along) who I was. I grabbed my shades and put them on. Damn... Ten minutes, later YoSaVon got behind the wheel. She didn't say anything to me. It was silent. Once we on the highway, I broke the silence, "That man..." "I know. You've met him before. Cute, huh?", YoSaVon asked. For a second, I thought she had her guard down. "Damn him being cute!

Who is he and don't give me that asking too many questions bullshit!", I stated. I was in a rage because I felt played. "He's a smoker.", Yo' said. "I know he's a smoker." "Well, he's a step down from being the boss. We had to make sure you were qualified for the session." "So, this boss of yours send somone to give him, her, it, or whatever to give them the okay?", I asked. I noticed she was going twenty five over the speed limit. "Slow down.", I said. She didn't. We passed a state trooper. He acted like he didn't notice that she was speeding. She never slowed down. "I told you who he was. I'm not going to tell you, again.", YoSaVon said. "Well, why did y'all have to met?", I asked. I could tell she was irritated by that question. She sped up five more miles. "We were talking about you." "What about me?", I asked. "He thinks we should make you a smoker. I don't.", Yo' stated. "How are you all going to make a decision for me?", I asked. "We can't. Do you want to be a smoker, Ava?" "I don't know." "Well, find out. You have two weeks to decide. Upon acceptance, you'll have to begin your training, immediately. Training will be one year and six months; six days out of the week. You'll be paid two hundred and fifty thousand for your training. You pay for your own living expenses. I suggest an apartment in the upper class Atlanta area.", She said. "Atlanta?", I interrupted. "Yes.", she said. "What about my current life? What about Ambrose?", I asked. Immediately, she slowed dow and pulled onto the shoulder. She put the vehicle in park and said, "Look, I don't know about Ambrose. He's just a man. I've never met a man that has a cash back, guaranteed, sign if you're not satisfied." "He just proposed, YoSaVon!", I yelled. "I understand that.", she said. I started crying. "Haven't you been in love? Don't you want children? I do.", I said. I wiped my face with a baby wipe. "Look, you have two weeks. It's your decision. I'm not aiming a gun in your direction. This is your decision and yours, alone. Ambrose should have no impact on your decision. That could jeopardize your life.", she said. She got back on the highway. "Two weeks."

Let&s Party

THEY ALL WERE THERE. I took over driving after we stopped to refill the Escalade with gas. I thought YoSaVon was asleep. I started to shake her, once or twice, to awake her. She caught me by the wrist and said that she was not asleep. "Damn, Yo', let my wrist go.", I said. She, basically, threw my wrist back to me. "Is that Ambrose?", YoSaVon asked. I forgot she never saw him before. He was standing behind mother with his hands on her shoulder. They, both, were smiling from ear to ear. "Yeah, that's him. That's my baby.", I said. "Damn, I see why your decision is so tough.", YoSaVon said. RoNao was holding Sympathy on her hip. Stecha was sitting in a lawn chair; counting money. She had shades over her eyes. They all look nice. They all were dressed nice. I was so happy to be home. I felt like I had just did four years in the military. I was glad to be home. Before I turned the engine off, I took a deep breath and exhaled, slowly. YoSaVon was, already, out of the vehicle. I got out, quickly, because I wanted to be the one to introduce Ambrose and YoSaVon to each other. "Y'all hoes look tired.", Stecha said. "And you look beat the hell up.", YoSaVon said. "Don't start.", Mama said. "Hey, Yo.", Rona said with a grin. Knowing RoNao, she, probably was glad Yo' said what she did to Stecha. "Hey... Come here, Sympathy. Come to auntie." YoSaVon said. "I'm glad y'all got here okay.", Momma said. "Yeah, thank God. Smooth sailing.", I said. "Well, y'all get over here and give Mama a hug.", Mom said. The three of us embraced with Sympathy on Yo's hip. "Damn, don't smush my baby.", Stecha said. "Girl, shut up. You know no one is going to hurt that child.", Mama said. I was about to say something sassy to Stecha but, Ambrose hugged me. He hugged me right after YoSaVon, Mother, and I embraced. "Damn, I missed you. I'm glad you're back. Let's go home", He said. "Slow ya' roll, guy. Let me introduce you to my sister, YoSaVon. YoSaVon, this is Ambrose.", I said. "Hey.", They both said in unison. "Now, that we've been introduced, I'd, really, like to chat with my mother.", Yo' said.

"Yeah, and I'd like to do that and then some with your sister.", Ambrose said. RoNao said, 'oooh..' like she was rehearsing to sing in a church choir. Mom shook her head and walked in the house with YoSaVon still carrying

Sympathy on her hip. Stecha rolled her eyes, turned up her nose, and put her money in her purse. "Are you ready to go, babe? I need you. My shit got solid as soon as you cut that corner. You, already, know it's time for a workout. Like D. Banner say, I want to see you drip sweat but, in my own words, I want to feel you grip that." Ambrose whispered. He said it very, seductively. He pressed against me so I could feel that his dick was hard. "Let's go. Let me tell Mom that I am leaving, though.", I said. "Alright.", He said. He licked inside my ear, simultaneously, with his words. "I'll be in the Escalade.", He said. I walked into the house looking for YoSaVon and Mom. I didn't see them anywhere. I walked into the backyard and they were sitting in lawn chairs. I watched them before I made my presence known. Mom was talking and YoSaVon was listening and shaking her head from time to time. Not once, did YoSaVon interrupt her. Then, what happened next surprised me. Mom was using a cell phone. It looked like one of the phones YoSaVon gave me to use while we were in Atlanta. When Mom got off the phone, I opened the door, a little, to eavesdrop. "It's all set up.", Mom said. "The rest is up to her. I hope we don't waste any money on this project. Ava, come here, baby.", Mom said. Now, how in the hell did she know I was standing there? "We were just discussing RoNao's party. We're going to have it next weekend because Yo-kat said she can't stay too long. Is that okay with you?", Mom asked. "Um... Yeah. Yes, ma'am. Look, I'm about to go home. I just thought I'd tell y'all that. Do y'all need anything?", I asked. "No. I'm going to rent a car and get a room; somewhere nice.", Yo' said. "A room? Why would you get a room when you can...", I was saying before Mom cut me off. "Now, Ava, this child is grown. If she wants to stay at a room, then lean back." "Lean back?", I questioned. I was looking puzzled because I have not ever heard Mom speak slang, before. "Yeah, and before you leave, put the things you bought me in my closet. Okay, baby?", Mom said. I said, "Yes ma 'am" "Okay, then. Now, come give momma a hug." I did. I, also, gave RoNao and Stecha what I bought them and Sympathy. "So, what's up?", Stecha said as I was getting in the Escalade. "Tell me.", I said. "How in the fuck am I going to tell you? You're the one going home and shit. I guess your ass is dull, now.", Stecha said. "What?", I asked. "Bitch, don't play dumb. You know Ambrose is going to wax that ass. I want to hear all about your ATL voyage. Every little detail.", she said. "Hmph. Well, speaking of details, I think I might have found a brother to wax your ass, permanently.", I said.

"Bitch, what are you talking about?", Stecha asked. "Just call me, tomorrow. Okay?" "Whatever.", Stecha said. "Call me.", she said.

Ronao's party was, exactly, as scheduled. The week passed by, too quick. I rented the Escalade for the rest of the week. YoSaVon rented a Mercedes. I gave Stecha Duane's number. They had been talking, faithfully, everyday. I couldn't believe how excited she was about talking with him. They made plans to meet the next weekend. The same weekend I was to give YoSaVon my decision about if I wanted to be a permanent smoker. YoSaVon had been spending most of her time with mother. I guess they had a lot of catching up to do. RoNao was just excited about having her party. She still worked at La Cocina de Comida. Her party was extravagant. All of her friends were there. They all took pictures with RoNao. There was so much food left. We donated what was left to a shelter. That was our good deed for the week. She had her own D. J. Everything was nice. RoNao bitched, all day, because no-one in her family gave her any cash. She calmed down when she realized that we all chipped in to buy her a brand new Lexus Jeep; fully loaded. The Lexus was paid for. Straight cash. YoSaVon tried to give everyone (that helped pay for the Jeep) their money back. Everyone declined. Everyone, except Stecha. She snatched those five g's, so quick. I didn't see her unzip her purse. RoNao laughed, cried, jumped up and down, and thanked us all. It was a day to remember and a night to recall.

Ambrose followed me around the house as I prepared to go to Apples. "Baby, why am I always second to everyone else?", Ambrose asked. "You're not. I've told you, all week, that we were going out. So, why are you tripping, now? Shit, why don't you put on some clothes? Instead of walking around with your dick slanging and hit up Jock's? Get the fuck out of the house.", I said. I looked in the mirror and put my earrings on. "Man, I'm not trying to go out.", Ambrose said. "That's your business. I'm hitting the slab. Shit, it's hard trying to get YoSaVon to go anywhere. She agreed to go. So, we're rolling out.", I said. "Well, this is hard, too.", Ambrose said. He rubbed pre-nut on the back of my leg. "Man, go on.", I said. I wiped my neck with a baby wipe. "Well, let me just get a feel.", He said. "Hell no! If I do that, I'll have to get dressed all over, again and I'm the last one to get picked up and you know it takes me the longest to get dressed." "Yeah. Well, I'm still not going out. I'll be here waiting on you. Just wake me up by riding this dick"

It was difficult trying to convince myself that YoSaVon was dressed like a high-class hoe. The shit was unreal. She had on Chanel from head to toe. Her tan Chanel shirt revealed her Chanel bra. The shirt was a snap button. All the buttons were unsnapped; except, the ones, directly, under her busom. The shirt lead into the tan, khaki, daisy duke, Chanel shorts. She had a thick, gold, rope chain around her neck. Her stilettos were dark brown and tan. They matched her belt. The bangles on her arm were silver, bronze, and gold. Her hair was pinned up to show her Coco Chanel earrings. She decided against wear the matching shades because it was too dark outside. We all looked good. We took two cars that night. Stecha drove the Escalade and I drove the Mercedes. We couldn't ride five deep to Apples. It would've been six deep but, Stecha didn't pick up LeBome. "Stecha, why didn't you go get LeBome?", RoNao asked. RoNao and LeBome got close when Ro' started working at La Cocina de Comida. "Because the bitch wasn't ready.", Stecha said. She walked towards Apples swinging her thick hair. "That's...", RoNao was about to say. "That's what, baby? In this pond, you either swim or drown and right now, that hoe is being resuscitated. Clear!", Stecha said. Everyone laughed except, RoNao. Instead, she reached in her purse, lit a blunt, and walked back towards the Mercedes. We all stopped and turned around. "Ro, what's up?", I asked her. "You, already, know what's up.", Ro' said. "Here we go.", Le ebo said. "Man, let's go, Le ebo. Let them hoes have their heart-to-heart. Yo', you coming with us or are you staying with the baby?", Stecha asked. "I'm going to see what's bothering Ro'. Go ahead.", Yo' said. "No doubt. She might need an extra tittie.", Stecha said. Stecha and Le ebo went into the club. "Ro', are you alright?", Yo' asked. "Yeah, I just need to smoke one to be around Stecha. She's cold as hell. I've never met anyone so cold.", RoNao said. YoSaVon looked at me. "Yeah, she is deep freeze but, what she said was true. This is a dog eat dog world...", YoSavon kept talking. I couldn't believe my fucking eyes. Stanley the angler was pulling into a parking space (right) beside ours. He turned his car's inside light on. He pulled his visor down and checked his appearance. I guess he thought because he didn't see Stecha's ride that she wasn't there. "Yo, kill it; for a second. RoNao, looky-lookie.", I said. "Oh, shit!", RoNao said. "What? Is that the dude that hit Stecha?", Yo' asked. "Hell, yeah. Change of plans. Ro', go into the club and tell Stecha that we're...", I got dumbfounded. I couldn't think of shit. "That we're what?", Ro' asked. "Tell her that I had an emergency meeting with some very important clients from New Orleans. Tell her that I will make it up to her.", Yo' said. "Okay." "...and Ro'.", Yo' said. RoNao turned around. "Enjoy the night.", Yo' said. She tossed RoNao a stack. "Advantage, get in the back seat of his car. Try to stay low; that way you will go unnoticed. Here take my necklace.", YoSaVon said. Being that she called me by smoker's name, I knew that the shit was about to get real. It was about to pop off. I crouched down low behind the passenger's seat. I reached up to turn off the light switch. So, that when the doors were open the car would remain dark. I held YoSaVon's chain in my hand that was starting to sweat because of the gold and sheer nervousness. What? Did you expect me to be calm, cool, and collected? That shit with John was a different situation. I just lured him to his death. Looks like this time, I'd play the grim reaper. YoSaVon worked fast. She had Stanley walking towards the Mercedes in under five seconds. As they got into the car, they were talking about Hemisphere's make believe home in New Orleans and how she was into sadomasochistic. As we pulled out of Apples, I saw RoNao, Le ebo, and Stecha coming out of the club just in time to see us burn rubber. Stecha had one hand on her hip; flipping her other hand through her long, thick hair. Now, that I think about it, they reminded me of Charlie's angels' silhouette. I laughed inside. Although, I was still shaking outside. YoSaVon and Stanley continued to talk. "So, why did you choose me. um... again to dominate?", Stanley asked. "It's like I said, I've been in that parking lot a full hour and all the boys that passed me didn't look man enough to stand next to a real woman; like myself.", Hemisphere said. "Um... I like that.", Stanley said. He rubbed his hand up Hemisphere's leg. She stopped him by putting her hand on top of his. "Yes, and you're going to love what I'm going to do to you, even more. But, first, you have to be patient. It's, only, three hours before...", Hemisphere said. "Three hours? Why three hours?", He questioned. "Oh... do you want to go back, yeah?", YoSaVon asked. She spoke in a New Orleans accent; just a bit. "No. I just want to know why I have to wait three hours.", Stanley said. YoSaVon burst into a sinister laughter and said, "Because I live in New Orleans, dear. That's where all my equipment is; in my house. Surely, you don't think I could bring such machinery with me. Do you want me to take you back to your car? Do you have some girl you have to return to? Are you..." "No, I don't have any girl to return to and no, I'm not married. Just drive. This shit better be worth my while or so God help me...", Stanley said. "Oh, what I'm going to do to you, only, God will be able to help you.", Hemisphere said; patting Stanley on his leg. We drove about forty five minutes. They chit-chatted, every so often. Stanley told Hemisphere about how he poured out his heart and wallet to this one bitch that didn't appreciate him. "She was smart. A smart little bitch. Anytime I would ask her to meet me at a hotel room, she would refuse. You know, the only place she would meet me was at restuarant or the bank. Shit, in less than a month, the conniving little hoe took over fifty g's from me.", Stanley said. "Aw... poor baby.", Hemisphere said. She rubbed his head. "Naw, it's straight because I got that bitch back.", Stanley said. He looked straight ahead and had a snarl across his lips. "Oh...", Hemi said. "Oh, yeah.", Stanley said. He rubbed his hands together. "Man, I got that bitch to come to the bank on a Sunday. Bitch wasn't as smart as I thought she was because banks aren't open on Sunday's. But, sure enough, she came. I walked to her car with a smile on my face. When she pulled her window down I pulled that bitch through her window and started pound that bitch. I pounded that bitch for every withdrawal I made out of my account. Then, because I felt I had paid her enough, I took what I had been wanting the whole time.", Stanley said. "Oh, my God. You raped her?", Hemisphere asked. "Hell, yeah. She's lucky that's all I did. Bitch, taking my cash. So, you see this better be worth my fucking time.", Stanley said. He squeezed Hemisphere's right leg. She just smiled and said, "Oh, it's going to be worth both of our time. Both of ours."

Okay, so you know I was crotched down for too long of a motherfucking time span. All I could think of was this punk ass bitch raping my sister and she didn't tell us. Of course, she wouldn't. Not Stecha. Not ever. Okay, breathe. Breathe. Hemi better do something and fast. Hemisphere turned on a back road ten minutes later. She made a left on this backroad. "What are you doing?", Stanley asked. "I just want to give you a sample. So, what do you think?", Hemisphere asked. She stopped the car on the side of the road and clicked on the over (inside) headlights. "Think about what?", He asked. "My Chanel bra. Chain or no chain?", Hemi asked. "What chain?", Stanley asked. "This chain, motherfucker.", I said, a I wrapped the chain around his neck and proved that it wouldn't break. Stanley started to reach for the chain as he choked with his tongue hanging out of his mouth. His eyes buck and he pissed his pants. "Don't fight it, motherfucker. You see, that lit' smart bitch that you raped is our sister. She was smart enough to drain your money and we're smart enough to drain your life. Goodnight, motherfucker.", Hemisphere said. She punched him in his mouth and gave him a good karate chop in the neck to make sure he was dead. She kicked him out of the car. We rode home with the windows down.   Being a killer was burning hot in my blood. I walked past my man; that was lying in bed naked. The T.V. was on and he slept with the remote in his hands. His hands were on his chest; interlocked. I walked into the bathroom and splashed water on my face. I looked in the bathroom mirror. What am I becoming? I kept asking myself. Who am I? I held my head down and watched the water drip from my face into the sink. The irony of it was... I knew who I was. I knew what I wanted to be but, most of all, I knew where I was going.

"Baby, are you alright?", Ambrose asked. I grabbed a face towel from the baby-blue shelf and walked past him. "Yeah, I'm fine.", I said. "I know you're fine. What I want to know is why didn't you wake me up to a rodeo show?" "Ambrose, I am not in the mood, right now." "Damn, what's going on with you? It's like it's a problem everytime I talk to you or even try to touch you, lately.", He said. "There's no problem, Ambrose. I just need some me time. Some time to think.", I said. My attitude was not at it's best. "What in the fuck are you talking about; you time? You just had you time for two fucking straight weeks. Where is all that shit coming from?", Ambrose asked. "It's coming from this, Ambrose." I held up my hand and took the ring he gave me off my finger. "Ava, wait a minute, baby. Let's talk about this. We can get counseling. What... am I... doing wrong?", He started to cry. My back was to him. He grabbed my hips and squeezed them. He had his head resting on my ass; sobbing. I walked into the living room. The keys to my Accord was resting on the mantlepiece above the fireplace. I grabbed them and walked out the door. Ambrose ran in the bedroom and put on some boxers. I was behind the wheel of my car when he came running out of the house. My windows were up and my head rested on the steering wheel. I jumped when Ambrose started banging on my window. "Baby, open the door. Open the door. Don't do this, baby. Ava, please. Please. Just tell me why?", Ambrose said. He had tears streaming down his face. I placed my left hand on the window and watched my baby beg for me not to leave. I faced forward, checked the rearview mirror, and thought to myself: It's now or never. I pulled out of the drive-way. Ambrose was screaming my name to the top of his lungs. You'll be amazed how people will wake up at four o'clock in the morning for bullshit. It seemed like every porchlight lit up. Ambrose dropped to his knees, his shoulders slumped, he had his head down, and that's how I would remember him. I rode to my mother's house in silence. My second voice kept telling me to go back to Ambrose. Something told me that I was making a major mistake. So, I turned on the radio and I'll be fucked 'It's Never the Right Time to Say Good-bye.' by Chris Brown was playing. I cried all the way to Blinkye's house. I just sat there with the car running. Immediately, my mother's porch light came on. My mother rushed out of the house. YoSaVon and RoNao followed. She was wearing silk pajamas with a silk overcoat. RoNao and YoSaVon wearing Nike jogging suits. RoNao's jogging suit was pink and YoSaVon's was dark blue. My Mom banged on the window and said, "Open this door, child. Open this door, right now." I turned the car off, unlocked the door, and started to cry. "Aw, child. Come here. Ambrose called and told us what happened.", Mom said. "Us?", I asked. "Yeah. YoSaVon bought me one of those high tech speaker phones, yesterday. Want to see it? It's real nice." "Not now, mama." "You, okay, sis?", YoSaVon asked. "Yeah, I will be, eventually.", I said. I released myself from my mother's grasp. RoNao just stood there with her left arm across her stomach and her right hand covering her nose and mouth. "Why did you do it, Ava?", RoNao asked. "Hush, child. Let's go inside. So the child can rest.", Mama said.

Inside, We all sat on the same sofa. "Damn. Can I get some breathing room?", I said. "Oh, yeah. Sure.", Mama said. Mama moved to the recliner. YoSaVon moved and sat in the loveseat and RoNao sstayed seated with me. They all stared at me. "RoNao, let me get a square.", I stated. She walked toward her bedroom. Before RoNao got back, we heard the loud thud of Stecha's music. When it got quiet. I looked out of the window and saw Stecha getting Sympathy from the passenger's side of the car. I watched as she walked on the porch and opened the door. "Ya'll won't believe this shit.", Stecha said. "Watch your damn mouth!", Mama said. "Listen, y'all remember that motherfucker, Stanley?", Stecha said. "Didn't I tell you to watch your motherfucking mouth, young lady?", Mom asked Stecha. "Hold on.", Stecha said and continued... "What's going on here and why wasn't I informed of this meeting?", Stecha asked. She gave Sympathy to Mom.

"Because, we weren't informed of this meeting. Ava left Ambrose.", YoSaVon said. She got up and walked towards Mom and Sympathy. "Damn.", Stecha said. RoNao returned with the cigarettes and a lighter. "Family reunion?", She asked. RoNao lit a cigarette and gave it to me. "Anyway, y'all remember that dude that hit me?", Stecha asked. "What about him?", RoNao asked. "How about they found his body on a back road in Hattiesburg. Dead.", Stecha said. "Oh, my.", Mother said. "When did you find that out?", I asked. "Tonight. It's all over the news. He left his car at the club, tonight.", Stecha said. Mama got up and said she was going to bed. "Mama, I love you.", I said and got up to give her a hug. "I love you, too, baby.", Mama said. She gave me a kiss on the cheek. "Mama, I'm leaving, tonight.", I said. "Leaving? Where are you going?", Mama asked. "Atlanta, mama." "Well, if that's sure that's what you want to do, take care of yourself." "Just like that, mama?", I asked. "Yeah, baby, just like that. You see, you're grown, now, and you have to live with the choices you make. Is this your final decision?", Mama asked. She placed a hand on my cheek. A tear rolled from my eye as I said, "Yes, mama." Blinkye kissed my forehead and said, "Well, like I said, earlier, take good care of yourself." She turned and went to her bedroom. The light from her bedroom stayed on and I could've sworn I heard her on the phone. She, probabley, was praying. "Bitch, are you stupid? What in the fuck is wrong with you? How could you leave Ambrose after he just proposed to you?", Stecha asked. "I don't, usually, agree with her but, I'm like damn, Ava. What is, really, up?", RoNao asked. She was trying to pull Sympathy from YoSaVon. "Damn, is the whole damn committee coming down on me?", I asked. "No.", YoSaVon said. "I agree with Mama; you're grown." "Oh, come on with that you're grown bullshit, Yo. You, probably, don't even know what it feels like to be in love. So, don't even try to encourage her to follow her dreams. You just waltzed your ass in here. After what, two years? You don't even know Ambrose. Matter of fact, you just meet him, last week.", Stecha said. She stood up. "And? I was here when Sympathy was born.", Yo' said. "Shit... barely, and she don't really know you. She's just attached because you're blood.", Stecha said. Yo' stood up and gave Sympathy to RoNao. "So, what in the fuck are you implying?", YoSaVon said. She stood, directly, in front of Stecha. "I'm fucking implying that, why don't you hop your dickless, happy-go-lucky ass in your shiny, new rented Mercedes and mob the fuck out. Trust me; you won't be missed.", Stecha said. "Y'all chill out.", I said. I stood between them. "Ava, back the fuck up.", Yo' said. "Yeah, please do.", Stecha said. "Hell, no! Y'all tripping.", I said. "Bugging.", RoNao said. "I'on know who go you thinking you're Mrs. Tyson around here but, you don't need none and don't want none of this.", Yo' said. "Girl... please, bring that shit.", Stecha said. She tried to push me aside. "Nah... I'm going to spare your ass.", Yo' said. She walked past us. She got into her new rental and drove off. We sat down. The phone rang. RoNao answered it and turned the speakerphone on. "Aye, Ava. I'm headed to Georgia. Meet me there and, uh... Stecha, my niece saved your ass." She hung up.

We Meet Again

I T'S BEEN TWO YEARS AND four months since I left Mississippi. It's been two years and four months since I left Ambrose. It's been ten months since I've been official. Two months ago, I went to Jackson and met up with Stecha, RoNao, Mom, and Sympathy. RoNao is, now, a sophomore in college. She still haven't made a B. Mom is still mom, of course, draining our pockets. Sympathy is almost four months old and is beautiful, as ever. She looks like YoSaVon, to me. Stecha hate for anyone to compare her daughter to YoSaVon but, it's true they look alike. Stecha and Duane are living together. They're engaged. Duane did, exactly, what he said he would do if met that special someone. He closed shop in Atlanta and opened shop in Mississippi. Stecha made him quit smoking and I heard he was giving Ambrose's father shop a run for their money. As for Ambrose, Stecha said she think he's a punk, now. Stecha thinks everyone is a punk. He hasn't been serious with anyone since we broke up. Well, since I abandoned him. He's one of the head detectives for his district. They say he's a force to reckoned with. He's, literally, a cop. A pig of the worst kind. He goes by, "Boss Hog". I haven't seen him in two years and four months.

I have an apartment in Atlant and New York. When YoSaVon called me from Paris, I was in New York entertaining fellow smokers. I didn't think there could be so many people involved in an international assassin ring. Famous people and all. There are so many anonymous smokers. I asked the D. J. to turn the music down a notch and went into my room. By now, I'm living lavished. Everything is plush. To disguise that we are legit. All smokers, only smokers, work at a cigarette factory to avoid the I. R. S. We, basically, sit around and wait for a hit. They come in, consistently. They came in from all over the world. That's why Hemisphere was in Paris. I closed my bedroom door, sat on my bed, and kicked off my hells. "What's up, baby girl?", I asked YoSaVon. "I'm at the airport. I'll be in, tomorrow. Are you having a party?" "A get together. So, why are you calling me? Did everything go okay?" "Good and smoked. I'm calling you to inform you that you have a cigarette, tomorrow. So, call your get together off and get some rest. I'll be there bright and early to inform you of the details." "Okay, but I don't understand why can't you just give me the pack, now. These lines are secure." "Because we're in on this together. CEO said it's top priority." "How much?" "Ten mil' a piece." She hung up. Damn, I've been official ten months, now. I haven't even put ten million in my accounts off-shore. I just reached my eight million mark, last week. I'm, definitely, about to cut this get together short. I jumped off the bed, open my door, and walked to the disc jockey. D. J. Dynamite, who is also a smoker, cut the music off and announced thta the party was over. I apologized to everyone and told them to take as much food and alcohol that they could carry. Leaving out the door, Dependable and this blonde bombshell named Firework, stopped to chat with me. "Over so soon? I was just about to seduce D. J. Dynamite.", Firework said. "Sorry but, I got an early morning schedule. Seduce him on the elevator.", I said. "Don't be such a bitch, Advantage.", Dependable said. "Don't start, D. I have a major pack in the a.m.", I rebutted. "Oh... top priority, huh? Since when do they give top priority to the rookies? Makes me wonder is showing favoritism.", Dependable said. "That's my cue.", Firework said. She rushed off to catch Dynamite. "Favoritism, D? How pathetic is that? That's the best you coul;d come with? How in the hell would the boss show favoritism to me? I never even met him. Maybe, he just likes my skills." "Your skills are still fresh. Top priority requires seasoned smokers. You are, oh so, bland. True, you haven't met the head huncho. Maybe, you should make an appointment to meet... her?", Dependable said. She looked me up and down. She looked in disbelief. She couldn't believe that I had a top priority. She looked at me, once more, over her shoulder and walked out. I closed the door; cursing Dependable in my head. She did give me some information. The CEO is a female. I looked at my living room and decided I will hire a maid to clean it up. I took a shower and went to bed.

"What the fuck?", I gasped. YoSaVon threw a glass of cold water in my face. "Put it down, Advantage.", Hemisphere said. She recognized that I was reaching for my twenty-five. I looked at the digital clock that was on my bedside table. It was three fifteen. I threw my legs over the side of my bed. My back to Hemisphere. "When did you get in?", I asked. I adjusted my eyes to the light illuminating from the bathroom. "Thirty minutes, ago. I would've been here, sooner. Traffic jam and coffee. Get dressed. It's time to go to work.", Hemisphere said. She tossed me a black, female style tuxedo. She walked out of the room. When I walked in the living room Hemisphere was checking our weapons. She closed the last suitcase and handed it to me along with a cup of coffee. We exited the apartment and headed towards the elevator. "The mark is Lit' Hut.", Hemisphere said. Inside the elevator's car, Hemisphere pressed the L button. "The famous rapper?", I asked. "None other. Since this is top priority, It's relevant for you to know who wants him dead." "Bingo. Right now, he is, currently, fucking a groupie. Our job is to do this mob-style, kick in the door, kill him and his groupie lover. Take a few articles. Toss some things around and leave.", Hemisphere said. "In other words, make it look like a robbery and leave." "In other words, make it look like a robbery gone bad." "Exactly.", Hemisphere said. She stepped off the elevator. "Don't underestimate Lit' Hut. There's two of us because I'm pretty sure he will be packing and so will his bodyguards. We have a room reserved adjoined to his with a peekhole. We'll case his room and decide when is the right time to strike.", Hemisphere said. As we drove toward the hotel Lit' Hut was staying, I couldn't help but wonder who was this mysterious C. E. O. "Hemi?", I asked. "Yeah.", She said. "Who's the C. E. O.?", I asked. "Why?", She asked. "Why not?" "That is not your mission. Your mission is to evaluate Lit' Hut. Are we clear?", Hemisphere asked. "Yes. I just want to know who she is.", I rushed out of my mouth. "How did you know?" "Know what?", I asked. "That the C. E. O. is a female.", Hemisphere stated. "Dependable told me." "This discussion is over."

I watched Hemi as she gazed throught the peephole. "What's wrong?", Hemisphere asked. She did not turn to look at me. She paid close attention to the activities manifesting, next door. "Nothing.", I lied. "We're sisters. I know something is bothering you. I can tell you don't believe I will help you." "You're right again.", I said. Hemisphere turned around and kneeled in front of me. "I tell you what; next week, I'll see if the C.E. O. will arrange to meet you. I promise.", Hemi said. She stood up and walked back to the peek hole. "Feel better, now?", Hemi' asked. She gazed, once again, through the peephole. "Yeah.", I said. "Good, because it's go time.", Hemi' said. She put her jacket on, and put her weapon together. We both had AK47's with silencer's. "There's two bodyguards situated in opposite corners of the room. Have a look. As you can see, Lit' Hut and the groupie are engaged in premarital activities. I will take the bodyguards. You take Lit' Hut and the girl. One shot. One kill.", Hemisphere said. "No problem.", I said. I screwed the silencer on my gun.

Outside the door Lit' Hut was behind, Hemisphere and I stared at each other. I waited for her to give the signal. Our weapons positioned. We burst in the room. Before the guards could unholster their weapons, they were dead. I watched their bodies slide agains the wall and hit the floor. I shot the girl in her head. Her mouth was still on Lit' Hut's dick. She was oblivious to what was going on around her. Lit' Hut was scrambling on the bed murmuring something unintelligible. "Please. I'm famous. I can pay you.", Lit' Hut said. He begged for his life. "Your wife, already, did.", I said. One shot. One kill. I began to kick shit over in the room. I pulled out drawers. Hemisphere took Lit' Hut and the bodyguard's wallets and jewelry. We went next door, gathered our belongings and left.

At my apartment, I took another shower. Hemisphere called me and told me she was at the airport; headed for Australia. Dependable and Firework would be accompanying her. She told me to take the week off; C. E. O.'s order. I turned the T. V. on. Lit' Hut's murder was broadcasting (all) over the news. The anchorman were saying the F. B. I. would be on the scene to investigate the crime scene. That's when I saw Ambrose's picture. They were flying him to New York to be the A. S. A. C. (Assistant Special Agent in Charge). My mouth dropped as I drawed closer to the television. They showed him giving a statement saying, 'that he is prepared to give his all to solve this brutal case. Shit, a vacation is well overdue, now. I ran to my room and packed a few items. I grabbed my wallet and the keys to my house and was, once again, on the move.

Stecha and Duane picked me up from the airport in Jackson. Sympathy was at my mother's house. RoNao was in school (college). I'd stay in her room. That was more convenient than paying a hotel. "Hey, Stranger.", Duane said. "Hey.", I said. I gave him a hug and a peck on his cheek. "Watch that shit. Don't get too damn friendly.", Stecha said. "Well, y'all, already, been introduced. So, save the hospitality.", Stecha said. The ride to our hometown was peaceful; peaceful, Stecha kept asking me a million questions. "So, what brings you here?", Stecha asked. "A much needed vacation.", I said. "From what? You don't do shit. You work in a cigarette factory. Acting like you got an important job and shit.", Stecha said. Duane laughed. "I just needed a break. I know you're going to let me take a break.", I said. "You do what you want but, answer me this: How do you manage to live so fly and luxurious off of that chump change?", Stecha asked. "I make do. My ends meet and expand.", I said. "Yeah, but how? I heard you just bought a brand new Escalade.", She said. "Where did you hear that?", I asked. "Mom told me. She finds out everything. YoSaVon tells everything.", Stecha said. "That's cool. How's Sympathy?", I asked. I tried to change the topic. "She's three almost, four.", She answered. That's Stecha. Some things will never change. Seeing Ambrose, again, made me realize that I never stopped loving him. I had to leave New York. It was best for me. The chances of me running into Ambrose in a spacious city are slim. I didn't want to weigh it.

Inside RoNao's bedroom, I unpacked my things and decided to watch some television. Blinkye knocked on the door. Sympathy was hugging mom's leg. "Come in.", I said. "Well, the door is, already, open. How was your trip?", Mom asked. "It was okay. Come here, Sympathy.", I said. Sympathy ran and jumped into my stomache. "Oh, you've gotten so big.", I said. "I'm three, auntie." "Almost four.", I said. "Uh-huh, almost four. I know my alphabets.", Sympathy said. She was full of excitement. I listened as she sang the alphabet song. I have her a cino for knowing all of her alphabets. "I know mine, too.", Mamma said. "Here, mama.", I said. I gave her one hundred dollars, too. "So, how is work?", Mama asked. She placed the money in her back pocket. "It's work momma. I'm thinking about quitting." "Don't you dare.", She said. It seems she hated the idea of me quitting. It seemed not to be an option. "Mama, I am tired. I want to go back to school; move back home, you know." "I know, baby. It's just sometimes we are born to what we do." "I wasn't born to work in a cigarette factory. I'm sick of it! Two years;

ago, I recall you saying that I was grown and I make my own decisions, in this very house.", I said. "I know what I said, Advantage.", Mamma said. "What did you call me?", I asked. "I called you Advantage. Hemisphere told me that you wanted to meet me. The CEO of Smokers Inc. Well, baby, the CEO raised you." "Mama!" "Don't give me that mamma crap! You would've found out, next week, anyway.", She said. "But.", I said. "But, what? You wonder how I could put up this masquerade; walking around like a do-good mother? Well, it's easy. I'm just playing it safe. You know, y'all have different daddies; all three of you. Your father was Irish. He founded Smoker's Inc. He brought me in as an accomplice. Busy man. Very busy. Always traveling. Always, out of the country. Well, you know, he and I were never meant to be together. He was just, sort of, a fling. Well, when I got pregnant with you I told him that I was pregnant. It was too late. He was, already, serious with someone else. A lady in China. He said that they were to get married and that I should quit Smokers Inc and raise our daughter. Our daughter. You. Hmmph. I could accept the fact that he was with someone else. I couldn't accept the fact that he wanted me to quit. So, I went to China where he was with his daughter and wife-to-be and killed him and his fiance. I took over Smoker's Inc, immediately, after his death was announced. I, even, paid for his funeral.", She said. She stared straight ahead like she was in a trance. "I'm going to watch Dora Dora, ganma.", Sympathy said. She hop out of my lap and ran into the living room. As she ran, she sang the theme song to, 'Dora the Explorer'. "What happened to the girl?", I asked. "Your sister? Oh, she's an agent for Smokers, Inc.", She said. I was out of words. This whole time I had another sister that my didn't tell me about. "Who is she, mother?", I asked. I didn't expect an answer. "Dependable.", She repied. "Does she know that I'm her sister?" "Of course not. How could I tell that child that I killed her father and gave birth to her only sister?" "Mama?", I said and started to cry. She hugged me as I sobbed in her arms. "So, what now, mamma?" "I don't know. That decision is yours. You continue to work or quit. Take a couple of weeks off. Let Hemisphere know your choice.", She said. She stood up and walked towards the open door. "Mama, why do you ask us for money. I know you have millions in off-shore accounts. So, why ask? I don't understand.", I asked. "Baby, mama's going to leave everything to y'all. Y'all have to learn not to showcase. Besides, you all are making a small investment into a large allotment. Very large. Neither of you will have to work another day in your life. You, really, don't have to work, now.", Mom said. "Why haven't you bought yourself a bigger house?" "Baby, I have several mansions. I've sold a few and kept a few." "Why don't you live in them?", I asked. "I'm comfortable. I get by. I visit them like I would visit a neighbor; every so often. They're kept up.", She said. "Dependable.", I said. "What about her?", Mom asked. "Will you ever tell her that I am her sister?", I asked. "One day. Just not tonight. Good day, baby.", She said and walked out. I couldn't believe what I just heard. My mother the CEO. That explains why she was talking on 'the phone' when YoSaVon and I came back from Georgia to celebrate RoNao's party. That, also, explains why she didn't try to stop me from leaving Ambrose. Whose money was YoSaVon sending her? Her own, perhaps? It all makes sense.

They found nothing about Lit' Hut's death. They said it was a robbery. Case closed. Ambrose flew back home from New York, the following week. I was still visiting my mother. I was babysitting Sympathy when someone knocked on the door. "Yeah, give me a second.", I said. "Bitch, unlock the door.", Stecha said. "Don't you have a key?", I asked. I open the door and let her in. "And what? I knocked, hoe. That means get the fuck up and open the damn door.", Stecha said. "Whatever. I'm not going there with you, today.", I said. "Yeah, whatever. Where's my baby?", Stecha asked. "In her playroom.", I said. "She's four. ", Stecha said. "Three.", I corrected her. "The poin is you don't leave a three year old unsupervised." "The whole room is childproof. She's in the back, Stecha.", I said. Stecha walked to the back to get her child. "What are you doing off, so early?", I yelled behind her. No answer. Someone knocked on the door, again. "I'm coming. I'm coming.", I said. I answered the door. "I can't remember the last time I heard you say that." "Ambrose? What are you doing here?", I asked. I was so shocked. It felt as if my eyes were bulging out of my head. I had to force myself to close my mouth. "Your mom called me and said you were in town. I just thought I'd stop by to say hi.", Ambrose said. Damn, he looked better than the last time I saw him on T. V. "Well, hi.", I said. I tried to close the door. He placed his hand on the door and said, "I just wanted to say that I forgive you and that I did not ever stop loving you." He walked off. "Who was that?", Stecha asked. "Nobody.", I said. "Whatever. I'm out. Say bye, Sympathy.", Stecha said. "Bye, te te.", Sympathy said. "See you, later, baby.", I said. I gave her a kiss. Mom came home thirty minutes, later. "Ambrose came by.", I said. "Did he?", she asked. "You should know you told him I was in town.", I said. "Call him, baby.", Mom said. She walked to her room. "No. Besides, I don't know his number." "It's still the same.", She yelled from her bedroom. I picked up the phone and was surprised that I still knew his number. "Ava?", Ambrose questioned. "Yeah. It's me. What are you doing?", I asked. "Watching T. V. What's up?", he asked. "Can you come pick me up?", I asked. "I'm on my way.", he said.

Things happened the way they should. I stopped working at Smokers, Inc. Ambrose and I got married in a double ceremony with Duane and Stecha. RoNao graduated medical school and received her Ph. D. Sympathy is in first grade. Mama is still the CEO. YoSaVon is still Hemisphere and guess what? Trinity is a new member of our family. She's one, now. Ambrose's father named her. Ambrose still doesn't know about Advantage. I know I love him. I, always, will. He's my husband, for now. My mother always taught me to not ever let anyone know everything you do. As far as the money, I told him I won a lawsuit against the cigarette factory. Things couldn't go sweeter. This is our second year anniversary. We decided to stay at home to a candlelight dinner. "I love you, so much, baby.", Ambrose said. "I love you, too, baby.", I said.

My cell phone rang. "Don't.", Ambrose said. "Just give me a second. They know it's our anniversary. Hello?" "Advantage. Tomorrow, be at the airport. We have another Johannesburg situation. You and RoNao are scheduled for the same flight.", Hemisphere said. I looked at Ambrose. "Okay.", I said. "You'll be briefed during the flight. Fireworks will be joining you all on this excursion. It's an one-day event and Ava, Happy Anniversary."

Printed in the United States
by Bookmasters

Printed in the United States
By Bookmasters